For Penney

A New Era for Manny Youngman

by Mike Murphy

First published 2015 by Mike Murphy
Reprinted 2021

ISBN 978 0 9944148 5 4

This is a work of fiction.
None of the characters or places in it are real or have any relation to existing people or places.

Also by Mike Murphy:
The Man Who Didn't Like People
A Life in Short Stories

ACKNOWLEDGEMENTS

To Michael Robotham, who urged me to write again when I had almost given up. To my late wife Penney who always believed I had to write. To Paula Boer for her critiquing, editing and friendship, and to Pete Boer and Cal for supporting her. To my daughter Bec for supporting me, and to my son Darren, my daughter in-law Kerren and my grandchildren Bradley, Tina, Jasmine and Chelsea because family is what everything is about.

Chapter 1

He would be attacked first, Manny calculated, by the handsome woman in the left aisle six rows back. From his chair on the stage, his eyes had been drawn to her among the two or three hundred people, predominantly women, shuffling into positions on thinly padded seats. A blustering wind was hurling unseasonable rain at the outside of the town hall, which would have made the size of the audience flattering if he thought they were there to listen.

Experience had shown they were mainly there to attack. At one of his first speaking engagements he confessed that he was only partly convinced by what he was saying, still trying to light his way down a dark path. He opened his heart and the audience turned on him, tasting blood. He learned to treat them as adversaries and make his words a barrier behind which his uncertainties could shelter.

Sizing up the opposition helped to take his mind off his dry throat, tensed neck muscles and the dozen or so butterflies in his stomach. He began with a scan of the faces around the handsome woman, deciding none of them appeared too threatening.

No. There was something. He reversed the scan. Katie Frank. For a few months in his twenties they had a lot of vigorous sex and passionate arguments. She had left him. The wound of it still itched after a decade and a half.

Her hair was shorter, cut below her ears instead of cascading to her shoulders. The face was as he remembered, more interesting than pretty, full of character, nose engagingly crooked between well-defined cheeks above a full mouth and a firm chin. It could change from an angry frown to a mischief-loving smile. Not chalk and cheese compared with the handsome woman, a different cheese with a more subtle flavour. What was she doing here?

She appeared more collected, more polished than in his memory, no longer unsure and arguing to assert herself. She sat shoulders straight, head held high. If she attacked him it would be with sharpened barbs designed to penetrate the holes in his argument and open them into gaping wounds.

The technique for dealing with that was to ignore her questions and repeat his main argument. For the handsome woman, who was more likely to attack with a blunt instrument, he would act confused and ask her to repeat the question. That would annoy her and she would hesitate, giving him time to prepare his answer.

He continued assessing the audience. He preferred men's groups but Tony, who organized these appearances, said he was better with women because he had Prince Harry's tousled red hair and the cheeky-boy face they found irresistible. So he had been allocated the Women's Service League. In a few minutes its president would introduce him.

The thought turned another screw on the vice constricting his diaphragm. Now it wasn't just a few butterflies in his stomach. A million crazed bats battered against each other in a panic to get out of one tiny hole in the roof of the belfry, or in this case, the dry, constricted passage in his throat.

"Ladies and Gentlemen." The president rose to her feet. "I do wish to thank you all for turning out on such a dismal evening." There were nods and murmurs of agreement. "I am sure we are all going to think it worthwhile when we hear our guest speaker. While Mr Manny Youngman has a well-established reputation as an architect, he also has a certain notoriety in a different field. In his book, 'The Male Conundrum', he espouses the views of the New Era Men's Support Alliance, the organisation of which he is president and which has been described as having unorthodox opinions on the role of the male in post-feminist society."

This was a cue for more wriggling on seats as heads nodded at each other. Perhaps he was wrong in expecting the attack to come from a woman. Men sometimes jumped to their feet to show the women how sensitive they were. He studied a man in the third row from the front. In his forties, about his own age. The man grinned back at him and began clapping. Manny realised the president was also clapping and looking at him expectantly.

Standing carefully, as he had taught himself to do after the time he jumped up and kicked over his chair and a jug of water, he moved to the lectern. The bats gave one last flap and settled down. From all around the hall whispered the sounds of people settling back in seats.

"Good evening. Can I say right from the start that the New Era Men's Support Alliance is not anti-women. We are not what I shudder to hear called 'sensitive new age guys' acting the way we think women want us to be. We are not red-necked macho males swilling beer, burping and rushing off into the forest to shoot anything that moves as a substitute for raping and pillaging. If I were asked to put our beliefs in a nutshell, feminism achieved considerable advances for women but it shifted the relationship between men and women, and that created consequences we at NEMSA believe need to be addressed."

He reminded them of the greater focus on men's health in recent years, particularly clinical depression and the rate of suicide among some groups of men, how this had resulted in dedicated men's health services, the Talk to a Mate phone line and growth of the Men's Shed movement.

"While we at NEMSA welcome these developments, we do not believe they address the root problem. They do not define a new role for men in today's society and they apply only band-aids to the scars left by the changes that have occurred, scars suffered not only by men but also by women. An increased number of divorced and unmarried women struggle alone to raise their children. Older divorced and widowed women face a lonely life in retirement and, as do men, suffer an increased rate of depression and other mental health issues.

"NEMSA is trying to find a new way, not reasserting the old. We do not preach a new male-dominated society but a society in which females and males are truly equal because they have a new type of relationship which they both understand and are comfortable with."

He spoke for the hour he had been allotted. When he stopped there was a brief silence followed by applause. Not a rolling wave of acclamation but more than just a polite clap. The president invited a small number of questions, because time, she advised, was running out and the weather outside was worsening. Manny sat back, sipped water and waited for the attack.

A large number of heads in the audience turned towards the sixth row back in the left aisle. The handsome woman rose to her feet.

Everyone seemed disappointed. Their eyes were directed to where Katie Frank studied her finger nails. She looked up, shook her head and gestured to the other woman to speak.

The handsome woman responded. "Well, Mr Youngman, you men will try to talk your way out of anything. We know the truth. Men still want to dominate. Always have, always will. You've done it for centuries. Until we stopped you. Now you're trying a new way."

She surveyed the audience as if gathering support. "His new society won't be any different. Men and women won't be equal. Men'll make sure they keep the power, just like they've always done." She sat down, making the movement an exclamation mark.

"I'm sorry," Manny responded without getting to his feet. "I don't quite understand. Is that a question?"

A few people laughed and the woman tossed her long

hair in annoyance. "It's what I feel about it," she asserted. "What's your response?"

Manny took up position again behind the lectern. With battle engaged, the bats were sleeping if not yet in hibernation. "I'll be happy to respond," he assured her. "I just didn't want to be impolite and fail to answer a question if you had asked one." He smiled. "I don't want to dominate. Domination brings responsibility and stress and a whole lot of other undesirables. I do want power, I don't deny that. However, the power I want is over my own life, not over anybody else's."

"Bullshit!" The flanking attack came from a red-headed woman near the front. "Men won't let women have power." The word 'men' was a spit. "You act as if you're being reasonable and rational but what you're saying is the same old bullshit. Men are so bloody condescending. Now you are going to tell us how it should be. Well, I've got news for you, you misogynistic sod. The world has changed. Women are going to tell men how it's going to be. Of course the pill has liberated you. You think you can screw women more often—and I'm not talking about having sex."

This won loud and prolonged laughter from a coterie of people surrounding her. It was not sustained across the whole of the audience. Manny addressed himself to the back rows.

"For the first time in history," he continued as if there had been no interruption, "we can have power over our own lives; we are all liberated. There is the opportunity, indeed the necessity, for changes in our social structures and in the relationships between people. I don't think women have recognised the full implications of this."

The single sound which followed this remark acted like a stimulant on the audience, as if the red-headed woman had been a sideshow to what they had really come for. Heads and eyes now turned back to where Katie Frank was sitting with her head thrown back in a mocking laugh.

"Very clever Manny." She stood and moved along the aisle to the side of the hall, where she could turn to see and be seen by everybody. She chuckled, and added, "Much more clever than I expected you'd be."

He'd been wrong to expect sharp barbs, he realized. She was a more skilful fighter than that.

"I'm fascinated by the name of your group," she continued. "The New Era Men's Support Alliance. NEMSA. Were you trying to identify yourself with MENSA? From what I've heard some of their ideas are quite as laughable as those we've been hearing this evening. As for men's support, isn't that one of those protection things cricketers wear under their pants?"

Manny smiled in the face of the laughter this provoked and decided it was time to take back control of the debate.

"It's gratifying to be having a good-humoured discussion instead of having it degenerate into an acrimonious argument," he began. "If we can joke and laugh together like this I think we are on the way towards better understanding. I've never believed the cause of men or women is helped by a 'them and us' approach. That's one of the reasons I prefer not to call people feminists."

"Oh no!" There was no laugh voice now. "You are not taking our name away. I am a feminist, and proud to be one."

"Going to prison to prove it," a voice interjected.

Applause greeted this affirmation. Manny was startled and only managed narrowly to recover and continue.

"Isn't it significant that men don't have a similar word to describe them?" he suggested. "The men's movement is not yet as defined as the women's movement. Men do not have a common text to work to. Women had that text. It said to men, 'You use your physical strength to impose your will, you use your economic and social position to gain advantage–you oppress women.'

"If men were to say to you, 'You sell your bodies to control men, you use your sexuality to gain advantage for yourselves, you nag your husbands.' Wouldn't you be offended?"

Katie smiled. "I'll say yes, because that's what you want me to say, but don't go offering to buy me just yet."

The audience laughed. They were enjoying this and sensed even better was coming.

"Thank you, I won't." He was becoming irritated by the way she turned his arguments into jokes. "As I was saying, some men may have power, but not all men. As an individual I don't have much power at all. I don't control any institutions, just as I accept you as an individual woman don't sell your body, nag your husband or use your sexuality to gain advantage."

"Thank you," Katie replied, the tone of her voice changed to counter the sharper edge in his. "Although what it has to do with you what I do with my body, my non-existent husband and my sexuality is quite beyond me. Men as a group do have power. Women as a group don't sell their bodies. There are still many instances of injustice towards women that have to be exposed and eradicated. There are men who resent the gains women have made and would turn back the tide of feminism if they could. Powerful men, and there are a lot more of them than there are of women who can claim in any way to have real power. That's why I..."

She stopped. A silence seemed to move across the room like a wave that advanced and receded, replaced by murmurs of surprise and dissatisfaction. Katie took a breath, lowered her chin and hooded her eyes. Her fingers curled into fists and she tapped her knuckles together as she controlled whatever it was that had overtaken her. She opened her eyes, unclasped her fingers and lifted her face towards him.

"You're right. Acrimonious argument isn't going to achieve anything." She walked back to her seat and sat down. The murmurs became a hum and the audience regarded each other with puzzled expressions.

Manny was unsure how to respond. Usually he made sure he had the last word, whatever arguments had been thrown at him. Now he felt the pulse of his audience and decided against it. He sat down and looked towards the president, who brought the proceedings to a close.

The applause was again subdued, a reflection of the audience's confusion rather than a response to his presentation. As soon as it ended, Katie left her seat and hurried to the exit, forestalling any attempts to question her. Her head was bowed, her expression unreadable.

Several among the audience began to talk animatedly and shake their heads, turning to each other for an explanation. Most began to follow Katie into the cold night, disappointed the heat had gone from the debate and eager for the warmth of their own homes.

Chapter 2

A week after his talk to the Women's Service League, Manny drove home relaxed and happy, singing a duet with the car radio. It was a tune from the personality-forming year of his seventeenth birthday, twenty six years before, and he got most of the words right.

He stopped when he saw the pink car in his carport. It wasn't just that the car was pink; it glowed beneath his carport light, like a glutinous blob in an ornamental lamp.

His eyes flickered to the front window of his upstairs apartment and scowled at his light glowing without his permission through his curtains. He swung his legs out of the door of his own car and closed it as if he didn't want to disturb someone he cared for.

His office, which occupied the ground floor, was in darkness, its door locked and no sign of broken windows. He went up the steps to the front door of the apartment and found it also locked. Whoever had got in didn't have a key or had locked the door again after using it. From the balcony, he could see in through a gap in the curtains. Not all the room, just the corner of it where he had his big, comfortable green armchair. A girl sat in it.

A shapeless black hat of soft felt with a narrow brim was jammed on her head. He was unable to see her face but he could make out she was wearing a loose green pullover and had her feet tucked up on the chair under her skirt.

She was talking to someone sitting opposite her in the

animated, unrestrained way in which females talk to each other even when they're angry or upset, one of which this youngster certainly was.

He moved closer to the window. The voices were just a murmur. No clues to be gained there. Even without seeing her face he was sure he had never seen the girl before. What he could tell about her was that she was ill at ease. The way she held her head and kept her arms wrapped around her knees spoke in a language he understood. The girl didn't like being there and was gearing herself to deal with a situation she expected to be painful.

That was a feeling he knew. Better than he wanted to remember. Twelve years old and standing in the long, empty, disinfectant-and-sweat-smelling corridor outside a classroom in a new school. Late because Dad got lost driving there. Mum sitting in the car telling Dad he's useless as usual and she's too embarrassed to go into the school and why should she because it isn't her fault.

Dad takes him as far as the classroom door and leaves him there with instructions to knock and go in when someone calls him. "It'll be all right. They won't eat you. Not 'til lunchtime, anyway, ha ha." Then he walks off along the corridor, stops, glances back and gestures again to knock on the classroom door. The boy Manny had no choice other than to put on his bravest face, hold his head high, wrap his arms metaphorically around himself and endure it.

Another time, fifteen years old and sitting with Mum

outside the room where he was going to be interviewed for his first job. Mum telling him how to stand straight, how to sit straight, what to say. Other boys sitting with their Mums. On the other side of the door a man who'll study him like a zoologist examining a warty frog and make judgments that will decide his future.

That was what this girl reminded him of, someone who was expecting to be judged, knowing it had to be endured, determined to pass the test and frightened to death that she might not. He related to her, which was almost as unbelievable as finding a pink car in his carport. Judged for what? Who by?

He had to go inside and find out, despite himself starting to feel very much like the girl. What was he going to be judged for? Who by? Something writhing around in his stomach knew the answer. The girl. It didn't make any sense. Nothing did.

He put his key in the door and opened it.

They stopped talking. On the girl's face, shadowed beneath the brim of the silly hat, he thought the features froze and waited for a cue to decide their next configuration, but it was only a fleeting impression before she turned away and looked at his bookshelves.

The face of the woman sitting in the other green chair didn't turn away but had a similar difficulty in arranging itself. He was not surprised. Katie Frank was right to be uncertain how she was going to be received.

"Hello, Manny." She made an attempt to be composed

and didn't succeed. "We, uh, um, came to see you."

"How did you get in here?" He was too intrigued to be angry. That could wait.

"Jenny got us in, didn't you, Jen? You left your loo window open at the top and she climbed up on my shoulders and wriggled through."

His office downstairs had a toilet at the back.

"I said we should have waited outside," the girl now named Jenny said to the book shelves.

"I suppose you're wondering what on earth we have to see you about?" Katie's laugh was too unsophisticated for the elegant green slacks and tailored jacket she was wearing.

"It had crossed my mind." He walked into the room, reclaiming his territory. He wished he could be closer to his books but the girl was sitting there. She had half turned her head towards him again and she had pulled her skirt tighter round her knees.

Katie laughed again, still with that awkward uncertainty. "Could I have a drink?"

"No." He stood on the other side of them so that they were nearest to the door and on their way out as soon as he could persuade or force them. "What did you break in for?"

"I told you we shouldn't have," the girl said again.

The woman shrugged at her. "I was bursting." The next shrug was to Manny. "I really did need to use a loo."

"You don't break into people's houses for that."

"We had to come in anyway, to see you."

"You haven't explained that either. What's this all about?"

"Something I have to talk to you about. Could I have a drink first? I'm gasping."

Manny considered it and because he was basically kind-hearted, agreed. "What would you like?"

"You always used to drink beer. Would you have anything else these days?"

She was recalling when he was twenty-eight. Now he was forty-three and there was a good chardonnay in the refrigerator and a variety of spirits on a side table. She chose a brandy with a mix of dry ginger which he also offered.

"What about you?" It was the first time he had addressed the girl and she flinched. "Orange juice? he suggested, softer to her. "Coke? Or there's ginger ale of course. Taste's quite nice with some lemon in it."

Jenny swallowed and said "Coke," in a controlled voice. "Please," she added.

Manny fetched it from the fridge with a beer for himself and took the time to get his thoughts back into order. After the Women's Service League meeting he'd asked around and learned Katie Frank wrote a column under the pen-name Sybil in a feminist magazine, organised rallies and attacked anything she regarded as evidence of male domination. While he was surprised he had not heard about these activities, it seemed it was just one of those things. What he hadn't been able to learn was why she would be going to prison.

Perhaps he was going to find out, as soon as she got round to explaining what she and her teenage companion were doing in his apartment.

"This is all a bit difficult," Katie stated when they had glasses in their hands and were supposed to be more relaxed. "I thought I could handle it more easily."

"Handle what?" Manny asked, struggling to sound reasonable.

"Coming to see you like this, with Jenny. Take your hat off, Jen."

Manny looked at Jenny for an explanation and saw it the instant before she spoke. The hat came away and revealed the red hair, green eyes and wispy ginger eyebrows familiar from every mirror that he had ever stood in front of.

"You're my father," the girl said as toughly as her fear of rejection allowed.

He didn't bother to deny it. Couldn't when his features and his father's stared back at him, accusing and beseeching. He gaped at her and back at Katie and back at her, his eyes out of focus and his lips apart in the rictus of an unasked question. What was he supposed to do? Hug her? Rush forward and take her in his arms and tell her that he loved her despite the fact that he hadn't known she existed?

"Hurhuh!" he gave a nervous half laugh and stopped. Her eyes still bore into him, waiting to be wanted or rejected, to be judged. He had to say the right thing.

"Sorry I gave you the wishy washy eyebrows," he said.

"The rest's all right, don't you think?" It was stupid. He knew as soon as he said it. The grin his lips tried to give birth to was so weak he let it die. "You her mother?" he asked Katie, trying to regain ground he had lost.

"Of course I am. What else would we be doing here?" She sounded more combative now, partly he suspected to protect the girl and partly because she was over the hurdle of revealing her existence.

"I haven't got the slight idea," he retorted with aggression of his own. "I suppose she was born after you left me."

"Obviously, or you'd know about her, wouldn't you?"

Suddenly Manny was angry. He straightened up his body and his face, his back and his mouth both becoming rigid. "You turn up on my doorstep, park your bloody car where I can't get in, break into my home and tell me I've got a daughter I don't know anything about. None of it's bloody obvious to me."

Katie seemed about to snap back at him with equal venom but fought for control and succeeded. "I didn't want you to know anything about her. I wanted to bring her up myself."

"Eh?" Memory stirred. It was one of the things they'd argued about. God, it was so many years ago. "You were a mad bloody feminist even then," he growled. "I should have remembered that when you turned up at that meeting the other day. Was that how you learned where to find me?"

"No. I went there to see what sort of a person you were

and make a decision."

Jenny must have wanted to meet her father, Manny thought. That was something he would have to deal with after he had got to grips with how he'd been deceived fifteen years before.

"You used to speak garbage about how much better girls would be if they were brought up by their mothers without the influence of men. Your father raped you or something, so you hated all men. I remember now. I wondered why you went out with me, although it explained why you argued with me all the time."

"He didn't rape me." Her answer was tightly controlled as she restrained herself from getting into another argument with him. "I went out with you because I wanted a child and I chose you for the father."

That stopped him again. He swung his gaze to Jenny. She appeared to have lost her nervousness and was watching them as if a drama was being played out before her and she was observing it from the front stalls.

"Don't look at me," their child said. "I can't imagine why she chose you either."

"For fuck's sake." Manny sat down for the first time since he had walked into the apartment.

"You don't have to swear," said the girl. Since he hadn't rejected her she appeared to have assumed the right to claim him and, being a woman, to criticise him.

"I'll swear if I fu..." He stopped. "Yeah. Well, I'm a bit confused by all this. That makes you swear a bit."

"More than usual?" She was being childishly bitchy which was understandable since she was a child and would have inherited the bitchy part from her mother. She hadn't got it from him. He started to tell her that, then stopped. It would be an insane conversation.

He turned back to Katie. Even if it didn't make for any greater likelihood of sanity he felt the ground he could fight on with her was just a little firmer.

"You deliberately got yourself pregnant? By me? To have her?"

He had to look at the girl again. His daughter. His mind couldn't grasp it.

"Well, I didn't know for sure it was going to be a girl but of course that was what I wanted," Katie answered, also looking at Jenny. Her expression was soft and loving, a mother's look. He had no idea what a father's look should be like. Not the inane expression he had on his face.

"I decided on having a baby, but I didn't want to get married," Katie continued. "I didn't fancy being artificially inseminated so I looked for a moderately reasonable man to have sex with and get pregnant. I found you. The only problem was you being Jewish."

"I'm not Jewish."

He had poleaxed her. Eyes popped. Jenny giggled.

"Never have been. What made you think that?"

"Your name. Emmanuel Youngman. That's Jewish."

"Emmanuel might be. My name's Robert."

"Robert?"

"Manny's a nickname I got when I was a kid. From the Youngman."

She frowned, then exclaimed with obvious clear recollection, "You're circumcised."

Jenny giggled again and turned her gaze to his flies.

In spite of himself Manny blushed. "Lots of men are. You don't have to be Jewish."

Suddenly Katie saw the joke and laughed at herself– and him. "Anyway," she said between giggles, "It didn't matter. My baby wouldn't be Jewish because it's passed down through the mother. You could still be the father and I wanted her to be like you in some ways. I never thought about the baby having your features, especially when it was a girl. I thought a girl would be like me. I got that wrong too, didn't I?" Another brittle laugh.

Manny didn't laugh back. He was still trying to wrap his thoughts round something solid. "What ways? You said you wanted her to be like me in other ways."

"Strength. Character. You knew where you were going, or seemed to. Had firm views about things, though I didn't agree with some of them. You were healthy. I figured your genes were good. I hadn't met your father."

She had this habit of saying things that left his brain grasping for something to hang on to, like someone thrown off the back of a speeding boat.

"What's my Dad got to do with it?"

"Weak. You got your looks from him but you must have got your strength from your mother."

Dad could seem weak if you didn't know him too well and Mum, well, strong was an inadequate word for her. Overpowering, domineering, combative, belligerent, nagging, bossy and bloody-minded were all appropriate, as well as loyal, good-hearted and loving. Manny didn't think any of her aggressive attributes could be applied to him.

"I decided it was going to be you when I saw you staring at me," she was explaining. "Bloody man, I thought. Can't keep his eyes off my boobs. Then I saw you were looking at my face. So I chose you."

Manny would take odds it was the breasts he noticed before her face. "I don't remember it," he said.

"No, don't suppose you do. Once I'd decided, I got you to take me out."

"How did you do that?" He was interested. It had never occurred to him that any woman had set out to lure him into a date. It always seemed as if he had to do all the work.

"Oh, there are ways," she said off-handedly, keeping him ignorant. "Anyway, you did. Took you a long time to get me pregnant. I had to hang around with you longer than I meant to."

Thanks for nothing, he thought. Still, she could be right. It made him think about a few other women he could have got pregnant. Luck, he'd thought at the time. There was one who thought she was pregnant and turned out not to be. He'd got as far as almost talking himself into marrying her. Christ. Maybe he was sterile. Well, no, he couldn't be because there was Jenny. That meant... For God's sake.

This woman had him worrying that he wasn't firing on all cylinders.

"What about the pill?" he attacked back in self-defense. "It sometimes takes a while when you come off it."

"Crap," she said. "That had nothing to do with it."

"Oh," he said, thinking he understood. "Was that when you met my Dad and decided our genes could be too weak for your needs?"

"Nearly gave up on you."

"But I snuck one in there anyway, did I?" He grinned, then looked apologetically across at Jenny who tried to appear as if what he had said had nothing to do with her. When he turned his gaze back to Katie she was giving him a thin smile to tell him how coarse and pathetic that remark had been.

"We hadn't been getting on anyway. I discovered too late you were a typical chauvinistic male and wouldn't listen to a word of sense."

He wasn't taking that. "Which, of course, was every gem of wisdom that dribbled out between your lips."

She glowered at him. "I'm beginning to think coming to you was a mistake."

Manny stared back at her and let her think it. "Could be. Since I still don't know why you're here."

He could tell she was frustrated. She wanted to argue with him and again something was stopping her.

"Why don't you tell me what you came for?" Then shove off, he felt like adding. Instead he demanded, having just thought of it, "You're not after me for money? Not after all this time?"

"It's Jenny."

He'd gathered that. She was his daughter. Okay. So what? Did Jenny need money?

"Can you have her for a while?"

He was aware of the girl again, trying not to appear hurt, not to be hurt. Being judged. Hell, this had to be a lot worse for her than his first day in that school, or going for that job that he'd got anyway. Katie had no right to put her daughter through this. Or him. The girl shouldn't be there while they talked about her.

"I have to go to prison."

Manny had forgotten about that. "Prison?" he responded.

"Yes."

"What did you do?"

She hesitated, glanced at Jenny, and said, "I threw a bomb in a men's toilet."

That was it. Over the top. Far too much. Manny began laughing.

After a while he controlled himself.

"She threw a bomb in a men's toilet?" He addressed the question to Jenny as if she would share his mirth. His daughter stared back at him and said nothing.

"It was a fake," Katie asserted, "not a real bomb. The men who were injured did it themselves trying to get out. They charged me with assault causing injury and I'll have to go to prison."

"Yes, I imagine you will." Manny erupted into laughter again and took another minute to bring it under control. "Sorry." He looked at the girl and her mother. "Why me?"

"Because I was worried they would put her in a detention centre, especially after the other time."

"The other time? You've been in trouble before? Another bomb in a men's toilet?"

She nodded and shook her head at the same time. "Yes we have and no it wasn't. We nailed up the door."

"The door of the men's toilet?"

"No. The men's club. The front door. The toilet was there too. In the club. They won't let women in."

"No, they wouldn't. Not in a men's toilet."

She bit her lip.

The part of his brain that was not worrying about what he would do with a daughter was enjoying this.

"You were angry because they wouldn't let women in the men's club," he prompted.

She nodded.

"And you nailed up the front door of the club so men couldn't get in either?"

Another nod.

"They let you off that time with just a warning?"

Another nod.

"And this time you go to prison."

"They're all men," Jenny interjected with a venom that caught Manny by surprise. He had considered her out of this part of the conversation. "The police, the lawyers, they're all men. Half the members of the club were their friends. Not that it makes any difference. They had it in for us right from the start. Pigs."

"Umm," said Manny. He couldn't mock Jenny the way he could Katie. "A bomb's a bit serious, you know, whether it goes off or not," he said to her. "People did get hurt."

"Wish it had been real," said his daughter. "Blow a few penises off. That'd be no loss to the world."

He wasn't even shocked. It was on a par with the rest of the evening's madness.

"So. Can you have her?" Katie smiled at what Jenny had said, raised her eyebrows at Manny and shrugged her shoulders as if this new insight must convince him she was what he had always wanted in a daughter.

"Let me get this right," he said. "She won't be put in a detention centre if she stays with me? Why? She wasn't…" Realisation dawned and he glared at the girl. "You were there."

She nodded, not looking as shamefaced as he could have hoped for.

"You should have seen…" she began brightly. Katie shushed her and she stopped, turning away again towards the books.

"Okay," Manny said. "I can understand that. So they won't charge her as an accessory."

Katie gave a little shrug which seemed to mean yes.

"Why me? I don't even know her."

"I didn't tell them that."

He took that on board with the rest. It seemed to make sense.

"How long will you be in prison?"

"My lawyer thinks six months. Perhaps only four."

"You haven't been tried yet?"

"No. But I'm pleading guilty."

"Why?"

"I did it."

"When's your trial?"

"Tomorrow."

Another punch to the stomach. He stared back at her in horror. "You left it all a bit to the last minute."

"Yes. I should have come to see you earlier." She hesitated. "I still wasn't sure after I saw you at that meeting. I was hoping there would be some other way."

"Didn't you like what you saw? Is that why you left in a hurry?"

She shrugged. "Quite the contrary. I decided I did like you, as a person, even if I didn't like your ideas. I didn't go there to confront you, just to observe, and it was silly of me to be drawn into the debate. Suddenly I realised how stupid it was, so I stopped."

"But you still weren't sure?"

"Not entirely. I think I was also putting off making the decision because I didn't want there to be a time when Jenny was still with me and you knew about her. It would have been more awkward."

He could see that. The logical part of his brain still functioned, and appreciated that she had had a very difficult decision to make.

"What do you think about it?" he asked Jenny.

"Being stuck with a man or put into a detention centre. Some choice." She tried to look aggressive and failed. Her face sagged and she scowled at the floor.

"Yes, I can see that," he told her, and then, as he realised how small and timid she now appeared, he at last thought to ask "How old are you?"

"Fifteen," Jenny almost whispered. "And eight months."

That was something he would have known if he had been around at the time. That and a lot of other things.

"All right," he heard his mouth say. "She can come and stay with me after the trial."

He thought that was the end of it, which proved to be another mistake.

"I'd like her to stay now," Katie murmured.

"Now?"

"I'm sorry. I know I've left it late. It's just that I'm going to be in court tomorrow and I may not be coming home afterwards. Her things are in the car."

Chapter 3

He heard her sobbing in the night. Twice he stood in the dark outside the door of what used to be his spare bedroom and was now his daughter's. He didn't go in, having no idea what to say, and her sobs had a stifled sound as if she didn't want him to hear them. She stopped eventually. He lay awake for the rest of the night.

He had a daughter. There was softness in him, deep down, unlike any feeling he had ever had. Was this what every man felt when his first child come into the world? While Jenny wasn't newborn, her arrival had been a birth of sorts for him and for these feelings he was experiencing.

What was going to happen now? How would he relate to her, she to him? How would they spend their time together? Should he buy her things, take her places, introduce him to his friends, to his mother and father?

What was Mum going to say? He knew what Dad's reaction would be, and that thought brought another, more familiar soft feeling. For all Dad's faults, weaknesses Katie would say, there was never any doubt about his inner feelings.

These thoughts spun in the darkness between his face and the ceiling, repeating themselves, taking different forms while providing no answers. The sound of his alarm clock was a relief, promising routine daily activities he knew how to handle.

As soon as he got out of bed he knew the promise had

been broken. Nothing could be routine anymore. At least not for the next six months. For a start, he couldn't stroll naked to his bathroom.

He got dressed, hesitating over the colour of his socks and whether they matched his shirt. He had no idea what Jenny liked or didn't like but it seemed important to make the right impression.

The bathroom door was closed. He always left it open. He called, "Good morning. Have a good sleep?" and made it bright and cheerful to show that having instant daughter for breakfast was as non-threatening as having instant coffee. "I'm putting on coffee. Do you fancy some and what else would you like for breakfast? Are you a corn flakes person, bacon and eggs or just toast? Jam or marmalade?" Breakfast preferences were one of a thousand things he had to learn.

His cordless kettle was already grumbling when he realised there had been no answer from the bathroom. Returning to the door he knocked hesitantly, producing only a rattle from the loose handle on the inside.

"Jenny?" He could see her shadow through the opaque stippled glass. No movement. "How long are you going to be?" Lightly. A question, not a demand. "We'll have to leave soon."

Katie had asked him to drive Jenny to school as she did every day. "I want to keep everything as normal for her as possible," she had said, and that was a complete nonsense. How could anything be normal anymore? Yet he would try. He had made that promise to her, meaning it for his daughter. She was the innocent victim in this. Whatever else happened he was going to try and make it easy for her.

He would make sure she arrived at school at the usual time and he would return at lunchtime so that they could ring Katie's lawyer to hear what had happened in court. Jenny was not allowed to take her mobile phone into school.

"Not long," a small, timid voice ventured from behind the bathroom door. The bravado she had displayed the previous evening had ended when Katie left. She snatched up her bag and flew like a frightened bird into the bedroom he pointed out to her. She locked the door and didn't come out when he asked if she wanted some dinner, so he ate alone, with ears straining, trying to interpret the muffled sounds.

"Do you eat breakfast?"

The thought of food seemed to strengthen her spirits and her voice. "Yes, please."

"Cereal, or eggs and stuff? Tea or coffee?"

"Cereal." A pause. "Can I have orange juice?"

"Sure. You like it straight or with water?"

"Water."

"Plain, mineral or soda?"

"Plain."

"Ice in it?"

"Thanks."

Banal yet effective. Communication had been established. He found the cereal and the orange juice, put bread in the toaster for himself and made up his usual industrial strength morning mug of coffee. Small sounds behind him announced that she had entered the kitchen.

"Take any chair you like." He turned to look at her, as casually as he could manage, again aware how much she looked like him. "Why didn't you answer straight away when I knocked on the bathroom door? You're not scared of me?" His joking tone was an attempt to ease the tension. The chair she had taken was as far from him as possible at the other end of the table.

She had on a school uniform. Blue jumper with a yellow stripe around the neck and a grey shirt and skirt. They made her appear younger and somehow less vulnerable. Also less threatening and less attractive.

With no response he continued in a jocular vein. Be friendly. Joke about the weather, his daily routine, the arrangements they would have to make to fit in with each other. Make a game of it.

"Not much for cereal myself but I always keep some in the cupboard. Never know what..." His mouth stopped before he explained that women friends sometimes stayed for breakfast. "...I might feel like one morning."

Despite the poor start he had to keep going. "Sometimes I just scramble out of bed, grab a coffee and run. I'm my own boss and work from home so it doesn't matter if I'm late most mornings. No-one to tell me off, although I do like to be self-disciplined about my work. Keep regular hours, that sort of thing." He was aware he was rambling, filling the silence between them with empty words. The toaster rescued him by rejecting its well-browned contents. He fussed over them while he considered what to say and do next.

He moved half way along the table towards her, closing the gap a little. "I have a feeling you're finding this as difficult as I am. You don't know me and I don't know you but we're stuck with each other." He hoped he was moving closer emotionally as well as physically, although he saw no response to confirm it. "I guess it's a bit like that for every father and daughter. I know our situation is a bit different, but any child is stuck with the parents it gets and any parent with the child or children he or she gets."

"I've never lived in a house with a man." It was said so quietly he almost missed it.

"Never, with a man? Well... I don't suppose it's all that different."

She looked at him as if he had said something silly.

"I know it must be strange," he told her. "The thing is, I'm not any man, I'm your father." He grimaced as he said it, trying to make it less inane than it sounded, and he almost missed the next thing she said as well.

"Some fathers rape their daughters."

"Most fathers don't," he said. "And not all men are bad. There are good people and bad people, or people who do bad things."

She grimaced as if struggling to express something she was not sure of. "If you're a girl you have to be careful with all men. You can't tell straight away which are good ones and which are bad ones."

"Mmm." He remained silent for a beat to give her words the serious consideration he felt she needed. "I can see it is a problem for you and I'll try to bear it in mind. I hope you'll find I'm one of the good ones."

She finished her cereal and looked up at him instead of down at her plate. "Could you hear me last night?" Her voice was still very quiet.

"No," he lied. "What were you doing?"

"Nothing."

He tried to read her face but she lifted her glass in front of it to drink her orange juice. Perhaps he had missed an opportunity. If she knew he had heard her she might admit she was crying and open up a bit more about how she was feeling.

"Anything you want to ask me?" he suggested. "You must have a lot of questions. Who I am, what I do? My parents? They're your grandparents. Knowing that sort of thing might help you to get to know me a bit better."

She hesitated. "I am interested in all that, of course. Do you mind if I ask you something else first?" There was a firmer note in her voice now and she was speaking almost at a normal level.

"Not at all. Ask away."

"Is having me going to be a problem for you?"

He shook his head although he was not sure if that was true. It could depend on a lot of things.

"I mean, do you want me around? I don't want to be in your way."

"Well, I'm going to have to make some adjustments. That's okay. I also don't know much about you, you know."

"Do you like me?"

Another question he should have prepared an answer for. If he simply said yes it would sound trite. "I like everything I've seen so far," he said. "You seem bright, intelligent. A nice person." He was going to say 'and you've got my good looks' but decided that was too flippant. It was like walking on a slippery slope, each step a potential stumble. "I've never lived in a house with a daughter," he added. "I think we're going to get along well together."

She nodded as if satisfied and he felt a shift in the air between them as if she had moved closer.

"I'll need a note for school. Telling them I'm living here for a while. Katie was going to write it but she forgot."

"You don't call her Mum?"

"Just Katie. Do you want me to call you Dad?"

"Hadn't thought about it. Up to you."

She shook her head as if she hadn't made up her mind.

"A note." He took up a sheet of paper headed with his name and phone number and a new thought occurred to him. "What's your surname?"

"Frank, of course."

He felt cheated. "Do I need to explain that in the note? Why we've got different names."

"No, I'll explain. Could you just say I will be staying

with you for a short time while my mother is away?"

"Who do I address it to, the headmaster?" For a moment there was a flash of something in her eyes. Again he had the feeling there had been a shift in the air between them, except that this time she had drawn back. He saw his mistake. "Or is it headmistress?"

She nodded but her eyes remained narrowed.

"Glad I checked," he lied. "Best to get these things right. Dear Headmistress. What do I say next?"

A few minutes later he shut his front door and followed his new daughter down his front steps. His car was now parked in its rightful place and its doors clicked as they should when he pressed the remote switch on his key ring. He was starting to feel confident after what had been a shaky start. He had everything under control. He was in tune with what she was thinking, ready to be reasonable yet firm, acting like any normal father would. He was doing fine. It was all going to work out.

An hour later his best friend told him how wrong he was.

Chapter 4

"You're mad. There is no way it's going to be that easy," Tony McKendry countered when Manny expressed his confidence over mid-morning coffee in the café on the ground floor of the converted former hotel where NEMSA held its meetings.

He had met Tony ten years before when he had employed his company to build the apartments in which he now lived. The discovery that Tony had similar feelings about feminism and the changing role of men had led to the creation of NEMSA and a close personal relationship.

"You're going to be dealing with a volatile mix of emotions," his friend said. "This girl's a teenager trying to be an adult and that's bad enough to start with. On top of that she doesn't know if she's supposed to be loyal to her mother, feeling guilty because she's not going to prison with her, worried what her friends are going to say, unsure how to relate to a father she knew nothing about and scared shitless what is going to happen to her. Whatever she says or does, she's a young kid defending herself against threats and feelings she's never experienced before. She's a time bomb waiting to go off."

Manny laughed in an attempt to sound confident. "How can you say that? You haven't met her."

"I don't need to. I've got two daughters and six nieces and I grew up with sisters. I know, believe me. You were an only son. You even have girl cousins?"

Manny shook his head.

"Well then. You've got no idea."

Manny thought he had. "We're getting along very well," he said. "I know those things must be making her a little edgy but I can handle it."

"The edge she's standing on is the edge of a precipice. You think you can stop her falling off? Her mother's put you in a dangerous situation, for you and for the girl. Do you have to take her in? You didn't even know about her."

Manny was uneasy at Tony's strong words. "I know about her now."

"That doesn't mean you've got responsibility for her."

"I think it does."

"Ah…" Tony looked deep into his coffee mug as if it might tell him the future. "What's she like?"

When he tried to describe Jenny, Manny realized he didn't have a lot to go on. He could repeat some of the things she had said, some of the things she had done, the way she had held her head and stared into her cornflakes, and he could add generalities like "intelligent", "confident", "knows her own mind" and "nice". None of them did justice to what he felt. She was like a new part that had grown onto him and he knew of no way to describe that feeling.

"It's like it's just my job to look after her," seemed to be the next best way of explaining it as an image of his father came into his mind and he experienced a reassuring echo of generations of ancestors having said and felt the same thing.

"Until her mother takes her back," Tony reminded him. "What are you going to do after that?"

"Keep on seeing her and getting to know her more. I'm only worried Katie may not want me to see her again afterwards. She doesn't like men much." This was a doubt that had begun to nag at the back of his mind, around where he had stored questions about why Katie had sent Jenny to him. None of that quite made sense.

"Must have liked you fifteen years ago," Tony responded, grinning.

"Only for what she wanted out of me. What do you think of that? Going out with a man to get his sperm?"

"She had no right. In fact, it's a deprivation of your rights." Tony spoke half-seriously and laughed. "What if you went to the police? Reckon they'd charge her with theft?"

"Bit hard to show them the evidence," Manny grinned back, falling into a comedy act they often played. "Whip out the old fellow and say 'Here your honour, I tender Exhibit A, the receptacle from which the aforesaid items were stolen'. That should cause a bit of a stir. The charge could be carrying an implement suspected of being intended for use in a robbery, to whit, one vagina. We could charge every woman in the world with that one."

Tony spluttered into his coffee. "The only way they could prove lack of intent was if they'd had a hysterectomy, or were on the pill, or carried a condom in their purse." He pulled a comically sour face. "Trouble is most of them already do, now it's all safe sex. Sorry, Manny. I don't think we can bring a class action here. Just have to be satisfied with putting your ex-girlfriend behind bars a bit longer."

"I mightn't mind that." Manny stopped laughing. "I'd get to have Jenny longer. Give me more time to get to know her."

Tony also became serious. "Have you thought about going to the courts, getting some sort of access arrangement?"

Manny shook his head. "Hardly the way to have a good relationship with your daughter, would it, dragging her and her mother into court? That's what they came to me for, to keep her out of one. Maybe if I can establish a good relationship with her during the time I've got, it won't matter what Katie says. Jenny'll want to see me and there won't be too much Katie can do about it."

"I'd still get legal advice. Talk to Neil Blighton." Neil was a NEMSA member and a lawyer who did a lot of work for the association and for individual members. It was good advice. Manny told himself he would take it when the opportunity arose.

They were silent for a time. Usually they'd be casting an eye round the coffee shop, noting who else was there, what was going on. This time they were both reflective.

"So how do you feel about it?" Tony asked.

"Not sure. I want to do the right thing by her. I'm just not sure what it is."

Tony examined what was left of his coffee. "No man

knows what the right thing is for his children and you've got even less chance, not having seen what she was like as she was growing up. You're not going to get far trying to be what you think a traditional father should be because it's something that grows on you, not something you can learn in a crash course." He smiled. "In some ways you're going to have to be a real new era man."

While he said it almost as a joke, Manny saw he had hit the nail on the head.

"You're right," he exclaimed, punching Tony lightly on the shoulder. "God, I've spouted it out enough to all these meetings I talk to, you'd think I'd see it straight away. I keep saying men have to find a new role for themselves, to break away from the old models, and here I have that opportunity."

When he left the coffee shop the confidence and enthusiasm he had walked in with were back in abundance. It was going to work.

Chapter 5

Manny stepped from a glass lift which had brought him up though a multi-layered building and crossed in front of a large window facing out onto a roof-top garden. As always when he came there, he stood for several seconds and enjoyed the feeling of spaciousness and energy he had created for one of his biggest clients, Claire O'Connell. This was what being an architect was about, the creation of something unique and beautiful while at the same time functional.

In its own way, the garden's mix of trees, shrubs and groundcovers mirrored the building beneath it in which split-level spaces with mezzanines and atriums opened out onto each other, creating an open, breathing organism filled with light and life. The garden was where Claire brought her visitors to impress and relax them, where she held staff meetings on days when the weather allowed it, where her staff took breaks and unwound between projects, and where inspiration for new projects was born and nurtured. He would bring Jenny here soon, Manny promised himself as he walked along to Claire's office. It would tell her more than words what he did and the sort of world he worked in.

Claire O'Connell was a planning consultant who became tired of clients' conservative ideas and turned developer in her own right. Manny admired the way she was hands-on with her projects and worked face to face with her consultants and contractors, in which he had a favoured place as someone who spoke her language and could match her with innovative ideas and ways of achieving them.

Listening to her thoughts on their latest project as they sat in front of a wall screen on which his drawings were projected, his imagination began to layer ideas onto hers. They spent the next two hours deep in discussion until an assistant came in to remind Claire it was after twelve and she had a lunch appointment.

"I'll keep going," Manny told her. "There are some things I…" His mind registered the time the assistant had said. "Shit! I've got to meet my daughter." The explanation came out so naturally that he didn't think about its implications until he saw the question in Claire's eyes. "I'll explain later." He left her office, sprinted past the garden window and stabbed at the button for the lift to hurry up from the ground level. Claire must be thinking he was either mad or lying. He was half turning to rush back and explain when an image of Jenny standing at the school gate pushed everything else out of his mind. The lift doors opened and he stepped inside.

Jenny was not standing at the school gate. She sat slumped on the footpath with her back against one of the gate pillars, tears streaming down her face. His reaction was so intense he nearly drove the car onto the footpath. Something kicked in just in time to enable him to bring it to a more controlled halt, but the motor was still slowing down as he threw open the door and stumbled out.

"What's happened? What's wrong?"

The eyes that looked up at him seemed hollow and sunken in a face wet with tears, but it was the expression of despair that grabbed at him most. He directed his gaze up and down the footpath and through the mesh fence into the school grounds. There were children everywhere, laughing, walking or running together, continuing their lives as if one of them were not sitting here, desolate and alone, crying. What sort of heartless creatures were they?

What did he do now? If it were a young girl he didn't know he would call for help. Physical contact would be invasive and dangerous. What would a father do? Reach down and pick her up? Offer her a tissue to wipe her face?

He sat down beside her, ignoring the litter of chocolate wrappers, screwed up pieces of paper and other detritus in the dusty strip between the edge of the concrete footpath and the fence. "Sorry I'm late. I'm here now."

"Nine months!" Jenny erupted in a wail of hurt and anguish. She turned into him and buried her face in his shoulder. Through the folds of his jacket sleeve he could hear her sobbing more words and felt the despair radiating out of her.

He curled his arm around her shoulders and pulled her close. Immediately she tensed. Too soon. Too intimate. A tissue was a better idea after all. He unfolded one from the handypack he kept in his pocket and she took it with gratitude, pulling back from him to blow her nose and wipe at her eyes. He handed her another.

"How did you find out?" Her phone was in his pocket.

He had felt it when he was bringing out the tissues.

"Betty had her phone."

A small group of girls some distance away were giving them sidelong glances while talking animatedly. He nodded towards them. "Why didn't they stay with you?"

"I told them to go away. I didn't want them to see me crying."

She seemed a little calmer. The tissues had been a good move but he had liked the feel of her pressed against his shoulder, even if it was too close too soon. He hoped there would come a time in the future when putting his arm around her would be natural.

"Who did you ring to find out?" He was keeping his tone conversational, trying to continue the calming process.

"Chloe. She's Mum's lawyer."

He didn't ask how she got the number. All it would take was a call to directory enquiries if she didn't know it already.

"You must have known it was likely."

"I know." She said it dejectedly, not trying to deny it. "I thought… maybe…"

"Maybe only four months?" he suggested. "Katie seemed to think it wouldn't be more than six."

For a moment it seemed she would crumple again. Manny's heart contracted. "She'll be okay," he said, knowing it was meaningless. "You will too. It will turn out all right."

Jenny shook her head as if he didn't understand. "She's

there all alone in that horrible place and I won't even be able to see her."

"You can visit her, can't you? Visitors are allowed."

Another shake of the head. "She doesn't want me to."

Manny felt he was getting into deeper water. Katie hadn't mentioned not visiting the prison, or a lot of other things. He hadn't been given the complete instruction manual.

"Well, look on the bright side. You and I have got nine months in which to get to know each other," he suggested, doubting the wisdom of the words even as they emerged.

She blinked at him uncertainly, as if part of her expected never to see the bright side of anything again.

"Do you want to go back to school now?" he asked to keep the conversation moving and prevent another slump into despair. "Or I could text them and make up some excuse." He held up his own phone. "They already know you're with me instead of your mother so they won't be surprised if there's a change in the normal routine."

She nodded and gave him the school's number. He was careful to text it attention of the headmistress.

"Done. Have you had lunch?"

She shook her head.

"Okay. I have a place I often go. You want to try it?" He got up from his seated position and brushed the dust from his pants. Jenny scrambled to her feet beside him.

"You want to say goodbye to your friends?" He nodded in the direction of the group of girls. Again she shook her head. "Okay, let's go."

As she was getting into his car he sketched a wave in the direction of the girls without being sure why he was doing it. To reassure them Jenny was alright? That he was not some pervert running off with her? For a second he stood beside the car, experiencing a feeling of alienation, of being in an unfamiliar landscape. All he could do was press on and cope with each situation as it came along. So far, he felt, he wasn't doing too badly; it was just that the terrain seemed to have a habit of being unpredictable.

"What classes are you missing, not being at school this afternoon?" he asked as he drove the car towards a place near the river where there were a number of cafes.

"Nothing important." The dejected, defeated tone had returned. She was slumped in the seat staring out of the window.

"All education is important," he told her, determined to stay upbeat. "What are you working towards? Any ideas of going on to university or what sort of career you might go into?"

He felt rather than saw the small shake of her head. Still, that was better than no response at all.

"I can't believe that. A girl as bright as you. You must have plans." Still no reply. He pressed on through the alien territory. "No point having plans with your Mum in prison, is that it? I doubt she'd want you to think like that. In any case, telling me about them isn't making it worse for her. She'll survive better in there if she thinks you're getting on with your life and not moping about her."

It was a long speech but it seemed to work. He saw her glance across at him and she pulled her body more upright on the seat.

"Literature first period. After that maths and science."

"Sounds like a good academic sort of programme. So what do you want to be?"

He could feel her wriggling, as if she was fighting with herself, making up her mind how to react to the pressure he was putting on her to come out of her dark mood.

"I'd like to be a writer," she said after a silence, "but Mum says I'll need some other job as well, in case the writing doesn't work."

"Sounds like good advice." She had called Katie 'Mum' a few times now. He wondered why she had insisted before that she always called her Katie. Still, that was not important. He had to keep this conversation going. "So if you want to be a writer, I guess literature is your favourite subject."

She nodded.

"Who are your favourite authors?"

She seemed to brighten and he had the oddest feeling that he had thrown her a lifeline she could hold onto.

"Margaret Attwood, Virginia Woolf, Simone De Beauvoir. Germaine Greer, of course, and Eve Ensler, and Jessica Velenti." She stared out of the window as she had been doing before but her mood was different now. He sensed she was waiting for his reaction. There had been another of those shifts he continually felt occurring in the balance between them.

The writers she had listed were all women, which was understandable. They would be at the top of any list of popular feminist literature. So, her choices or Katie's?

"The Vagina Monologues and Full Frontal Feminism don't sound like the kind of thing you'd be studying in a literature class," he commented as if seriously considering the possibility. "The Female Eunuch maybe and some of Virginia Woolf. Which of hers have you read?"

Without taking his eyes from his driving he knew hers had shifted back to him. He had the impression they showed surprise. She hadn't expected him to know the names, let alone what each one had written. After a pause she answered hesitantly "To The Lighthouse".

"Ah, well, that is a classic. Written before A Room Of Her Own made her famous. However, I suppose you know that. It won the Femina Vie Heureuse prize."

Jenny was silent, again staring out of the window. Had he been too clever? What was he trying to prove, showing he knew more about feminist literature than she was likely to?

"I was thinking Jane Austen and the Brontes would have been more likely in a literature course, which probably only shows how out of date I am," he added to water down the effect he might be having. "I imagine schools like to offer a more varied diet of reading these days."

There was another silence and Jenny said, "Mr James,

our literature teacher, is more old-fashioned even than that. He wouldn't know those books like you do. I keep telling him that there is a feminist interpretation of literature which is more valid than the traditional male distortion of reality."

She waited, as if expecting an immediate response. Manny remained silent. No time to be clever now. Undoubtedly Katie's words. Even the intonation of her voice had changed.

"I can't even get him to recognise that what he calls classical literature is written in sexist language. Like you say, he quotes Jane Austen and the Bronte sisters. Austen was besotted by men and lived in a male-dominated society. Even when her heroines are being strong it's in terms of their relationships with men, not themselves. Their attitudes to their sisters are all male-oriented. Charlotte Bronte had to get published under a man's name at first. As for Emily Bronte! Kathy is a freak and Heathcliffe is the arch-typical male chauvinist pig, even if he is ill-treated by other men. Her chasing after him, calling out his name. It's sick-making. Him flouncing around sulking and being difficult. That scene where their bodies crumple together in the grave. That's what all men want, to totally absorb women so that we have no identity of our own."

Spoken with poise and self-confidence. Impressive in its own way. He didn't care if she was quoting her mother. Perhaps she was compensating for Katie being in prison, standing up for her and arguing the case she was unable to present herself. Whatever it was, she wasn't in a slough of despair anymore. He intended to keep it that way.

"What other classes have you got today?"

"Maths and history."

"Maths was one of my best subjects. You need it in architecture."

The response was a noise that sounded like "Hmpth!" followed by a pause. "Maths is full of sexist language. You can just tell it's been written by men. What sort of examples do they give you? If it takes ten men three days to dig a hole, how long will it take three men to dig ten holes? Men, and they're digging the holes. Not women."

Damn. He'd hoped she'd express an interest in architecture, ask him more about what he did, but Katie was still not so far away.

"All the examples are like that," she continued. "Nuts and bolts, pistons, mechanical things, men things. Not women things. Why don't they ask if there are 100 calories in three packets of cornflakes how many calories are there in ten packets?"

"Are calories and cornflakes women things?"

"Of course."

Weighing his next words, and almost deciding against them, he continued, "If men and women are equal, should girls mind examples with nuts and bolts in them?"

"Well..."

As he'd expected she was less sure of her argument now. She had strayed into thoughts of her own, away from the well-learned lessons of her mother. He needed to find a balance between sounding too clever and steering her into more thinking for herself.

"I can see your problem," he said in a tone he hoped would be encouraging. "You're right that most people would think nuts and bolts are men's things, so when girls do maths with those sorts of examples in it they might think it's not for them. What you're saying is there should be a mixture of all sorts of examples, nuts and bolts and calories."

"Exactly." She sounded relieved, and surprised to be agreeing with him.

"Better still, they could count non-sexist things, like bananas," he suggested.

She grinned. "Or they could dig small holes, in gardens, to plant roses."

They both laughed at the absurd turn their conversation had taken and, as he drove on, Manny allowed himself to believe that somehow they were finding their stumbling way into the beginnings of a relationship.

Okay, so it was alien territory and he had no doubt there was more to come. Before it did he needed to find out a little more about what had happened so far. Why had Katie been given a longer sentence than had been expected, why did Jenny think it was her fault and why wasn't Katie allowing her to visit the prison?

Chapter 6

Manny discarded the idea of a bistro and took Jenny to a café that offered crumbed chicken, cheese sausages, pies, pasties and sausage rolls. It seemed more appropriate for a girl in school uniform. He suspected she would not have felt comfortable in a place where most of the other females were dressed in designer clothes. Another missing page in the instruction manual.

He ordered a steak burger and took a bottle of tomato juice to go with it, asking Jenny what she wanted. It turned out to be a hamburger, her preferred drink being a banana smoothie. Now he was learning more about her, he told himself, only a little mockingly.

After they sat down at a table near the window, she sipped on the smoothie and examined him over the top of the glass. He tried to read her expression. The tears for her mother's plight seemed to have dried up. Was she sad, scared, lost? What had happened to the smart-assed girl who spouted feminist literature and derided maths for being misogynistic? Tony had been right, she must be on a roller coaster of emotions, trying to adapt to each new situation as it confronted her. In one day she had woken in a strange apartment, had breakfast with a father she didn't know, gone to school knowing her mother was going to court, learned the details of her mother's sentence, and held up her end in a strained discussion about what she did at school. How did he expect to know how she was feeling when he had no idea how he would feel in the same situation?

There was one way to find out. "Penny for them," he said.

She was puzzled. He could read that expression.

"Penny for your thoughts. It's an old saying, from the days when there were pennies and pounds instead of cents and dollars."

"Oh." Taking her mouth from the straw she examined the other people in the café. "It's weird being with you like this."

He waited for her to expand on that.

"Being with a man. It's very different."

"In what way?"

"Lots of ways. I'm not sure. The way I feel. The way people look at me." She took another sip from her smoothie. "It's like they're thinking 'there's a girl having lunch with her Dad'."

"What's so strange about that?"

"It's strange for me. It's not the same as going somewhere for lunch with Mum." The thought brought a frown to her face and a tear formed in the corner of her eye.

He responded quickly to wipe them both away. "I wonder if people are thinking I'm a Dad having lunch with my daughter? I hope so. Makes me feel good."

She half smiled and took the napkin that had come with her hamburger to do her own job of mopping up the tear.

"We should have badges on our chests," he suggested.

"Mine saying Dad and yours Daughter so that everyone will know."

Now it was a three-quarter smile.

"Your mum will be okay," he told her. "I can understand how you're feeling, and it's natural, but she won't want you to be upset. Eat your hamburger before it gets cold."

Her eyes locked on his for a second. He hoped he could read in them that he had struck a chord somewhere and made a connection. When she dropped her eyes again, took up her hamburger and began eating, he wasn't sure.

"Talk to me," he said. "Tell me about yourself."

"What sorts of things?"

"Everything. What do you want to know about me?"

She considered this for several seconds. "Why do you drink tomato juice? It's gross."

It was an odd beginning, but it was a start. He was soon learning some of the things he might need to know. Lemonade was her favourite drink when she couldn't get a smoothie, or something with crushed ice in it; she preferred Pepsi to Coke and liked it full strength, not one of the low sugar versions; didn't like onions in her hamburgers; thought wedges were much better than chips; and didn't like any fish that was not disguised in batter. She had been a vegetarian for a brief period after they had been shown a video at school about how meat was prepared, and thought the Japanese should stop killing whales and they shouldn't send Australian animals like sheep and cows overseas if they were going to be mistreated when they got there. And they shouldn't mistreat the boat people when they came. That didn't mean they had to accept them, but they didn't have to be so horrible to them.

Manny listened in fascination. This was important information he needed to store away and weave into the fabric of their relationship. Other fathers assimilated this over years. He had nine months.

It wasn't going to be enough. His working and his social schedules were already laid out. He had clients to meet, projects to work on, NEMSA meetings to attend, talks to give, friends to visit. How and where was he going to fit in establishing a relationship with a teenage daughter? She might be expecting him at school functions, to take her to and from sports activities, to her friends' houses. He had to explain her to his friends and work colleagues, to his mother and father. His mind almost snap-froze as he tried to imagine explaining to his mother that she had a grand-daughter. A more immediate question entered his mind. What was he going to do with her for the rest of that afternoon? He hadn't thought of that when he suggested she take time off school.

Explaining to Jenny that he had to call on a client, he led her out of the café to his car and drove to Claire O'Connell's office. Claire was expecting an explanation and Jenny would be distracted. She would see something of the work he did and a lot more than that. He could score multiple goals with one kick.

He didn't go into the underground car park for which he

had a permit. Instead, he stopped some distance away from the building and invited Jenny to walk with him towards it. As he was expecting, she stopped at a place where the building could be seen in its full magnificence and gazed up at it in awe. The O'Connell Building was no phallic tower punching a hole above the city skyline. It was a flowing building of curves and openings designed to draw the eyes to its component parts more than to its overall massiveness and dimensions. He had spent many long hours studying designs considered masculine or feminine, avoiding hard angular shapes and instead seeking something which suggested power without strength and heaviness.

"What a beautiful building," Jenny said after a long examination. "It flows, doesn't it? I'm not sure if it's upwards like a flame, or downwards like a waterfall."

Manny glanced at her in surprise. She could not have known that thoughts similar to that had been part of his design process, a conflict he had sought to resolve with an impression of two-way power transmission, like the flow of energy between a woman and the world around her. No-one else had ever recognized that in the building, although Claire herself, who had been its unacknowledged inspiration, had come closest.

They went in through the wide, welcoming entrance and rose in the lift to Claire's floor where they stepped out into the light-filled space in front of the garden window and walked along to the softly luxurious opulence of the office area. Jenny halted again and stared around her in surprise.

"Do you work here?"

"It's not where my office is. That's at home, on the ground floor below the apartment. I come here to see my biggest client and to discuss the projects we're working on. In some ways it is my work, or at least an example of it."

She gave him a puzzled frown, clearly not understanding. He decided not to explain. It would seem like boasting, trying to impress and overpower her with his achievements.

Walking from the lift, they entered a large space containing more than a dozen people at computers. "Administration," he told her. "Drafting rooms and technical areas are at the back, and the surveyors and planners down the corridor. Come and meet my client."

He led her across to the management area where they were greeted by a male assistant. Jenny seemed taken aback, staring in surprise at the man and, as he waved them through into the inner office, at the name Claire O'Connell on a small panel beside the door.

"Hello." Claire rose from behind a small kidney-shaped desk and came round it with a hand outstretched. "Please forgive my rudeness for not knowing your name. It's one of rather a lot of things your father hasn't told me about you."

For an instant Jenny hesitated, seemingly taken aback, trying to decide whether she had to explain his odd behaviour, then she read the smile in Claire's eyes and grinned back at her.

"Jenny Frank," she said, taking the hand being offered.

"That's my mother's surname."

"Rightly so." Claire released Jenny's hand and moved across to a group of comfortable chairs along one wall, folding herself down into one with her long, elegant legs tucked under it, and beckoning her companions to join her. She was a tall woman with a strong face and an air of quiet authority. No-one had ever called her beautiful but everyone said she had class.

"I sometimes wish my children were Whittakers," she said. "That's the surname I was born with, but I took my husband's name and it was too complicated to change it after the divorce as I was already in business. I've got four children. Mack is nineteen, Dallas sixteen, Tony thirteen and Tina eleven. Dallas works here, doing her Certificate 3 in Business Administration. You may meet Tony and Tina later because they're coming after school and we're all going out together. We don't see much of Mack because he's at university and busy living his own life."

Manny admired the way she chatted so easily, putting Jenny at her ease. He knew she had also used the time to take in Jenny's appearance, noting the obvious resemblances and making other assessments as well. Claire was a shrewd judge of character.

"So that's my family. What about you?" Claire asked. "I know you have never lived with Manny or he would have told me. Am I right in guessing you have only just met?"

Jenny was staring out of the huge window that made up

the wall behind Claire's desk, providing a panoramic view of the city and the river that flowed through it.

"Yes," she answered. "Only yesterday. Last night, actually." She glanced across at Manny as if expecting confirmation.

"Jenny's mother needed someone to take care of her for a short time," Manny explained. "She asked if she could stay at my place."

Claire smiled. "To which you of course agreed. Who wouldn't with such a lovely daughter? I imagine you got a bit of a shock when you found out and now you are absolutely delighted."

Manny speculated on how much Claire had found out in the short time since he had left her. The young man outside her door, if not Claire herself, would have been on the phone to anyone they could think of who might have some answers. She was now observing him expectantly and he realized he had more explaining to do.

"I had to rush off this morning and we hadn't finished what we were discussing," he said. "There are a few details I'd like to firm up on so I needed to come back and see you. I didn't think you would mind if I had Jenny with me. She'll be able to see what I do when I'm at work."

"Not at all," Claire smiled. "However, Jenny might get bored just watching us pore over drawings." She turned to his daughter. "Would you like to see what else we do here?"

Jenny said she would and Claire pressed a button on a

console. A young woman came into the office and Manny was not surprised to see that it was Claire's daughter. He had no thought that it was a coincidence. She had been in the wings, waiting to be called.

"This is Dallas, my daughter I told you about," Claire introduced her. "Dallas, this is Jenny Frank who has just learned that our Manny here is her father and is a bit bewildered by everything. Do you think you could give her the grand tour and show her what we do here while Manny and I discuss some work for a few minutes?"

As Dallas said she would be delighted and came forward to shake Jenny's hand he saw she was uncertain again. The rollercoaster was taking her in yet another direction. "Will you be alright?" he asked. "If all of this is too much I can take you…" he was going to say home, then realized that was not how she would think of it and changed it to "somewhere else".

Jenny drew in a breath and shook her head. "I'll be alright," she said, and followed Dallas out of the office, only briefly looking back at him.

"She will be," Claire reassured him as soon as the door had closed. "As you say, we have work to do. I'd hoped you might bring your daughter when you returned so I asked Dallas to be here because I know they'll get on together. Your daughter's nervous of course. Who wouldn't be? So now, tell me the details."

He did, such as he knew them, and Claire's eyes widened. When he had finished she walked across and stood studying the panorama of the city.

"Her mother must have been faced with a very difficult decision," she said.

"Well, obviously. She knew she was going to prison."

Claire shook her head. "No, it has to be more than that. Think it through Manny. If you were her, would you hand your daughter over to a complete stranger, even if he is her father?"

Manny had to admit he probably wouldn't.

"There must have been alternatives," Claire continued, "Family, friends, even acquaintances if not close friends. Someone Jenny would at least know and feel more comfortable with. Why you, and with all due respect Manny, why a man whose views are contrary to those she presumably has passed on to her daughter? Does Jenny have similar views to her mother?"

"She says things which sound pretty much like they've come from Katie."

"As she would, especially if Katie has forewarned her what your views are. You may have a tricky situation on your hands, have you realized that?"

Manny nodded.

Claire had come back from the window as if she had seen out there whatever it was she was seeking. "If it were me," she said, "I would find out a bit more about the circumstances which led Katie Frank to bring her daughter to you. I think there must be some expectation there, of how it would affect Jenny and how she would relate to you.

Knowing what it is could be a big help in working through what is frankly a very unusual and potentially difficult situation."

Manny felt himself nodding again. This sort of analysis was one of the reasons he had decided earlier to introduce Jenny to Claire O'Connell. She never took anything at face value.

"I'd been thinking something similar without taking it quite as far as that," he admitted. "I guess to some extent I'm still getting over the shock of finding I even have a daughter, let alone examining the circumstances of why it has come about."

"Well, you're lucky in one regard. She seems to be a very nice girl, and intelligent I should say. It should be easier to establish a relationship with her than with a gawky, gum chewing teenager who thinks like everything is awesome, as if, and the latest fourteen year old pop star like has the x factor and is so sexy its absolutely amazing."

She had imitated an exaggerated nasal voice for these last words with the emphasis rising and falling as her eyebrows went up and down. Manny grinned and nodded in appreciation. He was indeed glad Jenny was not like some of the typical teenage girls he had seen around the place. Would he have agreed to take her in if she had been? The answer was probably yes, with a lot more misgivings, and that was saying something. Misgivings were already something he had a lot of.

"If there is anything at all I can do to help you know

you can call me," Claire said. "Any time, Manny. I mean that. Jenny could come and stay at our place if it comes to that, or I could have a woman-to-woman talk to her. Does she have any family or friends?"

"She said something about other kids at school. Nothing specific. Katie didn't mention any family and I don't remember any from when I knew her before."

As he spoke he looked at Claire and around them at her office. He wouldn't be having this conversation with one of his men clients. Although Claire O'Connell might have all the trappings of success, even of power, in a world where that was not all that common, she was still very much a woman.

Half an hour later, when he and Claire had finalized the work they had started that morning, Jenny returned from her tour of the offices and they said their goodbyes.

"Did you really design this place?" Jenny exploded as the lift doors closed and they were alone.

When Manny confessed he had she went on, "Dallas told me, and I couldn't believe it."

"Architects do design buildings."

"Not like this one. What else have you designed?"

"The place where I live. A few other places."

"Does that lady really own this whole place?"

"Claire? Yes. Owns the building. Occupies three floors. Has a staff of about two hundred. Annual turnover around the twenty million mark. That's their own revenues, not the total value of all the projects they handle."

Jenny didn't seem to be able to take it in.

"Did she inherit it?"

"Not at all. Studied as a town planner and worked for a firm for a couple of years until she set up on her own. Started with a few small projects and grew it from there."

By the time the lift reached the ground floor, Jenny seemed to have assimilated that and was thinking along a new track. "Is she your girlfriend?"

Manny laughed. "No. She's a little older than me, not that it would be a problem. Out of my league in a number of ways.

"There are a lot of women executives in companies these days," he went on. "Claire does happen to be one of the more successful. Why are you finding it difficult?"

"She doesn't act like a man," Jenny answered, wonderingly. "She doesn't even wear trousers."

Claire often did wear a pants suit, and jeans or even overalls when she was out on site. She happened to be wearing a skirt that day. He thought about explaining this but decided against it, instead echoing his earlier thought. "Claire is very much a woman."

Jenny turned on him sharply. "You mean she is not as good as a man?"

Stunned by the suddenness of the attack he almost gawped at her and had to work at controlling his expression and his tone of voice. "She is far better at what she does than any man I know in the same business, or in a lot of other businesses. However, she is still a female."

"What does that mean?"

This time he laughed. "She wears feminine clothes, walks like a female, has the same interest in fashions most females have, enjoys spending time talking with her friends, believes in networking and establishing strong relationships, tends to be more diverse in her thinking and less pragmatic and direct than men, and all that while still achieving her goals."

They were back at his car. He opened the passenger door.

"Would you open the door for her?"

For a second he was confused. "For Claire?"

"Yes."

He didn't know. He had never been in a car with Claire as far as he could remember.

"It's the gentlemanly thing to do," he said, without explaining.

"Only if the man thinks the woman is weak and inferior."

Manny sucked in a breath and made the best of a smile. "Not at all."

"Why else would you do it?"

He hadn't the slightest idea. "It's to show the woman she is valued and that the man wants to take care of her," he ventured.

"So if women don't open car doors for men, does that mean they don't value them or want to take care of them?"

This was turning into a silly argument. Or was it? At

one level it was very profound. However, getting into a car in the middle of a busy city street was not the place to be having it. He let go of the door and walked round to the other side of the car, leaving her to get in and shut the door by herself. Perhaps that was more appropriate with a teenage girl. He wasn't sure of the exact etiquette.

He was beginning to feel she was not the only one on the roller coaster. Where had all this come from? He had expected her to be awed by Claire and had hoped meeting her would counter some of her ideas about how men treated women. Somehow it seemed to have turned the other way around. He wondered what was coming next.

"Why aren't you married?" his daughter asked as if it had just occurred to her.

"Because I never met a woman I wanted to marry," he said, and a fleeting thought passed through his mind that it wasn't true. He might have married Katie Frank.

They didn't talk anymore on the way back to his apartment, both having a lot to think about. When they turned in through the gateway there was another car in his parking space.

Jenny looked unconcernedly at it while Manny took a deep breath, wondering how best to warn her that something else dramatic was about to happen in her life.

Chapter 7

"It's my Mum and Dad," Manny said.

Jenny's hand stopped in mid-air as she was about to open the car door. "My grandparents?"

"I was hoping to sort of ease you into them."

She turned back to him wide-eyed. "What do you mean? Are they terrible?"

Manny made a face. "Not terrible. They can be difficult. Well, Mum can. You'll like Dad."

The hand moved again, but not to open the door. It joined her other hand in her lap as she pulled back into the passenger seat. "What if they don't like me?"

He grimaced again. "Oh, they'll like you. That's something I've no doubt about." He had never had to explain his mother to anyone before. "Mum'll give you a hard time at first. That's just her. She can be hard to get along with if you don't understand her."

As he said the words he saw a shadow of dismay cross Jenny's face and became aware of a presence behind him.

"What's all this about?" His mother was standing behind him beside the driver's door window. "What's all this nonsense about you having a daughter?"

Manny looked up, smiling to calm her down, but she was already moving round to the other side of the car.

"Where is she? I want to see her. Someone's making a fool of you Robert and it's just typical of you to be taken in by it. Well, we're going to put an end to it, I can tell you.

I'm not having any nonsense like this in my family."

Manny glanced at Jenny and was surprised to see her eyes narrow and a calculating expression flicker across her face.

"Now young lady, you just come out here and explain yourself," his mother demanded, reaching the passenger door and bending her head to stare in the window. "For heaven's sake! Would you look at this!"

Over her shoulder Manny's father's face appeared and as soon as he, too, saw Jenny, he broke into a smile. "Well I'll be!"

"Wh... wh... what?" his mother stuttered, still staring in disbelief at the red hair, green eyes and wispy ginger eyebrows she could not deny were those of both her husband and her son.

Manny pushed open his door, walked round the car and eased his parents to one side so that he could open Jenny's door and invite her to come out. Damn the etiquette, he needed to stand between her and his mother until he was certain how this was going to develop.

"Let's get inside," he suggested to her. "It might be easier."

With his mother following close behind, her confused feelings written across her face and in every tense muscle of her body, and his Dad grinning ear to ear, he indicated to Jenny she should go ahead of them up the steps and into his apartment.

"Come in," he said to his mother who had no intention

of going anywhere else.

"This is Jenny. My daughter," he said when they were standing inside.

"Hello, Jenny," said his Dad. "I see you got the eyebrows."

Jenny giggled, nodding, with one eye on her grandmother who seemed to reorganize her resources and snapped "I can't see what that is to be happy about."

"Oh, I don't know Mum," Manny turned his back so she couldn't see when he wiggled his eyebrows at Jenny. She laughed again. Then her eyes became serious and she stepped around him.

"Would you mind if I called you Gran?" she said, facing up to his mother.

His mother seemed to first stiffen and then dissolve in front of their eyes and Jenny turned to her grandfather. "What shall I call you?"

Manny's Dad's face flushed. "That's something I've never had to think about." He caught his wife's eye. "Don't suppose it matters."

"Yes, it does. I want a special name only I call you. How about Gramps?"

"Gramps." He grinned with delight. "That'll do me."

"Gran and Gramps," said Jenny very properly. "Pleased to meet you."

Manny's mother swallowed and blinked several times, squared her shoulders, looked at her husband and her son and then back to Jenny.

"Well, I don't know. It's all a bit unusual. I don't suppose there's any denying you're a Youngman. Not with that face, pity help you."

She turned and picked out a chair to sit on, waving Jenny towards another. Manny and the newly-named Gramps also sat.

Manny took the initiative and related yet another version of Jenny's arrival in his life. He said Katie had had to go away and omitted to mention it was to prison.

"Doesn't she have any other family?"

The question was thrown at Manny, but Jenny fielded it.

"You're the only family I've got. My Mum's parents are dead and she was an only child, too, like Dad."

She thought on her feet, Manny thought admiringly. If she called her mother Katie, Gran would have something to criticise, and his mother hadn't failed to notice she called him Dad. Nor had he.

"Why couldn't she take you with her?" His mother was still on the hunt.

"It wasn't possible. I nearly did go but it would have created problems with school. So Mum thought of Dad."

"Bit strange isn't it, after all these years? Why didn't she get in touch with him before?"

"I don't know." Jenny's voice dropped in volume and tone. "I think she was ashamed, Gran."

A retort hovered on the other woman's lips and was suppressed. Instead she nodded to show she understood. "I see. So what happens next?"

Manny was caught off guard, busy admiring Jenny's performance. "How do you mean, Mum?"

"You don't intend for her to stay with you, surely? She'll have to come and stay with me."

"No. She's staying with me."

"Ridiculous."

Jenny opened her mouth but Manny looked hard at her. This one was his fight. "It's not ridiculous at all, Mum. Jenny and I have only just met and we want to get to know each other. You and Dad are welcome to come round as often as you like and I'd love to bring Jenny over to your place for dinner. She's already moved into the spare bedroom."

His mother gave in quicker than he'd expected. He guessed her insistence that Jenny should stay with her had surprised and disconcerted her, too, and she'd been happy to back out of it. "You take your Dad outside for a bit," she said.

Jenny glanced towards Manny, but he couldn't think of anything his mother could say or do that would be too terrible, or that his new-found daughter couldn't handle.

"Lovely girl," his Dad said as they stepped out into the garden. "Gave your Mum a run for her money."

Manny raised an eye at him in surprise. He'd never heard such sentiments coming from that direction.

"She'll give you a run for your money, too, don't you worry. Her mum a bit of a problem?"

When Manny looked at him quizzically the older man said "I thought so. Where's she gone, the mother? Run away with some fancy man?"

Manny shook his head. "No, nothing like that."

"Well, what is it? She in hospital?"

Again he shook his head.

"Ah, well, I suppose that's your business. Have you any idea what you've got yourself into?"

"I'm beginning to," Manny answered him. "How do you do it, Dad, establish a relationship with a young girl you've never met? She was so scared of me she locked herself in the bedroom and again in the bathroom this morning, and she was crying during the night. But you heard her with Mum. She sounds as if she's got it all under control. One minute I think it's going to be all right, the next I'm not so sure."

"Just work at it, son. That's the job, isn't it?"

It was said with a quiet acceptance of the reality. Not resignation to the inevitable, Manny sensed, but an uncomplicated understanding that was how life was and the way forward was just to get on with it.

"Make sure you do bring her round, Manny," his Dad was saying. "I'd like to see a lot of her. Not ever having had a daughter, a grand-daughter could be a bit of fun. Especially one all grown up and out of the crying and dirty nappy stages."

Not totally out of the crying stages, Manny thought, and as for grown up, he wasn't sure. He thought of a chrysalis emerging from a cocoon and turning into a butterfly, but that was a continuous process. Jenny seemed to fluctuate between being one thing one moment and another the next.

"What did Mum want to talk to you about?" he asked when his parents had left.

"She wanted to make sure I had enough tampons."

Another missing page. He hadn't even begun to think about that side of having a young girl living with him. "Have you?"

"Yes. Do you want me to cook dinner?" It appeared the subject was closed.

"Can you?"

"Of course. If it's not too complicated."

"Is taking a packet dinner out of the freezer and putting it in the microwave too complicated?"

"No, I can handle that. Mum doesn't cook either. You are very alike in some ways." She turned away and he had the impression of a tear glinting in one corner of her eye.

"What did you think of my Mum and Dad?" he asked her.

Before she turned back to him she dabbed at her eye with a tissue and there was no trace of the tear when she asked, "Do you think they liked me?"

"I'm sure they did. What about you? How do you feel about having grandparents?"

She seemed to need to think about that. After a while she said "I want them to like me." This was followed by another pause and she added, "I want you to like me, too."

Chapter 8

Manny had never noticed before how the sound of a voice travelled through the walls, but nor had he ever had anyone living with him, so he'd never been in the situation of eavesdropping on someone else's conversation.

He had enjoyed their first evening together. After Jenny had defrosted and cooked dinner in his microwave oven she wanted to know more about him, what school he had been to, what friends he had had, what food he liked. In turn she related the main events of her shorter but, to him, no less interesting life. They compared their hands and feet, finding that while they had matching fingers their toes were so dissimilar they might have taken different evolutionary paths. Jenny persuaded him to sit with her in front of a mirror while they compared faces. He took out an old photograph album and together they examined uncles, aunts and cousins for other evidence of consanguinity. The revelation that, with Manny's father, they were the only three of a kind delighted both of them.

They had been getting on so well together and sharing so much of themselves that Manny had found himself resenting it when the phone rang and he had to take time out to discuss with Tony the agenda for the next NEMSA meeting.

During the night he had heard no crying, despite staying awake and listening. In the morning the door of her bedroom and the bathroom had not been locked when he tried them. It had all seemed very promising.

Jenny had emerged in her school uniform and there was no suggestion she would take more time off from her normal routine. Over breakfast they had discussed whether they liked the same books and art. He had been impressed again with the quickness of her mind and the range of her interests. While he had to give Katie most of the credit, certainly on the nurture side of the equation, he felt satisfied his own genes had made a contribution on the nature side.

Jenny asked if she could use the telephone to call some friends and took the cordless phone into her room while he settled down with his newspaper in his chair next to the wall. He hadn't started on the first headline when he realised he could hear everything she was saying.

"How's Mum? Have you heard?"

How would one of her school friends know how Katie was? He refolded his newspaper and listened more closely.

"Is she? That's good."

There was another pause while the other person conveyed more information. Manny found himself glancing around guiltily, as if there might be someone to observe and condemn what he was doing.

"I bet she did. I can just imagine her standing there in the dock with that silly judge lecturing her. Did she laugh or keep a straight face? What did she say?"

The reply made her giggle and Manny would have given anything to hear what it was that Katie had said.

"I wish I'd been there." She seemed to think about that

and change her mind, "No. Maybe not. I'd have cried and that would have made it worse for her. When you see her, give her my love. Tell her I'd love to come and see her but I understand why she doesn't want me to. You'll ring me every time after you visit her, won't you? Before you go there, too, so that you can take messages for me. Thanks, Sweeny."

Thinking she was about to say goodbye and hang up, he lifted the newspaper in front of his face and attempted to focus again on the headlines, and felt stupid as well as guilty when she continued speaking.

"He's wonderful. I like him. We get on so well together and he says having me here isn't going to be too much trouble. Not that having me could be any trouble to anyone, of course, I'm such a wonderful person and so gay and witty." She laughed. "I wasn't so gay and witty at first. I got scared and stayed in my room. Even in the morning I didn't know what to say or do. I felt so stupid. I told him I was worried because some fathers rape their daughters. Can you believe that?"

Apparently the other person could believe it.

"Yes, well I guess I was a bit worried about that, but also about how we were going to get along together. It was exciting to meet him, but I didn't know what he was going to be like. Mum said he would be all right but she hadn't seen him for years. He could have been horrible. I mean, really weird, or anything. I didn't know.

"He's been good really. I guess he's finding it as difficult as I am. I mean, we don't know each other at all and it's a bit awkward sometimes, but I feel I do know him. Especially when I look at his face. I almost burst out laughing when I first saw him. Or crying. I wasn't sure which to do. He's exactly like me, Sweeny. I mean, exactly. No kidding. The red hair, the eyes, the eyebrows. Even his mouth's the same, and some of his expressions. It is so weird. We sat in front of a mirror and it was like there were two mirrors, you know, like you could see a double image of yourself? I made a face and he didn't, and it was so funny. His father, my grandfather, is the same too. Three of us, all the same. Isn't that incredible? I used to think I was the only one who looked as stupid as this in the whole world.

"Yes, well thank you. You don't have green eyes and red hair and these awful eyebrows. I think I look stupid.

"My grandfather? I only met them for a short time but I liked them, too. My grandmother came on a bit heavy so I had to play the young lady and sweeten her up. I called him Dad and both their eyes sort of went all teary.

"No, I haven't called him anything. I sort of avoid it. Seems funny calling him Manny and I can't call him Mr Youngman. Dad's someone you've known all your life, you know what I mean?

"No, I don't think he's got a permanent girlfriend. He obviously has some sort of love life. I nosed around while he was talking on the phone down in his office and there are some photos of him with women. Guess what? I found a pink dressing gown in one of the wardrobes that I'm pretty sure isn't his. But I bet he bought it. It's not what anyone would buy to wear at their boyfriend's place, you know? More what you'd wear if you were about ninety years old and had ten kids. Not sexy. Maybe he keeps it for emergencies in case someone stays the night and hasn't come prepared.

"Well, I don't know, do I? About three or four different women in the photographs. From all the signs I've seen, I'd say my father is a very contented bachelor."

For the first time Manny began to feel uncomfortable listening to this conversation. It had seemed alright when Jenny was talking about herself and her relationship with him. While he could rationalize that the better informed he was the better he could manage the situation, it was different hearing her discussing him in more intimate terms. This was the part where an eavesdropper might not hear well of himself. He wondered who Sweeny was.

"I met one of his clients. Have you heard of Claire O'Connell? Yes, that's her. Nice lady and not at all hard like you might think. Wears beautiful clothes. She had on a blue skirt with a primrose blouse with a ruffled neck. Very chic and elegant. Must cost pots of money to look like that. Gold earrings and a necklace and this beautiful bracelet which was gold with something set in it. Yes, I know, I was sort of expecting her to be a bit mannish, too. She wasn't at all. Very feminine. I thought maybe he was having an affair with her, so I asked her daughter Dallas, who showed me around the place, and she said they're not. She and her brother and sister keep a good check on what their mother's up to and she said they were very good friends and work well together but they've never even been out on a date or anything. Dallas said they were a bit surprised to find out I existed and she wanted to know all about Mum and me. I guess most of his friends will. He doesn't talk about them much. There's a lot more I've got to find out about him when I think about it. I don't even know what he would be doing if I wasn't here. I mean, he might go out to play golf or watch the football. Not golf. There aren't any golf clubs. Of course I've snooped around. You would, wouldn't you? I know you would."

Shortly after that the conversation ended. Manny's heart lurched again in guilty anticipation of being discovered. Casting aside the newspaper as possible camouflage, he was on his feet, heading for the kitchen to appear busy and otherwise occupied, when he heard more numbers being punched and Jenny saying "Hi, Betty. It's Jenny. I had to ring you. Have you seen Shane since the weekend? Did he say anything about me?"

He stopped half way to the kitchen, turned, hesitated and almost overbalanced with the change in his momentum. This was wrong, and ridiculous. He shouldn't be listening.

"Would he have said anything to Grant? I don't care how much you don't like your brother, Betty Polson, I think you owe it to your friends to keep the lines of communication open so that we can learn what we need to know about all the cute boys he hangs out with."

Perhaps he should have stayed in the green chair. If he went into the kitchen he would have to do something. That would make noise she would hear and realize that if she could hear him, he could hear her. He remained still.

The contrasts in the girl amazed him. The conversation with the person named Sweeny had been conducted by a more mature, almost adult side of her character. Now with Betty Polson she was being a gushy teenager. Where did the militant feminist fit into the picture, or was that just a shadow of Katie?

He looked towards the kitchen and back to his chair. The chair was safer. He could close his eyes and pretend he had dozed off. Much better camouflage than reading a newspaper. He could even give a snore or two. He stole back across the carpet and sat again in the chair. He opened the paper and held it on his knees as if it had dropped that way when he fell asleep, lay his head back and closed his eyes.

Jenny hung up on Betty and called Gillian, and after Gillian, Olivia and after Olivia, Rose. None of them had heard from Shane, or that he had taken the slightest notice of the attention someone named Billy Longford had been paying to Jenny.

"Maybe if I ring Shane myself," Jenny said. "I don't have to ask him outright. I'm not that silly. I'll be able to tell if he was jealous, won't I? I can just mention Billy's name. I'll hear his reaction."

She said goodbye to Rose and punched in the next

number. Manny had a crick in his neck and was starting to feel ridiculous. Enough eavesdropping was enough. Also, he felt he should prevent her making the call. Ringing Shane would be a tactical error. He rustled the newspaper. "Can I use the phone now? You've been on it a long time."

Jenny appeared in the doorway. She frowned at where he was sitting close to the wall on the other side of which she had been talking.

"Could you hear what I was saying?"

Manny shook his head.

"I could hear you, and you didn't yell or anything."

"I've been asleep. Anyway, I've got better things to do than listen to that teenage nonsense." He laughed to make it a joke and knew even as he did so that it wasn't going to work.

"How do you know it was teenage nonsense if you couldn't hear it?"

It was time to change tactics. He added a touch of annoyance to his voice. "You've been so long on the phone we're going to be late getting you to school."

Her eyes narrowed in an expression he knew well, using it himself frequently. "You didn't say there was a rule against it. Are there any other rules you haven't told me about?"

Now he could feel his annoyance becoming more real, and that would be unproductive. Keeping his tone conversational, he asked if there was anything else she had to do to get ready for school.

In reply she glared at him and went into her bedroom, not quite slamming the door. He wasn't sure whether he had made a successful escape or not, and suspected the verdict was still out.

A few minutes later, after she had re-emerged with her school bag in her hand and a steely expression on her face, he followed her out of the apartment. She stopped on the steps and glowered down to where a van was parked in the courtyard in front of one of the other units. "Huh!" She said, inflating the little three-letter exclamation with several puffs of scorn.

"What's wrong?"

"That van. It says Warren Williams, Master Plumber. How come they don't have Mistress Plumbers?"

It seemed they were about to have another conversation like the one about maths.

"Doesn't mean the same, does it?" he said without trying to sound argumentative. "It means someone who has mastered plumbing. Doesn't have anything to do with gender."

"Yes, it does. It's sexist. It says that to be the best at anything you have to be a man. If you're master at something, you're superior."

"A mistress is in charge too."

"Then why don't they say mistress craftswomen?"

Manny wasn't sure whether this conversation was happening because he had stopped her making more phone calls or because she was upset about the boy Shane. He considered explaining that historically crafts had been carried out by men, foresaw the new argument that could lead to and thought better of it.

Again he reverted to a joke as a possible way out. "Perhaps we should leave a note under his windscreen wiper to tell him."

She took him seriously, and began rummaging in her bag, "Good idea. I've got some paper."

"We really are running late," he said quickly. "We don't have time to stop."

"Okay." It was said uncaringly and again he was caught off guard. Had she been serious about the conversation or had she just been testing his reaction? Too many questions.

"Do you know any woman plumbers?" she asked as he drove his car past the plumber's van.

He didn't, when he came to think about it, but decided against making the admission. Instead he said, "You seem to have strong views about sexism."

"Women have been treated like second class citizens."

"That's true historically, I'll give you that, However, that situation has changed, and is continually changing."

"Not fast enough. Men are just chauvinist pigs."

"Not all men. Perhaps reform would happen faster if women selected their targets more carefully and stopped antagonizing most men."

Her eyes glinted at him. "What do you mean?"

"Calling all men chauvinist pigs not only makes those who are chauvinist pigs angry, but also those who aren't. It doesn't achieve anything."

Jenny laughed. "You feel better."

They were approaching the school and her laugh stopped. Apprehension filled her face until she saw the yard was almost empty. She hesitated. Was she going to kiss him goodbye? No.

"You'll pick me up here?"

The butterfly had turned back into a chrysalis, it seemed, the militant feminist into an uncertain schoolgirl.

"Yes. And don't forget what I said about not telling all the boys they're sexist pigs." He smiled, trying to make it a joke, but her face remained serious. She nodded, turned and followed the last of the other students up the steps. At the top she stopped and half turned back, moved her hand in a small wave before she hurried out of sight.

He stared at the space she had vacated, wishing she would come back.

Chapter 9

Over the next few days, Manny's life became a pattern of having breakfast with Jenny, taking her to school, going about his work, collecting her from school and spending time with her in the evening, usually watching television or one of the DVDs she chose from his collection. They didn't speak a lot and it was mostly the everyday communications they needed to live in the same space together and balance their different activities. It appeared the discussions about personal things, past histories, likes and dislikes, were not to be continued, and she made no more phone calls from the apartment. He had no idea whether she had called the boy Shane or what response she had received.

There were moments when he could sense sadness in her and guessed she was thinking about her mother. While he thought Katie was wrong to have cut off all communications between them, there was nothing to be done except keep her busy and happy so that her mind would not dwell on it.

Despite a heavy work schedule with several projects in planning stages or in progress, it was not enough to keep his mind fully occupied. It was as if he were on automatic pilot. Part of his brain made sure he was saying all the right things to clients while the rest argued with itself about whether or not he was being a good father and how this situation was going to develop. When he was not arguing with himself he thought about Jenny.

She was a great kid, and not just because she was his daughter. She was smart. Look at the way she handled his mother. His own life might have been a lot easier if he could have handled her as well when he was that age. In fact it might be a lot easier if he could handle her like that now.

Claire O'Connell said her daughter Dallas and Jenny had become friends and texted each other messages. "She's an exceptionally mature girl in some ways," she said. "Quite unusual." He agreed wholeheartedly.

On one occasion, standing on the scaffolding of a half-built building staring out across the city, he noticed workmen observing him and realized he was smiling. He turned away and became busy again while inside experiencing the soft feeling that was becoming increasingly familiar. It was as if his heart itself was smiling, relaxed and happy, venting a deep satisfied sigh.

His daughter was intelligent. She had a strong personality. Dad liked her. So did Mum, though she wouldn't let on. He felt good about that and it gave him more of that warm glow.

He reflected often on what Tony had said about this being an opportunity. Was he going the right way to develop a relationship with her based on innovative male/female roles? That was the plan. The process was not so easy.

At four o'clock one evening she was standing outside the school gate where he always picked her up, this time with a group of boys around her. She had her back against the wall and one of the boys was leaning over her, his hand propping him away but still so that they were almost touching each other. Manny parked the car about fifty metres short of them and sat watching.

The boy had shaved hair around the sides and back of his head and wore a school jumper over torn jeans. A second boy in a short-sleeved shirt was talking rapidly and gesturing with his hands. A third boy who had the sleeves of his jumper knotted round his neck hopped from foot to foot. Jenny was smiling at all three of them, but her eyes were mainly on the one leaning over her.

Jealousy? Is that what he was feeling? Manny shook his head. For heaven's sake, he told himself. She's a young girl and they're young boys. You were a young boy once. Stop and think. What does a new era man do?

He got out of the car and walked along towards them. The boys smiled cheerfully, unthreatened. Jenny also smiled, and walked towards him, her hand waving a goodbye. All very normal. All very natural. So be normal. Be natural.

"I thought you didn't like men."

He let the words escape without censoring them and knew immediately that he had made a mistake. Maybe it was natural to have the feelings he was having. That didn't make it wise to express them.

She stopped, frowning at him, her expression wary.

He tried to recover. "Never mind. How are you?"

"What did you mean?"

"Those boys you were with are males," he pointed out.

"Duh! Boys usually are."

"It was a joke. Some of the things you've said suggested you didn't like men."

"Do you like women?"

She had this habit of turning the conversation against him, much as Katie had that time at the Women's Service League.

"Yes, of course."

"You wouldn't think so from some of the things you say."

Manny took in the set, angry expression on her face and decided not to say anything more, with the result that as they drove home the usual silence between them was filled with tension. As they turned into the court yard Jenny said, "You designed this place too?"

He nodded. This was good. Normal conversation was being re-established. "It was an old warehouse. A big, open space, so there was plenty of opportunity to work within it, and the structural support was in place to extend the mezzanine floor that already existed over the offices at one end and create two floors with apartments above and offices below. This car park was part of the old loading yard." He turned to face her, expecting she would be impressed.

"A woman would have designed it better," Jenny said, "and Mr James wants to see you."

Manny was confused. "What does that have to do with what we're discussing?" He tried to remember who Mr James was. Her headmaster? No, one of the teachers.

Literature.

"I just remembered it. You might get angry if I forgot to tell you."

"Have I done anything to make you think that?"

"You were pretty angry the other day, about the phone."

She had turned the conversation to put him on the defensive again. He imagined he was now supposed to say he had not been angry, and let her have her own way. Instead he used her own tactic back at her and changed the subject.

"What does Mr James want to see me about?"

Jenny frowned and her lips pursed slightly. Manny again recognised one of his own expressions. "Some problem at school?" he prompted.

"No. I don't know what he wants to see you about. He didn't tell me."

"Didn't you ask him?"

"No. Do you have a girlfriend?"

She was very clever at this. He decided to go along with it and put the question of Mr James off until later.

"Why do you ask?" he said.

"If you have a girlfriend I could stay with one of my friends tonight, if you wanted to have her here. I don't want to be in the way."

Manny's brow furrowed and he made a conscious effort to stay with this conversation and find out where it was going. There was something going on he didn't yet understand.

"You're not in the way, Jenny. I do have some women friends I go out with occasionally, to theatres or restaurants. Nothing on my calendar at the moment."

He had a sudden inspiration. "Would you like to go to a theatre or a restaurant? We could even take some of your friends."

Another inspiration. "I've got an even better idea. Why don't you invite your friends here?"

"Could I?" Her eyes widened and glowed with excitement.

"Of course." Now he was getting their relationship right.

"When can I do it? Saturday?"

His instinctive reaction was to say no, to push the event into the future. Instead he nodded. "Why not?"

Jenny reached for the phone, stopped and looked at him. "I need to call people."

He went through to the kitchen where he could not overhear her. It was only when he was standing at the bench, clicking the button to start the jug boiling, that he took time to think about what had happened and wonder whether he had been manipulated.

No, he decided, continuing to pour the coffee and calling out to see if she also wanted one, making it loud to emphasise he could not hear her. He had control of the situation.

"Yes, please, and thank you," she called back. "Everyone's thrilled about the party. They're all dying to meet you."

A party! He'd been thinking of a few friends for a quiet evening sitting and talking together. Five, maybe six. What did a party mean? Twenty? A hundred? He took a step into the room to say something and was turned back by her delighted smile and the excitement in her eyes. Why shouldn't she have a party? Lots of young people. Laughter and youthful, exuberant life. It would be fun for both of them.

Later he asked her who was coming. "Tell me a little about them, so that I'm prepared and can talk to them when they get here."

This produced an uncertain expression. "You won't be talking to them much, will you?"

"I can hardly sit in a corner all evening not talking to anyone," Manny laughed.

"But... You'll be here? All evening?"

It hadn't occurred to him that he wouldn't be. "Well, I thought I..." He gestured with his hands as if seeking somewhere he could be. "I suppose I could stay down in my office."

Jenny sat down on the edge of a chair. The edges of her mouth compressed as she sought the right words to say. "This is silly, isn't it? I shouldn't have a party here."

"It has sort of rushed up on me," he admitted.

"I'll cancel it." She jumped to her feet and moved towards the phone.

"No." Manny surprised himself by disagreeing. "You

have your party, Jenny. I'd like you to."

Jenny remained ambivalent. "Well, usually when there's a party, the parents go out. Not that we're going to make too much noise, or wreck the place. It's just that..."

"I understand. I suppose Katie goes out when you have a party at your place."

"Sure. She always goes out." It wasn't said confidently. He suspected there hadn't been any parties at Katie's place or, if there had been, that Katie had stayed around to keep a watch on things. But he was playing by the new rules. He didn't care what Katie did.

"How long does one of these parties go on for?"

"One or two in the morning. Pretty late."

Again the over-confident assurance.

"How about midnight?" he suggested. "Start at half past seven. I'll stay till eight, go somewhere for a few hours and come back at 11.30. Everyone gone by midnight. Sound reasonable?"

"Could you come back at half past twelve? I'll make sure they go by one o'clock."

There was something magic about midnight, Manny reflected. Kids wanted to stay awake and kick on. It meant being adult, being free. It was exciting.

"Quarter past twelve. Gone by quarter to one." He put a twinkle in his eye to emphasise this was just good-humoured bargaining.

Jenny responded with an identical twinkle. "Deal."

She went back to phoning and Manny applauded

himself. He really was becoming good at this.

When she had finished telephoning, Jenny spent a long time in her room and he heard her cupboard door open and shut several times. Then she appeared in the doorway, her face shadowed by an uncertain frown. "Am I allowed to go back to my house? I didn't bring clothes for a party."

She was wearing old jeans and a t-shirt with "Women Are A National Asset" printed on it. This seemed to be her main outfit around the apartment but he wasn't sure whether she normally wore it at home or whether it was a statement for his benefit. The long skirt with the baggy top and the shapeless hat had not reappeared since the night of her arrival and were presumably for special occasions. Apart from her school uniform he had no idea what other clothes she had with her.

Katie had said nothing about a ban on visiting her house and he was curious to see the place. He suggested they drive there and find somewhere to have dinner while they were out.

Jenny ran to fetch her suitcase, empty now because its contents filled the drawers and cupboards in her room. While he thought it was bigger than she needed to carry just a simple change of clothes, Manny made no comment. An uneasy feeling had reawakened in the back of his mind that new era man was not sitting comfortably in the driver's seat and was being taken for a ride. He just wasn't sure where they were going, or how fast.

Chapter 10

Katie's house was the left half of a duplex set in a garden of well-trimmed flower beds in a tidy suburban street, not at all what Manny had expected. He had imagined a more utilitarian, functional place with only a lawn if it had any garden at all.

"There's Sweeny." Jenny let out a squeal, threw open the car door and ran towards a woman emerging from the other half of the duplex. Manny studied her with interest, pleased to have the answer to who it was Jenny had been speaking to on the phone.

Jenny threw her arms around the woman and gave her a tremendous hug, unexpected tears forming in her eyes and smearing down her cheeks. "Sweeny. I missed you so much."

Manny got out of the car and waited with one hand resting on the top of the door.

Over Jenny's shoulder, Sweeny smiled at him. "You've got to be Jenny's father. My goodness, you are alike."

Manny smiled back.

"My name's Alice Todd," she said, with Jenny still clinging to her. "Everyone calls me Sweeny. Hush, Jenny. It's okay. Come on now." She prised the girl loose while still holding her by the shoulders to maintain the contact. Manny watched in growing realisation of how much fear and confusion his daughter had been damming up inside herself, and experienced a touch of jealousy that it was another person who was calming it.

"Sweeny Todd," he said, to show that he had understood.

"The demon barber," she acknowledged. "I am a hairdresser, believe it or not. I had the nickname and it seemed inevitable."

She was older than he had thought when she emerged from the house. Thirty-five maybe. Short black hair sculpted over her ears almost elfin style, which suited her Audrey Hepburn face. She wore dark slacks and a pale yellow shirt with one of those extra-wide collars and the top two buttons undone.

"How have you two been getting along? Must have been strange for both of you."

"Fine," father and daughter said simultaneously, and laughed.

Sweeny's eyebrows lifted. "They not only look alike, folks, they talk alike," she pronounced in a showman's voice. "Roll up, roll up. See the famous double act. It's mysterious. It's amazing. They've only known each other a few days and they walk and talk in total synchronisation."

"Not quite," Jenny and Manny said again with identical grins. They looked at each other and began laughing again.

"Better get my stuff," Jenny said, grabbing her suitcase from the car and carrying it across the front garden to the door of the house.

The lawn had been cut not long ago, Manny noticed, and the edges of the cement path had been trimmed. Several low shrubs looked healthy and the flower beds had every sign of being well cared for.

"Katie keeps it well, doesn't she?" Alice asserted, following his gaze. "She fixed it all up before she went away and I'm just keeping an eye on it for her. Not that it needs much. Katie has been very wise and used plants that don't need a lot of attention."

Manny nodded, his question to himself answered, although he was a little surprised that it was Katie who had laid the foundations. However, with only a few pot plants to care for himself, he had no great contribution to make to a discussion on gardening, so that source of conversation seemed exhausted.

"How are you two getting on?" Alice asked him once Jenny was out of earshot. "Is it working out all right?"

Manny nodded. "Once I got over the surprise."

"How's she handling not seeing Katie or being able to phone her?"

He admitted he didn't know for sure, that she appeared to get sad at times.

"She's tough. It can't be easy for her," Alice said. "I know Katie thinks it's best, but I'm not so sure."

"It's not something I can influence," Manny told her. "All I'm doing is trying to ensure we stay on good terms and her life is as normal as it can be in the circumstances."

"Good." Alice nodded. "We wouldn't want her to be unhappy."

There was a threatening note in her words that made Manny uncomfortable. "Nor would I," he said, "so I'd better give her a hand." He followed Jenny into the house.

The interior was as unexpected as the garden and the street. The colours of the furnishings were muted, with a soft richness that promised comfort. A garland of twisted creeper stems interlaced with dried flowers hung on a wall, a diaphanous scarf draped through it with artful carelessness. An antique hallstand supported an array of hats which were mostly straw with coloured bands and more scarves tied around them. From the ceiling hung a plaited cane lampshade, matching a cane chair beside a telephone table made of blond wood with a green marble inlay.

Jenny had disappeared to the back of the house and Manny waited in a spacious lounge room in which two deep, plum-coloured sofas faced each other across a Persian carpet. Sofas and carpet were strewn with jewel coloured cushions. Low tables were scattered around, some with books piled upon them, one with an ornate backgammon board and another with a crystal bowl in which rose petals floated. A row of prints hung on one wall, all pastel treatments of the same subject, a dark-haired woman with a wistfully uncertain beauty. It was a warm room, comfortable and feminine.

The odd piece out was a wooden tool box, unvarnished and recently made, sitting on the carpet beside one of the armchairs. Manny picked it up and examined the careful workmanship. The wood, he thought, might be teak. The corners were dovetailed joints and the bottom and side panels tongue and groove boards.

"Right, I've got them." Jenny reappeared with her suitcase now bulging, a smaller one in her other hand and a rucksack slung over her shoulders.

"Are you sure you've got everything?"

"Yes, I think so." She hadn't noticed his sarcasm and when he thought about it, he was glad she hadn't.

"Who made the tool box?"

"I did. Got an 'A' for it at woodwork."

"You do woodwork?"

She frowned. "Are you surprised?"

"No and yes," Manny answered, seeing the pitfall. "Not because you're a girl doing woodwork. I was surprised because I thought I knew all the subjects you take at school, from when we talked about it the other day."

"Guess I forgot," she said, apparently satisfied that he hadn't shown a typical male reaction. "What do you think of Sweeny?" She turned for the front door, indicating no interest in showing the rest of the house to him.

"She seems nice," Manny responded, trying to peer into another room which seemed to be the kitchen as he followed after her. "Good to have as a neighbour, I imagine."

They were outside again and Alice was still there. A pleasant woman outside a pleasant house in a pleasant street. Jenny began gossiping with her about the latest dramas being played out among their neighbours.

The little pink car was parked in a garage at the side of the house. Out of curiosity and because there was nothing he could contribute to the conversation, Manny walked over to examine it.

Ignoring its pinkness, it had quite sporty lines and was unexpectedly roomy inside. A practical car, economical to run and obviously well maintained. A neat and tidy house, a well-kept garden, a practical, well-cared for car and a sensible, well-raised daughter. It was all out of keeping with the image of a mad woman who threw fake bombs into men's clubs.

Behind the car was a 250cc Honda motorbike. Who could be riding that? A boyfriend presumably, but he had seen no evidence of one in the house.

When they were back in the car and driving away he asked about it.

"That's Mum's," Jenny told him. "She got it to learn to ride on. She's going to buy a Harley Davidson one day and we'll go for a long trip on it."

Another piece in the complex picture of Katie Frank that was emerging.

"Did she?" he enquired. "Learn to ride the motorbike?" In the rear view mirror he could see Alice watching their departure and waving.

"Yes. We went on it when we boarded up the men's club door." She said it so casually he was taken aback. Like saying they had used it to go down to the corner shop.

"Why did Katie do that?"

Jenny became silent.

"Don't you want to talk about it?"

She seemed to think about that and make up her mind. "There was an article in the paper in which some man was spouting off about equal opportunity," she said. "Pompous old idiot. He mentioned this club and said it was a last bastion of male dignity, as if that was something to be proud of. Sweeny said wouldn't it be funny if someone did something to upset his precious dignity, so we went round and nailed up the front door.

"We?"

"Mum and me. Sweeny couldn't come because only two could ride on the bike and we went on the bike because no-one would recognise us with the helmets on."

Manny knew the club. It had substantial double front doors set in an imposing ornamental archway.

"What did you actually do to the door?"

"We made up an official-looking notice on the computer saying it had been closed by order of the Equal Opportunity Commission. Katie nailed boards across the door and we stuck the notice on them. They charged us with malicious damage to property. Men don't have much of a sense of humour, do they?"

"I can't imagine the members of a women's club would have felt any different."

Jenny examined him sharply. "Women don't have clubs like that."

"Not exactly like that," Manny admitted. "There are places that could be comparable."

"Like what?" She was looking out of the window, her

face drawn and defensive. Time to reverse tack.

"Pinning a notice on the door doesn't sound much of a criminal offence."

Jenny thought about that before answering, and when she did her voice had not lost its defensive tension. "Katie wasn't very good at nailing. The door splintered."

Manny decided against commenting how awkward some women could be with hammers. "How'd they find out it was you?"

Katie had gone to a newspaper to ensure the incident was publicised, Jenny explained. In effect she'd made a public confession. "Madge was furious."

Here was a new character. He was about to ask who Madge was when Jenny went on, "She said Katie could get herself into trouble if she liked, but it was not right to involve me. I said I wanted to be involved but she just said Mum should know better and it could hurt me in the future. She and Mum had a huge row about it."

Another neighbour, Manny decided, or one of Katie's feminist cohorts, although she sounded like a more sensible person. "What about you? What did you think?"

"I didn't mind. I thought it was funny. Mum did get a bit worried about it, especially when they said I had to go to court. I wanted to go. It wasn't as if we were going to end up in jail or anything. Not that time."

"Did you go to court?"

"Mmm. It was very interesting. The magistrate said Mum should know better and had been an irresponsible parent. He fined her two hundred dollars and made her pay for the door, but he let me off with a warning."

"Sounds like it was a pity you didn't listen. You and your mother. Did you go on the bike when she threw the bomb in the window?"

Jenny became silent. Glancing at her he saw her face working as if she had to make up her mind about something.

"It wasn't a bomb," she said. "It was an old alarm clock with some wires and a battery taped to it." She gave a brittle laugh. "You should have seen those stupid men diving out the back door. One was still trying to get his pants back on. They fell down the steps and knocked over the rubbish bins and made an awful noise."

So she had been there. Katie must have suppressed that information when she made her confession. As far as he knew there had been no suggestion of charges against Jenny on that occasion.

"Why did Katie do it? After she'd been charged the first time."

Jenny began to say something and then glanced at him. He had the impression she was torn between boasting about what her mother had done and admitting it had been wrong.

"That same man, the pompous idiot, called Mum a lot of names when he was interviewed by the paper after the first court hearing," she said. "He said the fine was too small. We were a disgrace to womanhood. That sort of stuff. I think he wanted us burnt at the stake as witches.

Mum said he needed to be taught a lesson."

"Did Katie go to the newspapers again, to get more publicity?" If she had it seemed a stupid thing to do after the first warning.

"No, the police came round to our place and said they knew it was us. I don't think they did, but Madge gave it away."

"Deliberately?"

"No. She just turned to Mum and said 'I told you you'd get caught again,' or something like that. She just didn't think. Of course, after that the police were certain and Mum told them it was her. I didn't think she'd go to prison, because it was only a fake bomb, but like Chloe told us, our lawyer, the courts are run by men."

If he had been the magistrate, Manny considered, the sentence didn't need to have anything to do with the culprits being women. The second incident had followed so soon after the first that it showed complete contempt for the court system. A fake bomb was just as bad as a real one. Someone could have had a heart attack or injured themselves falling down the steps. He was going to make a comment along these lines when he saw Jenny's face again take on that uncertain, defensive expression. He asked her instead what she wanted to pick up for dinner.

They stopped on the way home at a pizza parlour. "Which one do you want?" he asked her, pointing to the menu written on the wall. My favourite's deep pan gourmet pizza with extra anchovies."

For an instant he caught her eyes staring at him as if he had said something preposterous. Then she blinked, almost as if she was going to cry, and said she'd have the same.

What was that all about? He had no idea.

Back at the apartment, Jenny went into her room. There was a lot more opening and shutting of cupboards and drawers as she merged the clothes she had brought back with those that already filled most of the available space. After a while she emerged to show him one of the outfits she was considering for the party to ask his opinion. He said it was fine, but that didn't seem to be what she wanted to hear and she went back into the room to try something else.

Manny sat in a chair with his pizza on his lap and mused on the way his life had changed. And yet, in the strangest way, it all seemed natural. Hearing Jenny moving around and muttering to herself in the next room should have been alien and disconcerting. Instead it seemed familiar and comforting. When the phone rang, he was expecting it to be one of Jenny's friends calling about the party and was shocked when he heard the voice on the other end.

Chapter 11

He recognized her despite the way she spoke, as if she didn't want someone else to hear. "Manny? Are you in your office?"

"No." He matched her tone, glancing across to the door of Jenny's bedroom to see if she had heard the phone and come to find out who it was. "Why?"

"Could you take it there?"

"Hang on." Manny stood for a moment while he debated what to do. Jenny continued being busy in her room and didn't appear to have heard anything. Still carrying his plate with the now congealing pizza, he went downstairs to the handset on his desk, took it up and said in a normal voice, "What's going on, Katie?"

"Nothing. I just don't want Jenny to know it's me." She also spoke at a more normal level, but still sounded uncertain.

"Why on earth not?"

"I don't want to upset her."

"She's been waiting to hear from you. You should talk to her."

There was a pause and then she said, "Don't tell me what to do with my own daughter."

He had been standing up beside his desk. Now he sat down and held the phone at arms length while he contemplated replacing it on its cradle. He decided against it. "She wants to come and see you," he said, trying to sound reasonable.

In a quieter tone she replied, "That wouldn't be good. That's why I haven't rung until now. The trouble is I can't stand it. I need to know how she is."

"She's fine. She has been a bit nervous, but we're getting along well together, considering."

"Considering what?" Now she sounded suspicious and defensive.

"Considering we had never met before and didn't even know each other existed," he replied with a mildly critical tone. "You didn't think it would be easy for her, did you?"

"No, no." The defensiveness had gone and she now sounded contrite. "I just thought…"

"Did you? Did you actually think? Pardon me if I say I'm surprised."

There was a longer silence at the other end of the line. He imagined her taking a breath, reassembling her forces, making a decision how to respond.

"If you must know," she said. "I thought the two of you were so alike, not just the way you look, in other ways, too, I thought you might get on."

"Fine. We are getting on. She wants to know how you are, too. She's worried about you, if that's of the slightest interest to you."

"There's no need to be a bastard, Manny. Everything about Jenny is of interest to me. I haven't been a bad mother, you know."

"How could I know? I wasn't there to see it. Anyway,

the point is you are her mother, good or bad, and she wants to come to see you."

"I don't want her to see me in this place."

"You were happy enough to go there."

"That's different."

He felt like telling her that it wasn't, that she couldn't separate the one from the other so easily. He didn't. She was right. There was no point in being a bastard. "How are you, anyway?"

Again the silence as she assessed this change of tack. "I'll survive."

"Is that what you want me to tell Jenny, that you'll survive?"

"No. Don't tell her I called. I shouldn't have. I'm sorry. I just had to know she was all right."

"Not as glamorous and exciting as you expected?"

"I never expected it would be. Does it make you feel nice and superior to think I did?"

"No. But I'll say it does if you want to make a fight out of it."

After a short intake of breath she said, "I'm not going to fight with you, Manny. Please just tell me how Jenny is."

He waited to let her know he was controlling the conversation. "She wasn't too happy that first night. Cried in her room and..."

"What happened? What made her cry?"

What did she think had made her daughter cry when she was in a strange house with a father she had never met, knowing her mother was about to go to prison? "I imagine it was all a bit much for her. She was all right the next morning. Had cornflakes for breakfast and we were chatting like old friends by the time I took her to school." It was near enough to the truth. "She has met my Mum and Dad and we went round to your place to pick up some more clothes for her. Met your neighbour, Alice Todd. She seems nice. We've been out for pizza, she cooked us a meal one evening, we visited one of my clients where she got some idea of what sort of work I do, and she's been talking to her friends on the phone. I'd say she's adapting well to the circumstances and is as happy as you could expect her to be."

There was a long sigh at the other end of the line. He had a feeling she was conflicted between being happy for her daughter and jealous that he had got on so well with her.

"I bet she had deep pan gourmet pizza with extra anchovies," she said sadly.

He stared in confusion at the plate he was still holding. "How did you know that?"

"It's what she always has."

He had ordered the pizza, not Jenny. No wonder she had reacted strangely.

"I'm finding out we have a surprising amount in common," he said, "apart from the hair and eyebrows. An argument for nature against nurture."

"I already knew that," Katie responded with what

almost sounded like a concession of defeat, "despite all my best efforts."

He couldn't think of a smart retort. "We're having some of her friends over for a party."

"A party?"

"It seems like a good idea. Make her feel more relaxed and at home here."

"I wish you had asked me about it first."

"I couldn't, could I?"

"You could have telephoned me."

"You didn't exactly encourage communication. Anyway, having a party didn't seem an earth shattering decision that required consultation."

"She's my daughter, Manny."

"Yes," he said. It seemed pointless saying anything else. He was fast becoming tired of the conversation.

"You know nothing about her. Not to be making decisions that affect her life, and mine. You've got to remember I'm her mother."

"Yes."

"Why do you keep saying yes? What does that mean?"

"It means I know you are Jenny's mother and I will in future take more care to consult with you before we make any decisions I consider will affect her life and yours." He didn't mean it, but if it kept her calm until he could get off the phone he didn't care.

"Good," Katie retorted as if she had won the point. "Damn. I've got to go."

He had already heard a bell ringing in the prison room from which he imagined she was talking. "I think I should tell Jenny you called, that you asked how she was and that you are okay," he said. "I can say it happened while she wasn't here and that you were sorry you missed her."

"No, don't do that." She sounded uncertain as if she half thought it was a good idea. "I have to think about it. I'll call again soon."

The phone clicked dead. A vision came into Manny's mind of the barred door slamming on a prison cell and Katie locked inside, angry, uncertain, perhaps even frightened.

He sat for a long time with the phone in his hand, staring at a calendar on the wall without seeing it.

Chapter 12

Claire O'Connell said a strange thing to him the next morning. He had called in to show her some more of his ideas for the project and found her almost equally interested in how he was getting on with his new daughter. "You might have to watch her, Manny. She sounds like a girl who likes her own way and knows how to get it."

"Not surprising, with who she's got for a mother," Manny responded, and told her about the telephone call he had received.

Claire was surprised at Katie's refusal to allow Jenny to visit her. "I can understand her attitude to a point," she admitted. "However don't you think it's rather selfish? She's considering her own feelings, not her daughter's. I think I'd put my child's need to come and see me before my own preference not to be seen in such surroundings."

As she so often did, she was looking out of the window across the city. "But then I wouldn't have got myself in that situation in the first place," she reflected, turning back to him. "Do you think she is regretting it?"

Manny considered she might, adding that he didn't care very much one way or the other. Later, before he left, Claire reminded him again, "Although she's very mature for her age, Manny, she's still a teenage girl and they're a breed of their own. I know because I've got one, and another who is growing into that phase much faster than I want her to. Your one sounds even a little smarter and more capable of being manipulative than most."

Manny demurred. "If young people are treated as individuals in their own right, they'll respond accordingly. That's what I'm trying to do with Jenny."

Claire shook her head. "That sounds like something out of the Little Red Book of the New Era Men's Support Alliance. Be careful Manny. You don't let your NEMSA activities interfere with your work and it would be wise to adopt the same strategy in your dealings with Jenny."

"Would you say the same thing to a feminist?"

Claire nodded. "Or a theosophist. I have no bias in this matter, believe me. I speak only as your friend."

Later, as he was driving home from her office, he realised it was not so much that his NEMSA activities would impinge on his life with Jenny as the other way round. The next meeting was on Friday night. Could he go to it and leave her alone by herself?

To his considerable relief, the decision proved unnecessary.

"I have to go over to Sweeny's on Friday after school," Jenny advised him. "She's doing my hair for the party."

Manny studied her hair and wondered what Sweeny would do with it. Like his own, the carrot coloured strands tended to lie whatever way they wanted.

"What have you decided to wear?" he asked her.

"I'll show you. Can you wait a minute?"

He waited more like ten minutes until she reappeared dressed, as far as he could tell, exactly as she had been on the first night he had seen her. "Why do you need your hair done if you are going to wear that hat?" he asked, astonishment overwhelming prudence. "Didn't you get some other clothes to wear when we went over to your place?"

The look Jenny returned mingled resentment with uncertainty. "Don't you like my clothes?"

"They're fine." Manny backed away. "If you want to go over to Sweeny's, that's okay with me. Go ahead. It's very nice of her to offer."

"I have been worrying about it."

"About what?"

"My clothes."

"Look, I'm sorry. I didn't mean to say anything derogatory. Wear what you like."

"Not if you don't like them."

"I like everything about you."

"But not my clothes."

Manny tried again. "If that's what you and your friends wear, Jenny, that's fine with me. It's not what I would wear, but I'm a man anyway." His attempt to make a joke of it failed. Jenny seemed about to cry. "I'm just a bit surprised," he admitted. "I was expecting to see you in something nice you'd brought back from your place."

"I've tried them all on and I don't like any of them. Not for a party." She looked at him speculatively. "If I was still living with Mum she would probably buy me something new to wear."

Why hadn't he thought of that? "Well, that's not a problem. I'll buy you something."

"Would you?"

"I'd love to." He warmed to the idea. "The shops will still be open when I pick you up from school tomorrow. How about we go down and pick something out?"

She rushed across, gave him a big hug and went into her room where he could hear her calling Betty Polson and telling her about it. He stood for a long time absorbing the lingering sensation of having her arms wrapped around him. The next day they went shopping.

Manny had never shopped with anyone before. In fact, he'd never shopped in the sense that he went from shop to shop trying on everything and spending what seemed eternity to make a decision. His habit was to enter a shop knowing what he wanted. The concept of shopping for its own sake, of sampling everything before you reached your decision, was alien to his way of thinking. Men were hunters and women were gatherers. That's what it was. Hunters had to act quickly to get what they wanted. Gatherers had more time to make their selections. He was quite pleased with himself for having that thought.

Jenny was definitely a gatherer. He could see she loved shops, the things in them, the people moving through them, the sense of life and activity and high expectations that reverberated through them. Shopping was excitement and she was quickly caught up in it. She spent more than half an hour in the first big department store, leaving dresses, skirts and tops strewn on chairs and across the racks, attendants searching for their hangers.

"Do you like this?" she would demand. "Or this? What about this one? Tell me what you really like."

He pointed out some dresses. All of them elegant and sophisticated and a far cry from the ragamuffin look. Jenny raised an eyebrow.

"You don't think they're too old for me?"

"Not at all."

Jenny studied the dresses before adding them to the discard pile.

The next shop was the same, and the next, except that now all the clothes she was examining seemed to him to be moving closer to the style he preferred. She tried on long dresses and short dresses, different combinations of skirts and tops, even a pair styled like workmen's overalls, although no workman would have been seen dead in multi-coloured printed silk.

"What do you have in mind exactly?" he asked, laughing lightly to suppress his growing impatience with this long drawn out process of what should have been a simple decision.

"Something that's just right for me," she replied in a puzzled voice, as if the answer was obvious. "So that I can dazzle everyone and you'll be proud to show me off as your daughter."

They narrowed their target to smaller, more expensive boutiques. He caught Jenny turning her head to consider him questioningly as they entered one that had high priced gowns in the window. As he gave no sign of hesitating, she continued with a more confident step to meet the attendants who were closing in.

It was in this shop that they found her outfit, or rather, Manny did and pointed it out to her. It was displayed on a mannequin which had a slight, girlish figure, modest pose and a demure smile with red hair not unlike his and Jenny's own. Very simple and dark green, it was an off the shoulder dress similar to one he had liked in the first shop, though much more stylishly cut.

"How about that one?" he asked.

She frowned at him uncertainly. "Not too expensive?"

"Try it on."

She looked gorgeous in it. When she stepped out of the dressing booth to parade it before him, several people stopped to admire her, including a number of men. Manny glared at them and they grinned sheepishly, but glanced back once more as they moved on.

The material was clingy and had a slight sheen to it. Two simple straps supported it over her shoulders, crossing at the back. While its neckline was cut modestly, it left no-one in any doubt that his daughter had quite a striking pair of well rounded, youthfully firm breasts. Not only that, it curved in to her trim waist and out over her hips, falling from there in a series of soft folds to the floor. Its dark green colour, like the moss that grows in the darkest places among rocks and on old trees, was perfect for her hair and skin toning.

She stood before him, elegant, sophisticated, and uncertain. "Well?"

"Do you like it?"

She nodded hesitantly. "I love it."

He also loved it, and her. Without even considering the price tag he handed the attendant his credit card.

"Oh, thank you," Jenny cried exultingly. "Thank you, Dad. I really do love it."

If he'd said she loved him he couldn't have felt more pleased with himself. It was when she emerged again, back in her jeans and t-shirt, that the contrast gave him pause. Would Katie have agreed to such a dress, Katie who had selected, or at least approved, the baggy skirt and the floppy hat? Unless he was mistaken, Jenny had never had a dress like this before, had never looked like this before.

They found dark bronze-coloured shoes that toned well with the green, and two simple gold chains to go round her neck and wrist.

"Isn't it gorgeous? The dress?" They had finished shopping and were sitting on spindly chairs on one side of the shopping mall drinking thin coffee served by a matching waitress.

"It's very different to the other clothes you've been wearing. Would your mother like it?"

"Can't we buy you something?" She was standing off, eyeing him up and down. "A jumper or something? A big chunky cardigan would be very smart. One of those multi-coloured ones." They had seen them in several display windows on their peregrinations through the shopping centre. Multi-coloured woollens were the in thing.

"Okay," he agreed. "I guess I have to be presentable when I meet your friends."

Fifteen minutes later, after they had disposed of their coffees and found a menswear shop, Manny selected a jumper he wanted. Jenny still rummaged through the stacks.

"How can you make a decision so quickly?" she demanded. "You haven't seen everything yet. There might be something nicer."

Manny laughed. "Jenny, there might always be something nicer. That's just life. I like this one."

She didn't agree, one hand still resting on a pile of jumpers as she reluctantly relinquished the urge to keep looking. "Okay. Try it on. Let me see you in it."

He shrugged off the V-necked jumper he was wearing and pulled on the bulkier crew-necked one.

"There, it's perfect," he insisted, conscious of her only half-hearted acceptance as he hurried to pay for it before she could change his mind.

On the way back to his apartment she asked if they could call round to Sweeny's house to show her the dress. Manny liked the idea. Alice Todd's reaction to the dress would help settle the niggling doubts he was having and he had no objections to seeing her again.

As it turned out there was no opportunity to ask Alice privately what she thought of the dress. Jenny rushed out of the car when they got there, dashed into the house and called out "Don't peek, don't peek, I've got something to show you." Alice emerged from the front door calling back "I'm not peeking, I'm not peeking". She shrugged an amused grin at Manny, placed her hands over her eyes and whispered, "What am I not peeking at?"

Reaching back inside the car, Manny pulled out the new jumper and drew it over his head. "Me, for a start," he said, "Just a quick peek. You'll have to close your eyes again before Jenny comes out."

Alice spread her fingers to see through them as he ran his hands down the jumper and struck a pose.

"My. Mr Youngman about town. You do look smart," she laughed. "Have we been on a shopping spree?"

Manny nodded. "Jenny and I picked it out together. Wait until you see what I bought for her."

"I can't, but it seems I have to. I'd better not peek anymore." Alice closed her fingers without removing the conspiratorial smile from her face. "I'm still not peeking," she called out to Jenny.

Alice wore a light green dress with an abstract pattern of yellows and pale oranges which gave her a very summery appearance. Behind the closed fingers she had on glasses, Manny noticed, and he tried to remember whether she had been wearing them on the previous occasion. No, he decided, because he recalled he had admired the fineness of her features and the almost elfin look of her upturned nose. He wouldn't have seen that if she had been wearing glasses. She had a good figure, too. His imagination created a very alluring vision of her in the green dress.

Jenny burst out of the house calling "What do you think?" and pirouetted in front of them.

Alice dropped her hands. "Jenny! You look so grown up and elegant. It's the most beautiful dress."

"Dad picked it out for me." Jenny told her, continuing to pirouette. "Doesn't he have the most exquisite taste? I want to wear it all the time." She stopped and ran her hands down over the glowing fabric, her face a huge grin. "I suppose I shouldn't, should I? Come with me while I go and change, Sweeny."

She dashed into the house and Alice followed her.

Left to wait for them to re-emerge, Manny wondered why Katie had not left Jenny with Alice instead of bringing her to him.

Chapter 13

He wore his new jumper on Friday afternoon when he kept his appointment with Mr James at the school.

Entering the building provoked all five of his senses into a recollection of the unattractive brick edifice he had attended more than two decades before. The yells that echoed along corridors and through cavernous open spaces set up sympathetic reverberations along half-forgotten pathways to memories of his childhood.

How would he design a school if he were given such a commission? Would the functional requirements of moving large numbers of children through the structure and creating spaces for a variety of activities be limiting or leave enough scope to create an environment that enhanced the learning process?

He stopped in one of the open spaces, a bitumen courtyard with white lines marking out courts for a variety of games. This was Jenny's school, where she spent most of her time, learned, experienced relationships, was influenced in untold ways. He tried to absorb it, to understand more about her by her relationship to this space, but found it uncommunicative.

Mr James was waiting in a scarred classroom. "You're Jenny Frank's father?" He held a piece of paper in his hand and looked from Manny to it and back again as if there was some conflict between them.

"Isn't it obvious?" Manny gestured at his red hair.

"Not when your name's Youngman."

"I explained that in the note."

"So I see," the teacher replied and waved the piece of paper as if he was still having a problem understanding it. "We do have a responsibility to take adequate care, of course. Jenny could have written the note herself, or have one of her friends write it."

"I imagine she could have but she didn't, I assume, as her teacher, you're familiar with her writing. That's mine."

"Jenny is in fact staying with you?"

"As I said in the note."

"And her mother is away? That is Mrs Frank, by the way. We've always known her as that. Not as Mrs Youngman."

"Jenny's mother and I are not married and never have been." Manny was becoming annoyed by this man who seemed unable to get to the point and was casting aspersions on Jenny's character. "I am, nonetheless, her father, and she is currently staying with me. I don't see that this is any concern of the school's other than for your administrative purposes. My informing you was simply a matter of courtesy."

"Of course." Mr James nodded, narrowing his eyes and pursing his lips as if they had reached agreement on some deep truth. Then his lips straightened, his eyes widened, apparently satisfied with Manny's identity sufficiently to turn at last to the real issue at hand.

"We're having problems with Jenny. She's disruptive in

class. Especially with male teachers. She refuses to accept their instructions." He hesitated, as if making a decision. "She has called me a pig, to my face. She can be very rude, and it encourages the other girls."

Manny stared at him in astonishment. "Jenny?" he said, as if Mr James might be mistaken.

"On previous occasions I have spoken about this with her mother," Mr James continued. "I was hoping that, well, now you appear to have custody..."

"She's not exactly in my custody."

Mr James registered disappointment at this remark without being dissuaded. "The school can't be expected to put up with such behaviour, Mr Youngman."

Manny was no longer feeling annoyed. This sounded serious.

"No, I can see it can't."

"I am hoping for your co-operation."

"Of course." Manny had no idea what else to say.

"So you will do something about it?" Mr James still seemed to require reassurance.

"Er, yes. What did you want me to do?" He had no ideas of his own and hoped the teacher could give him some positive guidance.

"Parents have a responsibility for the behaviour of their children... Mr Youngman." The name was added as if an unspoken "even if they are not married" hung between the words.

"Yes, well. She is my daughter although she has not

lived with me until now. I had... not seen her in years," he added, not certain why he was not telling the whole truth. "To be honest with you I don't know her very well. I've seen one or two signs of her being a little difficult, especially about sexist issues. I had no idea..." His thoughts ran down to a halt.

"Something has to be done." Despite Mr James trying to sound immovable, the earlier determination in his voice was dissolving into a concession of defeat.

"I think it's really her mother talking. She's just repeating it." As he said it, Manny felt guilty of betraying both Katie and Jenny. "I'll talk to her," he promised. "I'll explain to her that it's not acceptable behaviour. She may listen to me, though I don't have much practice at any of this."

Mr James nodded as if he had already come to this realisation.

"Is it affecting her school work?" Manny asked, because it seemed the most important consideration.

Mr James was clearly uncomfortable. "She is a very intelligent student and able to achieve creditable results despite her attitudinal problems. That does not make them any more acceptable, however."

"How does she relate to the other students, and to other teachers? Are there problems there?"

"I would think the problems I have outlined are sufficient, Mr Youngman. Jenny is a disruptive influence in a classroom situation."

"I hear that. I am trying to get a broader picture of the situation, to see where I might be able to influence her."

"Perhaps if you spoke to the School Counsellor," the teacher suggested. "She has spoken to Jenny previously, and to Mrs Frank, and she may be able to suggest something else you can do. I must confess, Mr Youngman, I'm at the end of my tether with your daughter."

The School Counsellor's name was Bronson. She had blonde hair pulled back in a tight bun, thin lips and a peaky nose and she liked to be called by her first name, Ursula, which she pronounced Urs'la. His first impression that he didn't like her very much changed when he realised she was on Jenny's side.

"I've spoke with her at Mr James' insistence," she confirmed. "To a considerable extent I think the problem is of his own making. I'll be frank with you, Mr Youngman, Jenny is very mature for her age. That can be difficult in a school environment. She is also a strong-minded young woman with firm views of her own. Some male teachers find that threatening."

"What do you think I should do?" Manny asked her. "Give her a parental talking to?"

"Difficult in your situation."

"I've been trying not to behave like a traditional father. Quite apart from the fact that I haven't been her father in that sense, I don't believe in it."

"I wouldn't worry too much. Mr James is right to some extent. He can't allow it to continue even if he does cause a lot of it by his own attitude. There could be a reason for that. His marriage broke up recently. What I would do if I were you, Mr Youngman, is inform Jenny what Mr James has told you without condemning or criticising her. State it objectively and indicate you expect her to deal with it. She's an intelligent girl and, given your unusual circumstances, you will be a bigger than usual influence in her life at the moment."

Manny smiled brightly. James was an idiot. Treating Jenny like an adult would achieve far more than treating her as if she could not make decisions for herself. He set off to his NEMSA meeting with a light heart and no doubts that he was, indeed, putting his theories into practice.

Chapter 14

The NEMSA meeting was at the old converted hotel by the docks where Manny had met Tony a few days before, although it seemed like weeks with all that had happened in between. As it had once looked out over the ocean before the docks were built in front of it, some wag a hundred years before had named it "The End of the Earth". Manny had insisted on the name being retained when he supervised its conversion from a seedy corner pub to an up-market complex of offices, shops, restaurants and a conference centre where a variety of organizations held their meetings. "See you at The End of the Earth," or "it's The End of the Earth as we know it" were common exchanges between the members of NEMSA, which occupied one of the upstairs rooms.

This evening was a formal meeting, which meant a short, official agenda they would get through as quickly as possible. They had no speakers. When Manny walked into the room with its warm orange lighting and dark timbered, red leather upholstered chairs and tables, he saw Tony holding court in one corner, arguing a point with Bobby Carlsson while Tommy Bloffwitch and Neil Blighton urged him on.

They were a mixed bunch, he thought, not for the first time. Apart from all being men they would not have been considered to have a lot of common in another environment. They ranged from academics to tradesmen, outspoken bigots to shy introverts and politically conservative to left-wing radicals. What brought them together was a shared need to talk to other men without being concerned about societal expectations.

Bobby was a teacher and, after Tony, the richest source of advice and information on gender issues. He had recommended many of the writers whose books filled Manny's shelves.

"Manny," he called, beckoning him to join them. He was a tall, big-boned man reputed to be able to control the most rowdy classes at a high school in one of the poorest suburbs. His long arms seemed constantly in motion, perhaps to ward off attack, or to keep his students' attention focused on him and what he was trying to teach. "Come in, come in." He used his arms to carve a path through the group. "I need you to help me explain to this ignoramus why the fable of the Fisher King is an analogy of the male/female relationship."

"Manny's got something a lot more interesting than that to talk about," Tony informed the gathering. "He's had a baby since we last saw him."

Surprised faces turned towards him.

"Not a baby," Manny demurred. "She's fifteen."

"Good God. The mother must have found giving birth a bit painful," Bobby laughed. "Come on, old son, out with the sordid details."

As the news spread, more faces turned towards them. Manny felt as though he was being hemmed in, forced into a role he didn't want to play. Having Jenny was something he was still exploring. Relating the sordid details, as Bobby put it, seemed to be degrading it. He didn't want to do that.

Tony appeared to sense his dilemma and stepped in to help. "An old girlfriend had to go to jail and turned up on Manny's doorstep asking him to take care of his daughter he never knew he had."

"What did she have to go to jail for?" queried Neil Blighton, who was a lawyer. Manny was planning to get him aside later and ask about the rights of fathers to have access to their children if they hadn't raised them.

"She threw a fake bomb through the toilet window of a men's club," Tony continued telling the story.

"I didn't think they were allowed to have men-only clubs anymore," Bobby commented.

Neil contradicted him. "We're one for a start," he pointed out. "I heard about this incident and know the club where it happened. While its rules allow for women to be members, it's only with limited access to services and facilities. They are not encouraged and most women know it and have the sense not to push it. The membership is mostly professionals. Lawyers, judges, doctors, all right wingers. See themselves as some sort of power bloc influencing the government."

"Sounds like it served them right having a bomb thrown into their toilet," Bobby grinned. "Caught them with their pants down."

"It wasn't a real bomb." Manny was surprised to find

he was defending Katie.

"Doesn't make any difference," asserted Tommy Bloffwitch, pulling his two inch leather belt up tighter over the red checked shirt that never seemed to sit comfortably on his protruding stomach. "Whoever they were she shouldn't have done it. Was anyone hurt?"

Neil said no-one had been injured seriously, only cuts and bruises as they tried to escape what they had no way of knowing was not a real bomb.

"So there," Tommy proclaimed. "Imagine if some bloody woman did that to us? Serve her right going to jail."

"Still, you've got to admire her for sticking to her guns and going to jail for what she believes in," Bobby countered. "Even if you don't agree with her ideas you have to admit she's got guts."

"I might if she had achieved anything," Neil responded. "The reality is she didn't. The club continues to function with its rules unchanged. She has been incarcerated and there has been little reporting of the case so she hasn't even got publicity for her cause. Meanwhile, Manny is stuck with having to feed and house the child. No winners there as far as I can see."

"No, you're wrong," Tony interjected. "Manny's won a daughter, haven't you, Manny? From what he tells me she's a lovely kid and they're getting on well together."

"That so, Manny?" Bobby asked. "You've never had kids. Must be a bit strange."

Tommy gave an explosive laugh. "Never had kids?

You don't know you're own bloody luck." He had three daughters.

"He's approaching it like a new era man," Tony told them. "Treating her as an individual person and not as a female or as his daughter."

Tommy let out another laugh. "Shit," he said. "How's that work?"

"Sounds dangerous, old son," Bobby commented. "How old did you say she was?"

"Fifteen," Manny told him. "But she's very mature."

"Oh they all are, believe me," Bobby grinned. "Aren't they Tommy?"

"Too right," Tommy grinned with him. "My three are twelve, thirteen and sixteen and they all think they're thirty and know it all."

"So how does the new man deal with a fifteen year old individual female person?" Bobby added. "Come on, old son. Explain it to me. I'm fascinated." Bobby had two sons and three daughters from two failed marriages.

"As Tony said," Manny replied, "I treat her as if I had an adult friend staying in my house. You have to adapt and compromise to get along, and that's what we do."

"She adapts and compromises, too?"

"It's strange for her, and it has only been a few days. We're both learning."

"Can't be done," asserted Tommy. "Sorry mate. Teenage girls might be individuals but they are not reasonable adults and they're not just friends staying with you."

"He has a point, old son," Bobby agreed. "You could be mixing up two very different problems."

"No, he's not." Tony seemed to have taken on the role of Manny's defender. "It's just a different aspect of the same problem. Part of the conditioning for men is that we are expected to relate to daughters in a certain way."

"What way?" Bobby interjected. "I don't treat my daughters differently to my sons, and I don't think I should."

"I'll bet you do."

"Well, I assert that I don't."

"Do you tell your sons how pretty they are when they put on a new shirt? Do you put your arm around them and give them a kiss?"

"I hug my sons, as it happens. And kiss them. I'm not ashamed of it."

"Jeez. You wouldn't get me kissing my son, if I had one," Tommy growled. "People'd think we were poofters."

"That's what Tony's talking about," Manny insisted, breaking back into the conversation. "That's the conditioning, Tommy. Why shouldn't men kiss each other, if they want to? It doesn't have to mean we're queer."

Tommy grimaced as if he had a bad taste in his mouth. "It just doesn't seem right."

"Bet you don't even kiss your girls, Tommy," intervened one of several men who had joined the group, attracted by the animated voices.

Tommy grinned, but looked wistful. "Do you know," he said, as if confiding something that had been weighing on his mind, "I can't even get them to come fishing with me. Stick their noses up in the air and go all bloody prissy. Clones of their mother. They expect me to go to the ballet and crap like that then can't understand when I say if they want me to share in their interests they should be prepared to share mine. You know what one of them said? Going to the ballet was acceptable. Bashing round the bush like a red-necked macho throwback was not. That's what she called me, a red necked macho throwback. While her mother's standing there laughing. I nearly slapped the stupid little so and so. Jeez they make you bloody mad, don't they?" Suddenly he laughed again, as if expressing the thoughts had dispersed a cloud. "You'll find out Manny mate, now you've got one of your own."

Later, when Manny circulated around the other members, doing his duties as President, he found himself seeking out men with daughters.

"Can't see there's much difference between your situation and getting a step-daughter," said a man named Charlie. "When I married again I got two step-daughters. Never had a daughter before. It's not that hard. I find it harder to live with their mother than with them."

Sol Garfwicz had a daughter, but Manny found Sol had nothing to offer that was enlightening. Sol's was a stunted personality produced by a workaholic father and an alcoholic mother. He had lost his job in a government agency that had been forced into massive downsizing, his marriage was shaky and he was drinking. Tony said he was in a depressed state and had talked about killing himself.

"How's it going, Sol?" he asked, and declined the man's suggestion of 'just another one'. They all drank a lot, it occurred to him, and it had produced some riotous evenings in the snug comfort of The End of the Earth. Oddly, though, the thought of having to spend more evenings at home, and drinking less when he came out, was not as unattractive as it might have been.

Before he left, Manny caught up with Bobby Carlsson again in his role as membership officer. "You know a teacher named James? Teaches literature at my new daughter's high school."

Bobby shook his head. "Not one of my acquaintances. Your daughter having problems at school?"

"She hasn't been getting on with this teacher. I think it's more his fault than hers because he's got a few problems of his own. His wife's just left him, poor sod. I was thinking we might invite him to become a member."

Bobby said he would check it out and if nothing else pass on the free "Talk To A Mate" phone number and explain that advice on dealing with separation was one of the services it offered. "Maybe you should try them, too, Manny," Bobby said. "They give advice on parenting issues and building relationships. You know what they say. They're only a phone call away."

Manny grinned at him. "Why do I need them when I've got my friends?" he laughed, recognising as he said it that it was a typical cop-out response. "You're right. I will think about it." Continuing to circulate he thought to himself that he genuinely did feel very comfortable and among friends. This was putting their theories into practice and so was what he was doing with Jenny. That reminded him it was time to go and pick her up from Alice Todd's and that was someone he could feel comfortable with as well.

When he got there he was amazed by what Alice had been able to do with Jenny's hair. The wildness had been tamed, layered and cut shorter in places to create a sculptured arrangement which Jenny assured him was the latest funky, cool, cbo teenstyle.

Alice was looking good, too, and he told her so as well as complimenting her on what she had done for Jenny. Her response was a short moue of surprise followed by a sparkling smile. While Jenny retrieved her things he asked Alice what her favourite music was and her favourite food, and whether she liked up-market fashionable restaurants, charming little hideaways with discreet booths and subdued lighting or cute modern eateries with themed décor and fast service. By the time Jenny was ready to leave he hadn't invited Alice to go out with him but he had a fair idea where he would take her when he did.

He was still thinking about it going along in the car when Jenny asked him about NEMSA.

"What do you do there?"

He explained that it was a social meeting with an underlying agenda of men's health and wellbeing.

"We have one man who lives in a house full of women.

Wife and three daughters. While he loves them there are times, he admits, when it's gets a bit much for him and he wants to scream at them. Instead he comes to NEMSA and tells us about it. We sympathise with him, which lets his anger and frustration get defused. He's better off for it and so are his wife and daughters.

"Another man lost his job and now his wife is talking about leaving him and taking his children with her. He's in a very bad way. NEMSA is somewhere he can talk it through. We've told him about some services where he can talk to trained counsellors and get professional help."

He was aware of Jenny studying him with a tight expression.

"It's not that man's wife's and daughters' fault that he gets angry."

Which was very likely given the sort of man Tommy was, Manny thought. What did he do now to explain what he was trying to say without accusing her of missing the point. He was not giving one of his talks and she was not one of the audience.

"You're right," he said after a few moments thought. "It's not. However, he does get angry and we try to help him with that."

"Why did that other man's wife leave him?"

"Does it matter?"

"What if he did something terrible to her? Would you still support him, just because he's a man?"

"Not just because he's a man. Because he's in trouble

and he needs help. We do not condone violence. We would try to show him there was a better way to deal with his problems."

"So what about his wife? Maybe she needs help."

Manny was beginning to think he had given two bad examples and was digging himself a hole it was not going to be easy to get out of.

"Some men seem to find it harder to ask for help than women. All we do is try to provide somewhere men like that can come and talk to other men."

"And that's all NEMSA is?" She sounded confused. "Don't you talk about women taking jobs that men should be getting and destroying the traditional social and family structure by trying to be like men?"

Whoa! The hole had got deeper, and he wasn't the only one digging it. He glanced sideways at her and saw she was staring out of the window as if avoiding looking at him. "Is that what Katie told you?"

She went still. "I do think about these things myself, you know. I've talked about it with other girls. I have my own ideas."

"Good. As long as you know which are yours and which are your mother's."

Now she was looking at him.

"Obviously I have views that are different to the ones you were brought up with," he continued. "It's like you were brought up in a religious family and now find yourself living with an atheist. All I want is that you make up your own mind."

"Can I make up my own mind now?"

He nodded.

"I'd like to have pizza again," she said.

He turned the car to go in the new direction. Deep pan fried pizza with anchovies was something they could agree on.

Chapter 15

"I saw Mr James yesterday." He chose his words carefully, not wanting the slightest suggestion of criticism or judgment of any kind. They were at breakfast on Saturday morning.

"Did you?" She was pouring milk over her cornflakes.

"Why don't you like him?"

"What's to like? He's an idiot."

That seemed to be in line with what Ursula Bronson had told him, but he didn't think he should tell Jenny the counsellor's views. Nor was it appropriate to act the indignant parent and tell her she shouldn't talk about a teacher like that. "Is that a problem for you?"

"No. I just tell him what I think. He isn't a problem."

"It isn't affecting your schoolwork." He made the sentence a statement and not a question.

"Of course not." She was holding the toast with one hand and flicking the pages of a magazine with another. Something called 'Teen Scene' he hadn't seen before.

"Sometimes there's no point in upsetting someone else, no matter how much of an idiot they are," he said. "Most times it causes problems in the end and you have to think whether it's worth it."

Jenny paused in what she was doing, considered this, wrinkled her nose and returned to flicking through the pages. He wondered what she was searching for.

As if she had become aware he was watching her she

closed the magazine and laid it on the table. "I haven't been so tough on him the last few days," she said. "Not since I've been staying with you."

Manny had been holding a newspaper, without reading it, to give an added casualness to the conversation, and wondered whether her flicking through the magazine pages had been something similar. Now he frowned across at her, raising one eyebrow. "Why has that changed things?"

"After what you said about not calling all men sexist pigs, I've been trying it out. Being less aggressive. I think it works, you know? Anyway, some of the boys seem to like me more and I haven't made any trouble in Mr James's class." She was giving him a big smile and for a minute he wondered if she was sending him up. But there was something in her eyes that said she wasn't, and that she wanted him to approve.

"That's wonderful to hear, Jenny," he said.

She nodded as if that was what she had wanted. "I think I'm learning a lot from being with you. I was a bit worried when I first came, but I think it's been good for me. I'm seeing the world through your eyes, and learning a lot more about all sorts of things."

There was something about the way she said this that gave him pause. It was almost like when she was parroting Katie, except these weren't Katie's words.

When Jenny spoke again he got a clue whose words they were.

"I was telling Sweeny last night when she was doing

my hair. Just going shopping with you. You have such excellent taste in clothes. I would never have bought a dress like that for myself before you showed me what you liked. Then I could see that you were right. Sweeny loved it too and she's done my hair fabulously to go with it, don't you think?"

Manny agreed. Alice had done a great job.

"What sort of makeup do you think I should wear?"

He hadn't thought of that. "Not much at all. With young skin like yours you don't need much."

"Oh, you're absolutely right. But I do need something, don't you think? Just a little highlight maybe, and some eye shadow? Lipstick of course. What do you think of a coppery shade, like the shoes? Not exactly, but you know what I mean."

"That sounds like it." He hadn't any idea what she meant and wasn't sure what a highlight was.

"I knew you'd know what was right," Jenny was glowing at him. "The trouble is, I haven't got anything like that. I haven't got any real makeup at all."

"We should have got some yesterday, at the shops," he told her. "I'll run you down now."

"Would you? Could I call my friend Betty and take her with me? She can help me."

He had a couple of calls he wanted to make and they had an invitation from his mother to call in for lunch because she wanted to see Jenny again, but there was time to fit in a trip to buy her some makeup. On the way over he asked her more about Alice and how long she had lived next door.

"She was there when we came. I don't remember most of that time because I was so small. We lived in a flat before that, I think. Nan lived in the house where we're living now and used to babysit me while Mum was at work. She died when I was five."

"What about Katie's father? Did you know him?"

Jenny shook her head. "He died before my grandmother."

"Katie didn't like him, did she?"

Jenny seemed surprised at this. "Didn't she? She never talks about him much."

They reached Betty's house and further communication between them gave way to the barrage of gossip that began as soon as the two girls were together in the car.

He left them at the shopping centre while he ran some errands. When he returned they were still talking, standing at the kerb waiting for him. Betty was staying at the shops to be collected by her mother. Jenny waved to her as they drove away from the kerb, turning a smiling face back to Manny.

"Do you want to smell the perfume?" She held out a slim wrist and he sniffed it obediently.

"Smells beautiful. What's it called?"

"Midnight Fascination. Cool, huh? Not too strong. Betty and I agreed it's best to have just a hint. What do you think?"

"Smells fine to me. To be honest, I don't think men respond to the difference in perfumes as much as women think we do."

Jenny found this surprising. "Don't they?"

He shook his head. "I guess most men like a woman to smell nice. It's not all that important."

"You wouldn't think so from all the adverts."

"If you judge reality by what you see in advertisements, you'll find yourself living in fantasy land."

She smiled at him and again he had the odd feeling she was being condescending, as if he didn't know what he was talking about. He glanced at her as they drove along, trying to make the leap between the intellectual-looking girl with the hat she had been on their first encounter and this young fashionista who seemed to care more about eye shadow and lipstick than the feminist interpretation of literature. Perhaps she was a butterfly emerging from a cocoon, he wondered, or had she dressed like that for Katie and was now refiguring herself to be what she thought he wanted? Had she been repressed and was now expanding into her real self because he was treating her like a woman and not a child?

Her smile gave him no answers, except that she was happy. For the moment, he decided, that was enough.

In the street where his parents lived he pulled over and parked a short distance from the house so that he could point things out to her before they went in.

"I was born here and lived here all my life until I left home when I was nineteen. That was about five years before you were born. I used to play up and down this street. There was a vacant bit of land down on the corner where that big house is now. We used to play football and cricket there. The street was full of kids in those days. Mostly old people now."

His parents lived in an older style house made of dark red bricks with once-white-now-yellowing cement forming a decorative feature. The garden was neat and tidy, the lawn contained between cement paths he had helped his Dad lay when he was a teenager.

They entered through an iron gate and walked along the side of the house to the back garden where the sound of hammering came from a small shed.

"Dad," Manny explained. "Hides out here a lot."

Through a cobwebbed window they could see their older look-alike bending over something clamped in a vice. He looked up, lifted his sandy eyebrows in a smile and moved across to open the door.

"Jenny and Manny. Hello. Hello." He hesitated. Jenny moved in quickly, giving him a hug and a kiss. Manny felt something melt inside him and wanted to give both of them a hug and kiss.

Why not? He never had hugged his Dad before. He stepped forward and put his arms round both of them. His Dad tensed, surprised.

"Watch it," he grunted. "If we get mixed up they'll never tell us apart."

They all laughed. Manny felt his face soften into a smile that reflected the warm glow that was flooding his body. These two people were him. Why was he worrying about establishing a relationship? It was just there.

"What are you doing, Gramps?" Jenny asked with transparent curiosity.

They disentangled and Gramps stepped back to let them into his private space.

"Fixing an old chair. The leg's getting old and wonky like me and I'm putting some new dowels in."

"Can I help?"

"Sure. You can hold it..." He stopped when he saw Manny winking at him.

To the questioning expression on his face Manny said, "You hold it."

Gramps complied, watching with growing awareness and delight as Jenny took the dowel from the bench, tested it in the hole he had been cleaning out, handed it to him to hold in place and began applying the glue to its end. She found the clamps and screwed them in place, locking the dowel into the hole to set.

"Got any other jobs you need doing, Dad?" Manny smiled. "Jenny got an 'A' in her woodwork class at school."

Gramps grinned back at him. "Did she? You don't say? Well, come to think of it there are a quite a few things I've been meaning to get around to. How long have I got her for?"

"I'll go in and ask Mum if she can hold off lunch for half an hour," Manny suggested. "That give you enough time?"

"I'll say," Gramps laughed. "Get along with you then. Come on girl. We've got work to do."

He began reaching for a shelf and taking down something broken that was stored there. Manny left the shed and walked up to the back door of the house, his inner warmth still glowing. While there might have been a lot of Jenny's life he and his parents had missed, there was still a lot to be experienced.

His Mum would be difficult about the extra half hour, of course. She never accepted with good grace any changes other people imposed upon her way of doing things; he'd learned long ago to let the initial resistance run its short course and fade to complaining acceptance.

At lunch he watched with amusement and more inner glow as Jenny won his mother's heart as firmly as she had won his father's. After lunch, Jenny asked if she could stay there a little longer.

"Gran said she would drive me back," she assured him, revealing the topic of another private conversation she had had with his mother while he and his father had been in the kitchen washing and drying the lunch dishes. "I'll be there in plenty of time to get things ready for the party. Betty's coming early to help me."

So Manny was alone when he arrived back at his apartment to find a woman waiting at the foot of his stairs.

Chapter 16

Her car was parked nearby, a green Toyota Corolla polished as bright as her patent leather strapless shoes. It was not until he got out of his own car that Manny realised how tall she was. When he stood in front of her, he recognised the woman from the sixth row back when he addressed the meeting of the Women's Service League.

"Diana Strickland," she introduced herself, and handed him a business card which informed him she was a Children's Services Supervisor with the Department of Family and Children.

"You were in the audience when I spoke to that meeting a little while ago".

"Yes, I was, as it happens. However, that is not why I am here today, Mr Youngman. I have been studying the file on your daughter Jennifer."

"I didn't know there was a file." He was trying to remember what she had said at that meeting.

"Be that as it may, I am undertaking this visit to ensure that the best interests of the child are being served by the arrangements between you and her mother. Is Jennifer here?"

Manny shook his head. "We had lunch at my parents' house and she stayed on there. She'll be here in about an hour, I expect."

"May I see inside your apartment? The physical environment is always an important factor in these situations."

She was more relaxed than she had been at the meeting, probably because she was in a situation with which she was more familiar. There were none of the staccato sentences and pauses she had used to dramatise her assertions.

"I wasn't expecting you," he said, keeping his tone mild so that she could not take offence.

"That's standard procedure, to enable us to see things as they normally are and not re-arranged for our benefit."

When he let her into the apartment she moved through the lounge room and kitchen, stopped longer in Jenny's bedroom and noted everything in passing. It was done with such a concentrated intensity of movement and attention to detail that Manny wouldn't have been surprised to hear she would later be able to produce a complete inventory of his possessions with accurate estimates of age, state of repair and replacement value.

"Quite comfortable," she assessed. "You live alone, Mr Youngman? Under normal circumstances?"

He nodded, having decided that for this interview it would be wisest to speak when spoken to and answer only what he was asked. He recalled her asserting that all men thought they could talk their way out of anything.

"May we sit and talk for a while? It would help me to make my assessment."

They sat. She ran her eye down the sheet of paper she had taken from a slim black document case which matched her other accessories.

"You understand that it is part of the function of this interview to determine whether there is anything to contra-indicate Jenny's continued visitation with you?"

He acknowledged that with another nod. She was using longer words, he noticed, and official phrases to give her a protective authority.

"Normally of course it would have been more appropriate to conduct this inquiry before the decision regarding this arrangement had been made." Her tone was recriminatory, as if he been responsible, and there was a touch of something else about it. She was angry about something, or worried. He didn't ask what it was and waited for her to continue.

She looked for her next cue at the paper in front of her. "I have to tell you that preliminary inquiries indicate a number of matters which require a degree of elucidation."

This needed more than a nod. "What matters are they?"

"School holidays?"

"Yes." He wasn't sure what he had said yes to.

"You are aware that they are impending?"

"Impending?" Although he knew what the word meant, something recalcitrant made him respond as if he didn't.

"Will you be able to take time off from your employment to give Jenny the extra attention required?"

"Yes." He hadn't thought about it and hadn't discussed it with Jenny. That could be sorted out later.

"You understand, Mr Youngman, that it is a matter of which we are required to be cognisant?"

"Of course! Your cognisance is very important."

Her nostrils slitted. "Our client is in your care for a limited period, Mr Youngman. It is important that we remain informed of and agree with all variations of domicile."

"I understand." He had to avoid being flippant. She had too much power.

"Do you intend to take Jenny away during the holidays?"

"No." That was true because it hadn't occurred to him. Now she had mentioned it, it seemed a great idea. He began thinking where they might go.

"Will you be taking time off work to supervise her?"

"Of course." The south coast, he thought. It would be beautiful down there at this time of the year. He smiled at her. "There were other matters?"

She had laid one hand over the sheet of paper in front of her as if shielding the words from his eyes. "Your activities with the organisation called NEMSA, Mr Youngman. Would I be right in saying that its members express strong and in some instances quite violent views against women?" There was a peculiar stress on the word violent as if she were thinking of some personal experience.

Manny gathered his thoughts before answering, "We're not in favour of violence. Some men who come to us show a tendency to physical violence as a conditioned reflex to the emotional stress they are under."

"So you admit their natural response is to be violent." She made notes.

Manny leaned forward, pointing to the page on which she was writing. "Would you make that 'conditioned reflex' instead of 'natural response'. The two have quite different meanings and I do not wish to be misquoted."

Her nostrils flared as she pulled her head back and glared at him.

"Have members of your movement not referred to women in terms which could be described as derogatory and liable to provoke hostility?"

"Only in the same way some women refer to men as monsters or pigs, as I had hoped I had explained when I gave the talk at the meeting you attended."

The glare began to lose confidence. He wondered whether she was surprised that he had recognized her or concerned that he knew where her bias was coming from.

"The New Era Men's Support Alliance is not anti-feminist and it is not anti-women," he went on, deciding it was worth reiterating even if she had heard it before. "We've read the same articles, heard the same radio and television interviews and visited the same web sites I am sure you have, the ones that say professional women are suffering burn-out, that women have raised their expectations so high they can't find men to match them, that many so-called liberated women are ending up manless, childless and despairing, that they're suffering more stress, their health is deteriorating, that there is a higher proportion of divorces between couples who regard themselves as modern and equal with both contributing to their income and the man sharing in the housework. This doesn't mean women are to blame for any ills that have fallen upon them; we're not gloating or saying that they are being punished for some terrible wrong they have done to men. We are saying there needs to be another way."

He stopped, seeing in her face that he was wasting his time. "May I ask what you consider NEMSA's views have to do with my relationship with Jenny?"

The thin nostrils widened again. "You understand our concerns must be in the circumstance of your close association with such views, Mr Youngman. They beg the question of how your relationship with a young, vulnerable girl would be affected."

"Why? Because I hear other men say things?"

"We have your daughter to consider."

"Several NEMSA members have daughters."

She seemed to find this disconcerting and didn't make a note of it. She began to get to her feet as if preparing for departure.

"I think I'll come back another time to see Jenny, Mr Youngman. I have all I need for the present."

"Have I passed the test?"

"I beg your pardon?"

"Well, I have the distinct impression that one purpose of this visit was to determine whether I am a fit person to look after Jenny. Have you reached a conclusion?"

She sat down again.

"The premises are of a standard within the acceptable

range. I will need to talk with Jenny and make some additional inquiries. We are not only concerned with your fitness to have custody of her."

"What are the other considerations?"

"Her state of mind. Whether she needs counselling, and whether she needs any form of care that could be better provided in another environment. Having her mother sent to prison can be traumatic for a fifteen year old girl, Mr Youngman. At that age they are extremely conscious of what other people think of them. I understand you were called to her school and that there are problems there."

"Jenny and I have discussed that. She is doing something about it."

"Is she? She told you that?"

"Yes."

"And you accept that. Jenny has said she will do something about it."

"Yes."

She was writing in her notebook again. "I'll ask her about that myself when I call back. Will Monday morning do?"

He pointed out that Jenny would be at school and she seemed annoyed with herself for not having remembered that. She was definitely uncomfortable about something. They agreed she would phone on Sunday morning and see if something could be arranged for later that day.

"I'll make sure Jenny is here. Is it all right if she knows what it's about?"

"Oh yes, quite all right. Thank you, Mr Youngman." She drove away to the accompaniment of a mild popping from the Corolla's exhaust.

Manny had a lot to think about while he waited for Jenny to come home.

When she did she was later than he expected and arrived wild-eyed and a little flustered.

"Gran and Gramps are so lovely I wanted to spend more time with them."

"Never mind." He decided to leave news of Diana Strickland's visit to a time when they could sit down and discuss it. However, there was something from her visit he did want to discuss. "Remember we were talking about NEMSA and what we do there?"

She hesitated. "Yes."

"You do understand that we don't have violent views against women? We are not anti-feminist?"

"Oh yes. That's what you said in your book. I was a little surprised, because it isn't about men having trouble living with their wives and daughters either or being depressed because their wife has left them."

He wasn't aware she had read his book and asked her when she had.

"I found a copy on your shelf. You don't mind, do you?"

Quite the contrary. "What did you think of it?"

"I'm not sure. I'm still thinking."

"You must have some initial ideas."

"It makes sense, sort of, although I find it very hard to accept some of it. I haven't heard some of those ideas before."

"You don't have to have heard of ideas before in order to make up your mind whether they're right or not."

"Don't you? I think I do." She gazed at him earnestly and he was struck again how much more mature she looked with her new hairstyle. "I had very clear ideas about feminism, or I thought I did. Your book has made me wonder whether I need to think more about that, about what I really do think. Why did you write it?"

It was a question he had been asked before and was never certain if he had given an honest answer. Now, he thought, he had better make sure.

"The ideas in it are not all my own," he said carefully. "I met a man who said feminism had been a good thing but now we needed manism. The more I thought about it the more it made sense of a lot of things, including the fact that I had never found anyone…" he almost said 'except your mother', but edited it out before it became something he had to think about, "…I wanted to marry or have a strong relationship with. I wasn't the product of a bitter divorce or a domineering mother, although Mum can come on a bit strong at times. I guess there were a lot of influences. It was just something my friend Tony started me thinking about. One day I started writing down what I was thinking and it became a book."

Jenny's eyebrows knitted in one of his own familiar

expressions. "You must have thought about it a lot. Now you're making it sound sort of dry and academic, and it isn't. It reads like you are very passionate about it."

Manny decided not to comment on that. It sounded as though a seed had been sewn and the best course was to let it grow. "Now how about this party?," he said, changing the subject. "We need to get started. What would you like me to do?"

Jenny assessed the room. "We'll need to have some drinks."

"Right." He prepared himself for action. "I'll zip down the shop. What shall I get? Coke or Pepsi? Other stuff like orange juice? Shall I get a mixture?"

There was a long hesitation before Jenny answered. "Could you also get some other drinks?"

"Anything you want. Name it."

"Beer? And maybe some whisky or something."

Manny stopped in mid-stride and turned to face her. "Alcohol?"

"Just some. Not a lot."

"Jenny. You're only fifteen."

"Some of the kids are older. They'll expect us to have some beer here. It's normal. I promise I won't have any myself and I'll make sure no-one under-age drinks. I'll feel silly if I can't offer the older ones something."

Manny stared at her bright face and its beseeching smile. He really did love this girl who had crashed into his life and now seemed as if she had always been a part of it.

Inside his head he was listening to himself say "you are only fifteen" and accusing himself of playing out the old parental stereotype again.

"Okay," he said. "I'll get a carton of beer. I don't think spirits are a good idea."

Jenny stepped forward and hugged him. "Thanks, Dad. You're right. No spirits. Could you make it two cartons of beer?"

Manny went down to the liquor store wondering whether he was doing the right thing. There was a lot to being a new era father he wasn't at all sure about.

One thing he was sure about was that Diana Strickland, the social worker, wouldn't approve.

Chapter 17

Every light in the apartment glowed and the music blared to compete with the din of excited, chattering voices. Fragments of conversations, names and isolated words floated outwards. As Manny reached towards them they were absorbed back into the whole and he remained on the outer fringes.

His chairs had been pushed back, paintings and pictures replaced with posters of actors and singers. His books remained on his shelves obscured by the scrum of bodies filling the room and overflowing into the kitchen.

Jenny emerged from the press and came up to him, holding by the hand a very tall individual with the head and body of a mature man and the uncertain face of a boy.

"Dad, this is Noel."

Manny smiled. "Hi, Noel. Pleased to meet you."

"Yeah." Noel looked around in dismay as Jenny let go of his hand and darted back into the crowd. He stared longingly after her.

"Have you known Jenny long?" Manny asked.

"Yeah. Sort of."

"From school?"

"Yeah." Relief spread across his face as Jenny re-emerged from the throng, towing a girl behind her. "Hi, Sue."

"Hi, Noel," the girl smiled up at him from a face about eighteen inches below his.

"Dad. This is Sue. Sue, my father."

"Hello, Mr Frank."

The words hit him like a slap in the face. "Youngman. My name's Youngman," he blurted.

The girl blushed and turned to Jenny in confusion.

"My parents aren't married," Jenny explained with a shrug, as if it was of no significance.

"I'm sorry, Sue," Manny apologised, "That's the first time anyone has called me that."

"Of course. I'm sorry. I should have realised." Sue was looking desperately at Noel, as if he could help her.

"Yeah," said Noel. Then his eyes lit with a sudden inspiration. "You want me to get you a drink?"

"Yes, please. I'll come with you." They hurried away.

Manny turned to ask Jenny why she hadn't warned people that their names were different, but she too had disappeared. After a search he spotted her on the fringes of the group around the boy Shane, pushing her way in to get closer to him. What did she and the other girls see in a boy with unkempt long hair, too-thin face and arrogant eyes? Even the other boys seemed to treat Shane as some sort of leader and role model.

Jenny was far too good for Shane. She was beautiful tonight with her red hair, artfully arranged and tied with a ribbon, dramatically complementing the long green dress, so much more elegant and sophisticated than the other girls.

Beyond Shane he could see Betty Polson who had appeared an hour before the others, giggling, to help

Jenny put out plates of cheese and biscuits and decide the music to be playing when the others arrived. Beside Betty was a boy sufficiently like his sister to be Grant Polson, potential conduit to Shane. They were watching another boy balancing a cup on his forehead while he rotated his body beneath it in small jerks, somehow keeping the handle pointing the same way.

Manny waited to see that the boy hadn't faltered and spilled fruit punch on the carpet, then steered a route round the edge of the crowd to the fridge and took a can of beer from the bottom shelf. Of the two dozen cans he had installed there earlier only one or two had disappeared. There was more interest in the fruit punch Jenny and Betty had concocted in a large glass bowl which stood on a table just inside the kitchen door. For the first few arrivals they had filled cups from the bowl and handed them round. Now the guests were coming to get refills for themselves. Three extra jugs were prepared and ready in the fridge. More ingredients were ready for when those ran out. Jenny and Betty had proved highly organised.

He had also met Gillian, Olivia and Rose who had been the other targets for Jenny's phone calls, and Billy Longford, who looked and behaved to Manny no more odious than Shane.

Just a nice bunch of kids, having a good time. The girls' choice of music had been right, the fruit punch was flowing, talk was humming. It was time to go. He pushed his way across to where Jenny had broken into the ring around Shane.

"A quarter past midnight", he mouthed. "Have a good time."

Jenny turned and took his arm, squeezing it tightly. For a moment he stayed still, wanting to hold the moment, then she turned back to her friends and it was over.

When he got to the upstairs room at The End of the Earth he found the teacher, Mr James, with Bobby Carlsson.

"When you told me about Dick's marital problems I gave him a call," Bobby explained. "Us teachers have to stick together, eh Dick?"

Mr James nodded uncertainly.

Manny had the impression that it was more to do with seeing the father of one of his students arrive than with being in these new surroundings. Did teachers have a conflict of interest if they had a social relationship with their students' parents? Perhaps it could cause complications. He also wondered whether the man was comfortable being called Dick. He seemed more the type who would prefer Richard. Still, Bobby would have already made a decision about that.

"I've been explaining that we're just ordinary blokes who want to change things and are helping each other to do it," Bobby continued. "Dick thinks women want their cake and eat it too, don't you Dick?"

"Something like that." He was frowning, perhaps worried that anything he said would be passed on and come back at him in the classroom.

"Like they moan about doing the ironing but the man's still expected to mow the lawn?" Bobby pressed, making it a question that expected an answer.

James nodded, still not committing himself.

"They're always criticising," Bobby continued. "Men can't do anything right, don't wash the dishes properly, don't sit properly, don't eat properly, don't dress properly. Constant nagging. And if we say anything about them and the way they do things, we're sexist pigs who don't understand them. That right?"

Bobby was one of the intellectuals in the group and was capable of speaking about these issues at a higher level than a ranting complaint against women. This was all clearly meant to reassure the newcomer and show him they were all mates together.

"Every man who comes to NEMSA says the same sorts of thing," Bobby went on. "Women don't understand that with most men the personal hurts go pretty deep, that we experience being rejected and humiliated by women for being what we are – boys and men. We're called uncouth and clumsy, and dirty. Like the old nursery rhyme. Girls are made of sugar and spice and all things nice and boys are made of slugs and snails."

Dick James was nodding. These would be the sorts of things Jenny's teacher had been saying earlier, before he had arrived, Manny understood, and Bobby was repeating and reinforcing them to make the man more comfortable.

"You listen to Bobby, Dick," he told the teacher. "And

by the way, what's said in NEMSA stays in NEMSA. No-one will be telling tales back in school."

James's expression lost its edginess while still not being a smile. "Good. So, if we can talk out of school, how are you getting on with Jenny if you haven't been married and haven't any experience of raising a daughter?"

"Wonderfully," Manny assured him. "I treat her as I'd treat any young woman. I respect who she is and she respects who I am. We're getting on very well together."

Bobby claimed Dick's attention again and began introducing him to other NEMSA members around the room. Manny also began circulating.

Several of the men talked about a new Men's Shed that had opened in the district and were considering going along to see what it was offering. It was all part of a much wider movement, men solving their problems together. Perhaps he should develop a talk along those lines. It gave him a lot to think and talk about as he moved through the crowd.

The meeting ended too early for him to go straight home, so he decided to walk down past his apartment to check everything was all right, and then go to the docks and get a mug of coffee at an all-night stand. Ahead of him he soon heard a lot of noise and the closer he got, the faster his feet began to move. For the last few hundred yards he was running.

The tableau that confronted him in the courtyard at the bottom of the stairs that led up to his apartment was a picture that remained frozen in his mind for hours afterwards.

Two boys with bloodied, angry faces, each being held back from further violence by residents from other apartments. Jagged fragments from a smashed bottle on the ground. Other youngsters milling around in the courtyard and on the stairs. Jenny at the foot of the stairs, hands pressed to her breasts to support the ripped remains of her dress.

"What the hell?"

Faces turned towards him. Shocked faces, frightened and dismayed.

He recognised the two boys. The long haired Shane was more frightened than arrogant now, Grant Polson defiant.

"They were fighting," one of Manny's neighbours informed him. "Making a hell of a racket. We had to stop them."

"Anyone seriously hurt?" He looked down at the shattered bottle.

"Just a blood nose and some bruises. We got to them before they could kill each other."

Manny glanced up the stairs, at the audience of young people gawping down at them. Music blared behind them as if this was still a party and everyone should be enjoying themselves.

"Thanks," he said to the men holding Shane and Grant. "I think you can let them go."

They released the boys reluctantly. Shane flexed his shoulders as if he was shrugging them off. Grant clenched his fists, ready to fight again.

"I think we'd all better go back upstairs," Manny said. "Jenny, go and change into some other clothes. You two wash the blood off so I can have a closer look at you. One in the kitchen and one in the bathroom. Stay away from each other. Everyone else go home."

Chapter 18

The music still blared. Manny stalked across the room and switched it off. He glared at the mess on the floor, scattered clothes, crushed beer cans, chocolate wrappers, pieces of cheese and biscuit crumbs trodden into the carpet. A line of youngsters queued up for the telephone to call their parents. Others used their own phones. All had worried expressions.

Jenny had gone to her room, Betty Polson with her. Grant Polson emerged from the kitchen with the scowl washed from his face with the blood. He was still struggling to appear defiant. Shane was taking longer to appear from the bathroom.

The first parent to arrive was a woman who gave Manny a distraught look, grabbed her daughter and fled. The second was a man who wanted an explanation. Manny told him what he knew, adding that he was waiting for them all to go before he sorted out exactly what had happened. The man left with his daughter and two other girls, not at all dissatisfied. Only one woman wanted to blame Manny for what had happened, even though he pointed out that her son had not been hurt or involved in any way other than as a spectator.

"It was your responsibility to ensure this sort of thing didn't happen," she insisted. "I'm sure all the other parents are like me. We assumed you were keeping an eye on our children."

She was right. He knew that. He was entirely to blame for what had happened.

It took more than half an hour before the majority of Jenny's party guests had been collected, leaving Shane and Grant glaring at each other from opposite sides of the room. Betty had also stayed behind and was still with Jenny in her bedroom.

"Okay. What happened?" Manny demanded.

"Nothing," Shane said ridiculously.

"He tried to rape Jenny," said Grant.

"Bullshit." Shane was indignant. "I wasn't trying to rape her."

"You bloody well were." Grant was on his feet, threatening to leap across the room and hit Shane again.

"Calm down, both of you," Manny growled, fighting to stay calm himself. What the hell had happened? If Shane had touched Jenny… "Sit down," he told Grant.

The boy did as he was told, the rebelliousness back on his face with a vengeance.

"Jenny," Manny called, "come out here."

She appeared in jeans and the 'women are a national asset' t-shirt. Her head was held rigid, her face closed and not looking at anyone, as if she were somewhere else, or wanted to be. Betty came behind, less sure of how to compose her face and almost on the point of tears.

"What happened?" Manny asked again.

"Nothing," Jenny repeated Shane's assertion. "It was just stupid. The boys started fighting."

"What about?"

"Nothing. They were drunk."

Although the four of them were in different parts of the room, Manny felt them join together against him. The tension was palpable. Before Jenny and Betty had come into the room, Shane and Grant had sat poised, Grant to leap at Shane, and Shane to defend himself. Now they had half turned away from each other and fully away from Manny. Betty had taken the chair nearest the door where she and Jenny had entered, her hands clasped in a fold of her skirt, feet together on the floor, head down. Jenny stood awkwardly, still wanting to be somewhere else. She studied her bronze painted fingernails.

Manny walked through to the kitchen. The table and floor were scattered with empty beer cans, the cartons they had come from piled in a corner. On the sink were half a dozen or more opened bottles of spirits. Scotch, gin, Southern Comfort and something with a bright yellow label he didn't recognise.

The room was saturated with a stale alcohol smell. He was surprised he had not been aware of it before. When he returned to the other room he knew why. The smell there was more aromatic.

Manny scratched at his forehead and studied the four youngsters, then crossed the floor to where Jenny barred the way to her room. With a flick of his head he indicated to her to move aside. When she stiffened and seemed about to refuse, he reached out a hand and touched her on the shoulder. For a few seconds she held his gaze, then dropped her eyes and stepped away. Manny went into the bedroom.

The aromatic smell was more intense. On a small table beside the bed, a saucer was filled with the stubs of thin, weedy cigarettes. The covers of the bed were thrown back and crumpled. The new dress was rolled into a ball and thrown in one corner.

He returned to the other room. "Marijuana?"

Jenny sat now in a chair beside Betty. They both nodded.

"Grant," he said, "you said Shane was trying to rape Jenny."

The boy looked at the others. When none of them responded he seemed to take that as permission to answer.

"They were in there," he said. "Jenny screamed and I went in. I pulled him off her and he hit me, so I hit him back." He went silent again.

Manny turned to Shane. "Did you try to rape my daughter?"

Before the boy could answer, Jenny interrupted. "This has nothing to do with you. It's my business."

Manny glared at her. "Don't be stupid!"

His daughter's head snapped back as if he had slapped her. Her mouth began to open but he turned to Shane and cut off her words. "I'll ask you again. Did you try to rape Jenny?"

Shane shook his head.

"You're lying," Grant snarled at him. "She was

screaming."

"Shut up, both of you," Jenny snapped.

"No. You shut up, Jenny." Manny pointed a finger at his daughter. "Be quiet, or I'll send you back into your room until I get this sorted out."

She withdrew into a scowling silence and he turned again to Grant.

"You heard Jenny screaming."

"Everybody did. I went into the room and he had her down on the bed."

"Shane?"

"I wasn't trying to rape her. We were just… you know."

"Yes, I do know. Why didn't you stop when she screamed?"

"It wasn't a scream. I thought she was pretending. I mean, she was coming onto me. That dress she was wearing. I thought..."

"Okay." Manny had heard enough. More than he had wanted to hear. "You three go down and get in my car. I'll drive you home. Grant, you and Betty go down first and sit in the back."

He waited until they'd gone before turning to Shane. "You wait outside the door and come down with me. You can sit in the front. I don't want you and Grant fighting again."

"I didn't rape her, Mr Youngman, honest."

"If I thought you had you'd have more than a bloody nose," Manny growled. "Do yourself a favour and shut up.

Just go and wait for me."

After the boy had gone he turned to Jenny. "I'll talk to you when I get back."

She stared back at him defiantly. "I said it's none of your business."

"I'm making it my business."

"I won't talk to you. You can't make me."

"We'll see about that." He glared around the room. "I want this place cleaned up by the time I get back. Completely."

He didn't give her any chance to reply. Following Shane out, he pushed him towards the top of the stairs and down to where the other two sat in his car.

He drove in a contained fashion, keeping within the speed limit. At Betty and Grant's place they hurried together into the house, the girl first, her brother protectively behind her. When he dropped off Shane, in a bigger house in a wealthier suburb, the boy stood half-defiantly on the footpath to watch him go. Manny turned the car and drove slowly to the end of the street. As soon as he turned the corner he allowed the anger to flow through his body to his feet and stamped on the accelerator.

It lasted until he got home and found the apartment had not been cleaned up as he had ordered. Jenny was not there.

Chapter 19

She was not in her bedroom, the bathroom, the kitchen, his office. He searched all of them, calling out her name, opening cupboards, looking under beds. All it told him was that the house was in a mess. There was evidence of an invasion of party goers in every room. Empty drink cans lay everywhere and more cheese and biscuit crumbs. The bathroom and toilet stank of marihuana and the bathroom sink had a dark green stain.

As fear started to tie knots in his stomach, he considered where she could have gone. Katie's house, Alice Todd's, Betty Polson's? He reached for the phone to call those places and stopped, realising there was a better way. All he had to do was ring Jenny on her mobile phone. He dialled the number to learn that her phone was either switched off or out of range. No matter, he could text her. He punched in a message, "Cll me pls." For the next few minutes he stood in the lounge room waiting for her to answer. Slowly he realised that she wasn't going to call him back, even if she did get the text.

He again searched the house, no longer looking for Jenny but for some clue as to where she might have gone. The jeans and t-shirt she had been wearing lay in an untidy heap on her bedroom floor. What did that mean? She had changed clothes. Why and what into? Not the green dress. That still lay crumpled in the corner where he had seen it earlier. Not her hat because it was hanging on a hook behind the door. Several drawers were open and their contents pulled out. Not having any idea what had been in them, he couldn't tell what she might have taken.

Remembering what he had been going to do before, he searched the telephone directory and dialled the Polsons' number. Jenny wasn't there and hadn't called her, Betty assured him after a nervous start in which she tried to apologise for what had happened at the party. Yes, if she did see Jenny she would tell her to call him. Mrs Polson came on the phone and promised that if Jenny did turn up at their house they would hold her there and call him.

Next he dialled Alice, but the voice that answered was Madge, Katie's other friend. He asked her if Jenny had called Alice or gone over there.

"What's happened?" Madge asked. "You sound worried."

"We had an argument about something and she's gone off by herself."

"The party?" There was a knowing note in her voice. He admitted that was what it had been and told her what had happened.

"I did wonder. Alice said that dress was…"

"She said Alice liked it."

"As a dress. It was too old for Jenny."

"Did Alice say that?"

"Not to Jenny. I told her she should have."

It was no time to be doing a post-mortem on the mistakes he or Alice had made with Jenny. He needed her back safe and sound. "I've got to go and find her," he said and hung up the phone.

She couldn't be far away because she was on foot. He drove down the street outside his apartment, turned left and went round in a square, then right and round in a bigger square, quartering the area in search of a small figure walking in the shadows.

What if she had heard the car coming and ducked behind a tree or a fence? What if she was running and was already further away than he had calculated? He drove in a wider grid, checking every side street and even stopping the car and venturing into dark alleys and empty blocks between houses.

His phone rang and he grabbed at it. "Jenny?"

It was Alice. Madge had told her about his call and the pair of them were also out searching the streets, working the route towards his house, hoping that Jenny was heading home and they would find her walking towards them. "What on earth did you say to her?" Alice demanded.

"That I would talk to her later," Manny answered. "That I was disappointed in her."

"Madge says you expected too much."

"Yes, I should have been there. I shouldn't have gone off and left them. I know. I've got to find her."

"Where are you looking?"

He described the area he had covered. Alice said she would drive down closer to the river. Jenny might have gone down there to sit and stare out across the water. She suggested he cover the area around the school.

It was as good a plan as any. He drove to the school gates, stopped and sat miserably while he remembered picking her up there, then began again driving along one road and another, searching, searching.

Alice rang to say they had not found Jenny and were going home. Madge said they would be of more use there because it was the most likely place Jenny would go. Also, she might call them. Madge didn't think driving round and round was getting anywhere. She suggested Manny should also return home. He told her that he couldn't.

He drove past the O'Connell building, the shopping mall where they had bought the dress, the pizza parlour, all the places he had been with Jenny in the short time they had been together. So few places. So many other places she could have gone that he didn't know about.

As a wan dawn washed across the streets, he called in at home to check that Jenny had not returned. People had begun to emerge, raising his hopes every time he saw a figure moving along the footpath ahead of him, but it was never Jenny. As the numbers of people grew so did the number of cars. He could no longer crawl along, looking, looking. Instead he went again to the café where he had taken Jenny for lunch on their first day together. She had not been there when he had driven past its darkened and closed door earlier in the morning and she was not there now, although it was open and filling with customers. He parked and went inside, sat in the same seats they had sat in before and ordered a toasted sandwich and a black coffee while he stared out of the window and prayed she would walk past.

She didn't. Tommy Bloffwitch did. Manny became aware of his face staring back at him through the glass and then Tommy was inside, demanding to know what was wrong.

"You look like shit. What is it?"

After he explained, Tommy wasted no time, grabbing for his phone and calling Tony and Bobby and several other NEMSA members.

"You come with me," Tommy instructed him. "You're in no state to be driving around. I'll take you home. If anyone finds her, that's where they'll call."

"You don't know what she looks like," Manny protested, knowing Tommy was right.

"You said she looks like you, right?" Tommy retorted. "So she's a young red headed girl. Is she tall?"

Manny shook his head.

"What's she wearing?"

He admitted he didn't know.

"Right. We're taking the street directory and each doing a page, starting from your place and working out."

"You don't need to do this, Tommy," he protested when they reached his apartment.

Tommy leaned across him to push the car door open and usher him out. "I've got three girls."

When he'd driven away, Manny began to climb the

steps, stumbling and holding onto the railing, realizing how tired he was, and sad, and angry. Not with Jenny. With himself.

The phone in his office began ringing. He turned and stumbled down the steps again, desperate to get to it before she could hang up and he would lose her again.

"Jenny?"

There was a long silence and he began to wonder if he had picked up too late.

"Isn't she there?"

Manny's mind went as blank as the wall he was staring at as he recognised Katie's voice. What on earth was he going to say to her? From somewhere a lie surfaced. "She's gone down to the shop for milk. We ran out."

"By herself? Walking?"

Part of his mind was telling him that if Katie was calling and asking where Jenny was that excluded the prison from the list of possible places she had gone. Another part was saying he'd been stupid again. There was no shop within walking distance. Would Katie know that?"

"She said she needed the exercise."

"Jenny?" Katie sounded incredulous. He was digging himself in deeper.

"She's taken my bike." She couldn't know he didn't have one. "She's been riding it around. Says she enjoys it."

He could feel sweat forming on his forehead. His hand trembled where it rested on the desk in front of him. He was sitting now, staring out of the window, his thoughts churning as he tried to make sense of what he was doing and what it's consequences might be. Jenny was missing and he was lying to her mother about it.

"How was the party?" he heard Katie asking. "Did it go well?"

He was going to have to lie some more.

"Yes. No problems. Everything went smoothly."

"That's good," Katie responded with no sign that she had picked up any of the tenseness he was trying to hide. "I'm sorry I've missed her. I wanted to ask her about it myself. I was a little worried, but it sounds as if I needn't have been."

He couldn't respond immediately. His thoughts had stalled as they took in what she had said. "You want to talk to her?"

"I've thought a lot about what we said before. I've been wrong not talking to her, and I want to see her too, especially if she wants to see me, as you said. Would it be too much trouble for you to bring her to see me?"

How the hell could he take Jenny to see her when he didn't know where she was? The feeling of anger returned, directed at Katie this time instead of at himself.

"How come you suddenly want to see her now?"

This was met with a short silence, then, "It's hardly sudden, Manny. I've been turning it over and over in my mind since we spoke before. It hasn't been an easy decision to make."

"I thought you didn't want her to see you in prison?"

"I can't avoid it if I want to see her, can I? Is there something wrong, Manny? Don't you want to bring her to see me? I thought you did before."

"I did. I do," he stuttered. "She wants to see you."

"Good. Could you arrange it? Soon, please. Now I've changed my mind about it I can't wait to see her."

"I'll talk it over with her when she comes back. We'll have to fit it in with her school and my work."

"Of course." She sounded disappointed. "I'm missing out on a part of her life, aren't I? I don't suppose you know how sad that makes me. I feel like I've lost her."

Manny stared at the phone and hoped she would never know he had actually lost their daughter.

How was he going to stop her finding out? He was going to have to concoct a story with Jenny, persuade her to lie to her mother, about going to the shop on his non-existent bike, about the wonderful party she had had, about not running away from him.

As a wave of remorse swept over him and he was on the point of confessing it all to Katie, she said goodbye and hung up the phone. He was left staring at it, noticing that his hand had stopped trembling and that the beads of sweat were turning cold on his forehead.

Chapter 20

Tony was the first to report in, bringing Manny out of a half sleep full of frightening thoughts he couldn't remember the instant he jerked awake. Some teenage girls had been sighted. No red heads.

"There were half a dozen hanging out around that shop that's got a pinball machine," Tony told him. "I hung around there for a while in case she turned up." He laughed. "One of them had green hair and the most awful bloody clothes, all ragged and torn. She was a bloody sight. What do they think they look like?"

Manny didn't know and wasn't interested. He wanted only to hear that Jenny had been found and that she was safe.

Tommy called in next. He was further out, covering the docks area. Nothing to report.

Each time the phone rang his heart turned over and he felt a numbing confusion of hope and fear. Every time he answered it his heart slumped as he heard nothing except that there was no news.

He discarded thoughts of ringing his parents and Claire O'Connell's office in the hope that she might have gone to either of those places. His heart told him she would not be there. He would only be stirring up more trouble for himself and, in his parents' case, worry for them.

One of the incoming phone calls was from Dianne Strickland, the social worker. She reminded him that she wanted to see Jenny and asked if it would be possible later that afternoon. He told her it wouldn't, that Jenny had made an arrangement he hadn't known about to go to see his mother and father. He would discuss it with her and see if it would be possible the following evening. It would depend on her other plans, he lied. There might be school commitments, or she might be going to a friend's house. The social worker sounded put out, as if her requirements should be put first. She said she would ring the school the next day to see if she could make an appointment to see Jenny there.

As he replaced the phone Manny stared into the abyss he was digging for himself and wondered how much deeper it was going to get if he didn't find Jenny soon.

At mid-morning he told his friends to stop searching, that it was pointless. Jenny could have taken a taxi, or gone to the home of a friend he knew nothing about. "All I can do is wait until I hear something," he told them. "Either she'll call me or someone will. There's no point you driving around anymore."

He slumped in the green chair in his lounge room where Jenny had been sitting the evening he had come home, found a pink car in his carport and seen her for the first time through his front window. Several cars drew up outside and he turned to the window hopefully. It was only Tony and the others saying they had called off the search as he had asked and had brought his car back from the café. They asked if there was anything else they could do.

Manny shook his head.

"I don't think she's hurt or anything," he said. "Not in danger."

"You haven't called the police?"

"What for? They'll tell me what I already know. That she has run away because we had a row. They won't know where she would go any more than I do. I just wanted to get to her first, to explain…" He trailed off and they all nodded. He hadn't told them his real reason. Calling the police would ensure that Katie, Diane Strickland's office, the school and everyone else would be involved, and the most likely result of that was that she would be placed in the care of someone more suitable.

"Bloody awful not knowing," Tommy said. "If it was my girls…" He didn't explain what he would do or how he would feel.

Manny thanked them for helping him, and they all nodded and said "Any time". They went back to their cars and drove away.

He couldn't face lunch and the afternoon stretched ahead endlessly. He walked around the apartment from the phone to the door to her bedroom and back again, seeing nothing, thoughts whirling in his brain, recriminations against himself, against her, against Katie, against the world. Several times he contemplated going out to search for her again, knowing it would be pointless. There was nowhere he could think off that had not already been searched. Wherever she had gone would be where she didn't want him to find her.

He began half-heartedly to prepare a meal. Two portions so there would be one for Jenny. Anything was better than doing nothing. When the task was finished he covered both plates and left them on the kitchen bench to be reheated, perhaps, if she ever came back.

There were pointless sitcoms on the television and music he didn't like on the radio. He put on a favourite CD, found it irritating, switched it off. He went one more time to the doorway of Jenny's room, pleading with its contents to speak to him. Her clothes on the floor said nothing. Nor did her makeup on the dressing table. It was what she had bought for the party. He remembered that what she had brought with her from home had been in a pink box with a panda bear painted on the side and when he looked, found it lying with the clothes on the floor. As he bent to pick it up he could picture her wearing the green eye shadow she had worn the first time he had seen her.

The box was empty. Still bending, he noticed shreds of torn cloth under the bed on the side away from the door. Pieces of material appeared to have been torn from a skirt or a blouse. Further under the bed was a bottle. He pulled it out to examine the label, ran out of the bedroom and into the bathroom. Examined again the stain in the sink. Left the apartment in a rush, took the steps down two at a time and sprinted to his car.

The shop with the pinball machine splashed a harsh yellow light from its doorway into the parking spaces on the other side of the pavement. As he switched off the ignition, Manny was accosted by the blare of rock music. A boy leaned with his back against the glass of the shop window, a blonde girl pressing against him as they kissed. His hands cupped under her buttocks and drew her closer. They were oblivious to Manny as he walked past them, entering the garish light and raucous sound of the shop's interior.

Her eyelids were layered thick with the green eye shadow but Tony hadn't got it right about her hair. It was not just green. She had died a black streak across the top from ear to ear. He wondered where she had got the black hair colouring. The bottle under her bed and the stain in the sink had been green.

She wore what appeared to be a black velvet blazer over a torn yellow blouse, a blue and white football scarf wound several times around her neck. Three layers of ragged skirts, variously coloured the same as the scraps of material on her bedroom floor, topped black stockings with holes in the knees, one purple boot, and one green.

When he called her name she turned without surprise, as if she had been expecting him much sooner.

Chapter 21

"Where've you been? I've been searching everywhere."

The green shadowed eyes gazed back emptily. He wondered if it was drugs.

"Come home," he said, "please."

"I don't have a home," his daughter responded in a flat voice that made his skin crawl.

His mind raced, trying to think what words would reach her and convince her to come home with him. He didn't understand why she was dressed like this, acting like this, and a part of his brain was asking where she had been all night, where she had found shelter, where she had slept, who she had been with. He had to do something, say something. What?

One of the men spoke. "What are you bothering her for?"

They were men, not teenagers as he had first assumed, several years older than Shane and Grant and the other boys at the party. In their twenties. Bigger, heavier and more dangerous.

"I'm her father," he said, as if it meant something or gave him special authority.

"That right, babe?"

"He's my biological father," Jenny answered in the same dull voice. "Not my real father."

"Jenny!" The exclamation exploded out of him and he reached towards her.

The man stood in his way. "Back off, mate."

"She's my daughter."

"Yeah, well she doesn't seem to care much about that. I think you'd better leave her alone."

It was a situation outside Manny's experience or comprehension. Instinct wasn't any help. The impulse to ignore the man and reach again for Jenny was negated by the gut feeling that he would end up on the ground bleeding, and she wouldn't care.

"Please, Jenny," he said, trying to make it unthreatening.

She turned back to a group of girls dressed as she was. In the same, half whispered tone he had used he heard her say "I hate him."

It was as if he had been punched in the chest; the pain was just as agonizing. Although none of the men moved he saw the tightness around their eyes, the readiness in their arms and hands. Any move he made towards Jenny would be the trigger they wanted.

He turned and walked away, not looking back. There was nothing he could do or say, nothing that wouldn't make the situation worse. At least she appeared unharmed and he knew where she was. That was a small advance on his desperation of the long hours that had just passed.

It was weak, and he knew it. All men confronted it at some time in their lives. This was the reality of survival of the fittest. It would be pointless to stand up to these men and try to wrest Jenny from them. He would be defeated and she would despise him.

He stood beside his car and looked back towards the shop. Jenny had her back turned. The man who had confronted him put his arm around her shoulders. She pushed him away and he retreated, shrugging. Manny heard his laughter. The man came to the door, grinned and waved mockingly. He said something and Jenny looked out through the window, her face a mask of unhappiness and, Manny felt sure, fear as she realized she had been left alone. For a few seconds he thought she might realize the danger she was in, come out of the shop and run across to him. Instead, she turned back and he could no longer see her face.

He sat in his car and contemplated whether to drive away or remain there, watching and waiting until something happened he could respond to. At least in the car he was in a small way protected from attack by the men, not that they seemed interested in him anymore. They were back playing the pinball machine, ignoring Jenny, who stood with the other girls, responding in a listless fashion to their questions.

He couldn't handle this situation alone. He needed help.

He thought of Tony and of Claire O'Connell, of Tommy who had three daughters, of Alice, Dianne Strickland, the school counsellor, Ursula Bronson. All were impossible in these circumstances. None of them would be able to get through to Jenny if he couldn't, and confronting her with them would make her embarrassed and she would hate him even more.

He was clicking through the call list on his phone, desperately seeking a name he hadn't thought of, when he saw the perfect person.

"Dad?"

His father listened without saying anything until he had finished.

"Alright son," he said. "I'll be right over."

It took him just over fifteen minutes, during which time Manny remained sitting in his car. More people had entered the shop and he no longer had a clear view of what was happening. One of the men came to the door, looked across at him, went back inside. What might have been a head with green hair peered between some other faces until people moved across behind the window and hid it from his view.

His thoughts still raced, his stomach churned. What if his mother came? He hadn't considered that. She would charge in like a whirlwind, causing more havoc than he wanted to imagine. He was about to call again to tell his father not to come when the familiar car turned the corner and parked behind him. The panic subsided. Dad was alone.

"No point getting your mother in a tizz. Told her I had to go to an all-night service station for something I forgot to get earlier," he explained as he came forward to where Manny had got out of his car to greet him. "Jenny still inside?"

Manny nodded.

"You'd better go," his father told him. "I'll bring her round to your place in a little while."

Manny was aghast. This wasn't what he expected. He needed advice, moral support, something to enable him to go back in to rescue the situation. "What if she won't come?" he protested. "She's angry and upset."

"Not with me, she isn't." The older man smiled. "We're good mates."

"What about those men?"

"Jenny won't let anyone hurt me."

Manny shook his head. "I'm not going away."

"Alright. Get back in your car and stay there, okay?"

Feeling weak and foolish again, Manny got back into his car and watched as his father walked across the road and into the shop.

Nothing happened for five more minutes. His father came out, stood in front of the window and made a sideways gesture with his head which could only mean 'go away'.

Manny slipped his car into gear, drove to a side street where he was out of sight, parked, and hurried back to peer round the corner.

His father had crossed the road and opened the door of his own car. Jenny emerged from the shop doorway, glanced down the road, which made Manny duck his head back out of sight, crossed to the car and got in. His father walked around to the driver's side, got in and drove away.

Chapter 22

Back in his apartment he sat in his chair, stood up and paced up and down, sat in his chair again. He went into the kitchen, lifted the two plates with their dinner on them and moved them to a shelf in the refrigerator. He shut the fridge door, opened it, took out a can of beer, shut the door, opened it and put the can back where it had been. His thoughts raced in many directions but made no progress in any. Hours seemed to fill the half hour that passed before he heard the sound of a car pulling to a stop in the courtyard and feet coming up the steps to his door.

His father entered cautiously. "Jenny's waiting outside. How're you feeling?" His voice was gruff.

"I don't know, Dad, I…"

"Yeah. That just about sums up how she's feeling. I've told her you won't get angry and start shouting. You won't, will you?"

Manny shook his head. Whatever he was going to do or say, and he had no well-thought-out plan for either, there would be no place in it for anything that could drive his daughter away again.

His father turned as if to go back and fetch Jenny, stopped and shook his head at him with an expression that seemed both critical and understanding. "You're a right pair, the two of you. You both think you're different, but when it comes down to it, you revert to being a typical father and she responds by being a typical teenager. Trouble is, neither of you knows what typical is, so you've both got it wrong."

Manny nodded. "Okay. I accept that. So what do we do? What do I say to her?"

His father screwed up his face and scratched at his cheek. "Nothing for the moment. Go into the kitchen and shut the door while I let Jenny get through to her room without you seeing her."

When Manny began to protest a hand rose to stop him. "I've never been a grandfather before, son, and I don't know that I was ever much of a father, so don't expect miracles. I seem to have handled this pretty right so far even if I don't know how any more than you do. Don't say anything. Let her go into her room and get those clothes off. She'll want to use the bathroom, too, I think, to do something about her hair. Let her be while she sorts herself out."

It was one of the longest speeches Manny had ever heard his father make, and one of the few that had not been encouraging him to do what his mother said and avoid confrontation. Maybe if there had been more like it when he was younger…

This was no time to dwell on that. He retreated to the kitchen from where he heard the sounds of Jenny's passage to her bedroom and, soon after that, to the bathroom.

His father called to him to come back into the lounge room. "Both of you get some sleep tonight," he suggested. "No talking, and especially no arguing. Give yourselves time to calm down and in the morning you can both try getting back to where you were before."

Manny was not even sure where that was, and said as much.

"Well, maybe Jenny does, son, and you should let her show you. If you want to know what I think, you two have been getting on famously, except you have both made mistakes, like anyone would. Now you'll have to sort them out together."

Manny stared at his father for a long time, taking in the familiar face that somehow seemed to have taken on a maturity and wisdom he had never seen before.

"How come she responded to you, Dad, and not to me? How come you have the answers?"

"I haven't, Manny. Don't ever think I do. I've just had more years to learn a few more tricks."

"Older and wiser?"

"Smarter, son. I've survived nearly fifty years of being married to your mum."

Manny wanted to say he had often wondered about that. Instead he said, "How does that explain why Jenny came to you?"

For a few seconds his father looked at him as if choosing his words carefully and when he spoke it was with a depth of emotion Manny could not remember hearing in him before. "I'll tell you something, son, I'm still with your mum because I know the good things I like in her. She's like everyone else, good and bad. She shows the world a tough face, but I see her the other times. We brought you up and you could be a little bugger when you wanted to be. You have to accept the good and bad in your kids, too."

"What did you say to Jenny to persuade her to come home?"

"I didn't have to say anything. I wasn't threatening to her. I don't criticize her. She's not worried about being judged by me."

"How does she know all that? You've only met her a few times."

"She just knows. I told you I don't have all the answers." He looked around the room as if he might find some. "She's a young girl, right? She ran off because she upset you or you upset her, because she was in a situation she couldn't handle and needed to get out of. She was scared and confused. Didn't know what she wanted to do or where she could go. She'd made a mistake and she knew it. Hell, I don't know. I'm just guessing. All I did was go into the shop and ask her if she was all right. I said if she wanted to come home I'd be waiting for her in the car when she was ready."

"Did she say anything about what had happened, about me?"

"We chatted about a few things."

Manny realized he wasn't going to hear what they were. After a few minutes he said "Thanks Dad, you did good."

"Just doing my job, son, like I told you before. Except I'm learning as I go with this one. Anyway, I reckon it's done now, so I'll go home. Give me a call tomorrow and let me know how you get on."

After his father had gone, Manny went into his bedroom and lay down on the bed. He heard Jenny come out of the bathroom and go back into her room. Eventually there were no sounds except the creaks and snuffles all buildings make when it's dark and quiet. He tossed and turned until the sheets and blankets were screwed into a tangle and he had to get up and straighten them. At two in the morning a grey melancholy descended upon him and he got up again to break the mood, splashing water on his face and leaving the light on when he went back to bed, hoping unsuccessfully to keep his dark thoughts, self-recriminations and unresolvable anxieties at bay with the shadows. Eventually he gave up and turned off the light and around three o'clock drifted into a shallow, unsatisfying sleep from which the telephone dragged him up to consciousness five hours later.

"You find her?" It was Tony.

Aware that the telephone would also have awakened Jenny and she would be able to hear him, Manny grunted "Yes."

"Right. Understood. I'll tell the others. Good luck" Tony rang off.

He heard Jenny come out of her door behind him and go into the bathroom.

"Good morning. Have a good sleep?" He made it light and unthreatening as he had on the first morning she had come into his life. Not too bright, not too exaggerated.

Normal. "I'm putting on some coffee. Do you fancy some? What else would you like for breakfast? Are you in your usual cereal mood, or something else? Poached egg? Scrambled?"

She came and stood in the doorway in her dressing gown, with a towel wrapped in a turban to hide her hair.

"Cereal, please. The bran." She said it in such a small voice, and she looked so young and nervous, that his heart constricted and almost stopped.

"Lots of milk or just a little?"

"Just a little."

He busied himself bringing the packet from the cupboard, pouring the bran into a bowl and adding a dash of milk, trying not to look at her while desperate to read the expression on her face. A part of his mind wanted to apologise, to say it was all his fault, he had made a mess of trying to be a father and he was angry with himself, not with her. Another, sounding very like his father, said not to put any pressure on her, not to ask her to judge him or forgive him. His father had gone into the shop and asked if she was alright.

"How are you?" he ventured. "Alright?"

She was eating her cereal and had a spoonful halfway to her mouth. She replaced it in the bowl.

"Yes, thank you."

"Good. Anytime you want to talk about what happened I'll be ready. We don't have to if you don't want to. It's up to you." Was that putting pressure on her or giving her the freedom to make her own decisions? He had no idea, running on gut instinct and not at all sure his gut knew what it was doing.

"Thanks," she said again and, after another silence that began to grow so long he ached to fill it, "Do you think I'm alright?"

She was looking down at the plate in front of her and had gone still, waiting for his answer.

"I think you are everything I would have wanted my daughter to be before I knew you," he said. "I think you are more than alright. I'm proud and delighted to have you as my daughter."

"Despite what happened? Despite the party going all wrong, me running away?"

"Despite that and because of it. It's been part of my learning process in being your father."

"And what I said in the shop?"

"That you hated me? That too. I've heard all daughters hate their fathers at some stage. Sons too, I believe. Now I've experienced it for myself. Not pleasant, but I can handle it because I don't hate you back, and I never, never will."

'When Gramps came to get me I was so glad." She hesitated. "I hated myself for saying that to you, and for everything. I'd sort of painted myself into a corner. I couldn't come home although I wanted to. Then he came and I knew it would be alright."

She had said "come home" as if she were not aware the

words had any special significance. To Manny they had all the significance in the world.

"He thinks you're alright too," he said. "He told me so. Actually, because of you, my father and I have come closer together. You're something we are both delighted to have in our lives. You've given us a common bond we've lacked."

Jenny lifted her face to him. He thought he could see confidence and composure returning somewhere at the back of her eyes.

"Finish eating your breakfast," he suggested. "I'll finish cleaning the place up."

"I'll do it."

"We can do it together."

Several times while they cleared up the mess from the party, putting everything back in place, he saw or felt her turn her face towards him as if she wanted to say something. He resisted the impulse to prompt and left her to make her own decision.

At one point the phone rang, making Jenny jump. She stared at it as if it might be someone she didn't want to speak to. Manny answered it and when he heard the caller was Claire O'Connell's daughter, Dallas, raised an enquiring eyebrow at Jenny. She nodded and took the phone from him.

"Hi, Dallas. No, I'm okay. I was just being stupid."

After a silence while the other girl had quite a bit to say, Jenny told her, "You wouldn't have known any of them anyway. They're all from my school. It's just as well you didn't come."

More silence, then, "I know. I made a mess of it." She looked around the room and laughed. "In more ways than one. We're cleaning up the apartment now. Can I call you later?"

Dallas obviously agreed and Jenny put down the phone. She stood for a few minutes studying it. Manny had the intuition she was rehearsing how she was going to explain what had happened to her other friends. She put one hand up to the towel around her hair and he imagined she was also wondering how long the colour would take to come out and how she was going to explain that.

"Do you want to stay off school for a couple of days?" he asked, and was gratified to see the tension in her face relax.

"I would, if that's alright," she said. "It's only the last week, anyway."

The second part of the answer didn't seem to make sense at first. Then he remembered the school holidays were approaching.

"I've got an idea," he said, remembering the thought that had come to him when he had been interviewed by Diane Strickland. "How about I take some holidays, too, and we go away together? Down to the south coast? If you're not going back to school we could start tomorrow. Reorganising my work won't be a problem."

An expression of delight lit up Jenny's face before the

caution returned. "Could we? Are you sure?"

"Sure I'm sure. Give us a real chance to get to know each other. We'll hire one of those mobile homes and drive to different places. We'd never book in anywhere now, not with the school holidays. We'll be able to stop when we like and go where we like."

He was surprised when her face, which he expected to be at least a little bit pleased, if not exactly happy and smiling, became even more uncertain.

"What about Mum?"

For a moment he thought she was suggesting Katie should come too, then the reminder that Jenny's mother existed and needed to be considered dragged out something else he had forgotten. "I didn't tell you," he confessed. "She rang. She's changed her mind and wants you to go and visit her."

Suddenly he was seeing the happy smiling face he had wanted and was surprised at his reaction. It was jealousy. He felt envious of Katie for being able to produce that smile where he could not. One thing he could never doubt and should be careful never to forget, he told himself, was Jenny's love for her mother.

"Can we go and see her today?" she demanded

He was about to demur, changed his mind. "Why don't you ring the prison and tell her you're coming?"

"Can I? Can I speak to her?"

It was almost like a prayer. If he had been envious before he could feel only gratitude now for the mixture of relief and delight he could see in his daughter's eyes. He realized how much she missed her mother and how unhappy she had been behind the façade she had presented to him and the rest of her world.

Her face became serious. "When she rang… You didn't…?"

He shook his head. "It might be best if you didn't tell her about the party. It will worry her."

Jenny nodded as she went past him to the phone. She held it in her hand for several seconds before she dialled. He heard someone answer and the call was switched through.

"Mum. How are you? Are you alright?" She grimaced at Manny, and when he showed no sign of moving away from where he could hear her, turned her back so that she was speaking to the wall. "He said you called."

He felt as if he had been slapped. She hadn't called him Dad, or even by his name. Just 'He'.

"What's it like in prison?" she asked. "Is it horrible?"

He heard nothing for a long time while Katie answered. Jenny responded, "Can I come and see you today? Have you really changed your mind?"

After another silence while she was listening, Jenny turned and looked back at Manny, her eyes uncertain. She seemed to be seeking something from him. He didn't know what it was and could only shrug and lift an enquiring eyebrow.

"Yes, we're getting on fine," she said tentatively, and he realised she was beseeching confirmation.

He gave it by nodding and smiling and in return she half smiled back. Sensing she was not completely confident he said aloud "Tell your mother thank you for letting you stay with me."

Jenny repeated his words into the phone and her smile became more assured. "We really do get along well," she said. "Yes, it was great party. A lot of friends from school, and some of Grant's friends. No. There was no trouble." Again she looked at Manny and he gave her an affirming nod. "Why would there be, Mum? Well, you can ask him yourself if you like. I know he'll say the same thing."

Manny walked through to the kitchen, not needing to hear any more. He made himself a coffee and stood staring out of the window, not seeing anything in particular. Sometime later he heard her put the phone down and she came and stood in the doorway.

"She said it's okay to go this afternoon."

She had lied to her mother and he had been a party to it. More than that, he had encouraged it. The feeling that he ought to say something argued with the fear that it would be the wrong thing.

A knock on the door saved him from making the decision. When he went to answer it, Diana Strickland stood there.

"I decided not to wait until tomorrow," the social worker said. "Is Jenny here? May I come in?"

There was no reason Manny could think of to refuse and he assumed she had the authority to insist, so he stepped back and invited her in.

Jenny had come from the kitchen to see who was at the door, so there was no opportunity for him to conspire with her, issue a warning to say nothing about the party and what had happened after it, or make sure their lies coincided in other ways. With considerable misgivings he went down to his office and left them together. On the way down the stairs he stopped and waited, hoping he could hear something of what was said. While the walls might be thin, the floors weren't. He could hear nothing.

Trying to work was pointless. When the phone rang it came as a relief.

Madge demanded to know if Jenny was alright and he was able to assure her she was and apologise for not having called sooner. When she wanted more details he found he could not give them until he had discussed with Jenny what the full extent of their lie was going to be. He put Madge off by telling her that the social worker was there and he expected to be called into the discussion at any minute. She insisted he call later to relate what the social worker had said, as well as where Jenny had been and how he had found her. He agreed without being sure he meant it. Another lie.

Instead of putting the phone down he depressed the cradle and dialled the Polsons' number to tell Mrs Polson that Jenny was home safe and sound. Again he avoided any explanation that might have involved more lies.

The sound of a car door closing outside drew him to the

window to see Diane Strickland about to drive away. He hurried outside and stopped her.

"What did you say to Jenny?"

The woman gave him a look that appeared to be telling him he had no right to know, then relented. "We discussed her relationship with you."

"And?"

"She said it was good, but I have to tell you, Mr Youngman, I saw evidence of strain."

"It's possible your visit upset her. It's not an easy situation."

The social worker smiled thinly. "I'm sure it's not, and I know better than to upset my clients, Mr Youngman. Most of them are in stressful situations. I realise I may have come at an inopportune time with Jenny in the middle of washing her hair, but it was my impression she was upset before I arrived, and had been for some time. However, when I raised the matter, and I promise you I did it tactfully, she assured me everything was fine. Perhaps I should have pursued it further. Are you telling me she was not being truthful?"

The honest answer would have been yes. Manny shook his head.

"I understand she will be going to the prison to see her mother."

"That's right." He could answer that truthfully.

"I think it is perhaps the best course of action. I may call Ms Frank myself tomorrow, after their meeting, to get her impressions of her daughter's state of mind."

Manny remained silent, increasingly feeling he was not in control.

"What did she say?" he asked his daughter when he went back upstairs.

"I don't want her making decisions about me," she replied, by which he took it to mean she had told Diane Strickland nothing.

There was no point in pursuing the matter. Perhaps they would be able to discuss it later. If they were ever able to discuss anything later. He wasn't sure, about that or anything else, only that he had to try and maintain things on an even level. For a short time he had thought he was doing that. Now the ground seemed more uneven.

"We'd better start thinking about getting ready to see your mother," he suggested.

Jenny grabbed at the towel turban around her head. "What about my hair?"

Manny screwed his mouth sideways and nodded, almost glad of the distraction from his other concerns. "Not something I know much about. Could Alice help?"

She shook her head. "I don't want Sweeny to see it like this."

"A hat?"

"It's too long. It would stick out."

"We'll go to a hairdresser's. Get it cut."

They looked in the yellow pages and found a salon in a distant suburb where no-one would know Jenny or ever see her again. Manny drove her there still wearing the turban. Despite their careful choice of its location she scrutinised the passers-by before opening the car door and scurrying across the pavement.

While she was inside, he used the time to call clients on his mobile phone and cancel his appointments for the next two weeks. Only Claire O'Connell asked why.

He told her what had happened, adding. "You were right. I should have listened to you."

Claire laughed. "It's funny how men used to think because I was a woman I understood domestic things and nothing about business. Now they accept I know about business, so they assume I know nothing about domestic things."

Jenny had still not emerged so he walked down to a newsagent's and bought himself a paper to read. On his way back he tried to glance inside the hairdressers to see what was happening, but his daughter's head was hidden under something like the cowling of a jet engine.

After he had read the paper, he returned again to the newsagents and bought a paperback novel. Engrossed in this, he almost didn't recognise the figure that appeared beside his car. The turban was gone, and the once-red then green hair was now black and cropped very short.

"Is it alright?"

He was shocked almost into speechlessness. "You don't look like me anymore."

Jenny didn't laugh. "You think Mum will mind?"

He was sure she would. "She'll want to know why you did it."

"I'll say I wanted a change but something went wrong. She'd be more mad at me if I'd left it green."

She was going to be mad at him whatever colour it was, Manny expected. He'd have to go along with something having gone wrong. Another lie, or half a lie. The abyss was yawning wider.

To his surprise, Jenny appeared to be having similar thoughts. She gave him a rueful smile and said, "Dad. We need to talk about it, don't we? We can't just pretend it didn't happen."

He nodded. "Do you want to do it now or after we have seen your mother?"

She looked at him for a long time while she made up her mind.

Chapter 23

They approached the prison by a road skirting fifty metres of cleared ground fronting the first of its barricades. If Katie ever tried to escape, Manny reflected, she would be clearly visible and probably torn and bloody after struggling over four-metre-high chain mesh laced with barbed wire and topped with loose rolls of the same material. Ten metres behind the innermost barriers they could see windowless walls and a high-pitched roof made of a shiny material, with more rolls of barbed wire fitted over the guttering. Any inmate who climbed onto that roof was intended to slip off and break her neck if she didn't hang herself in the barbed wire. He was not surprised at the horrified expression on Jenny's face.

"I think that's part of why your mother didn't want you to come here at first," he said. "It isn't a nice place, is it?"

Jenny nodded. "I don't suppose it's meant to be."

"A woman would have designed it differently," he said, half flippantly to counter her mood, and instantly regretted it. She didn't seem to notice, staring instead at the grim sight with a deep sadness he intuited as a growing awareness of the reality her mother was going through. Perhaps Katie's first instinct had been right and Jenny should not be seeing this.

They hadn't had their talk. She said she needed to see her mother first, to know she was alright. He agreed because it was what she wanted and because until he saw the barbed wire and the walls he believed Katie was being unreasonable. Now he wondered what the experience was going to do to their daughter, how it would colour her picture of what had brought them there and the events of the past few days.

They were going to lie to Katie about their relationship, about how Jenny was doing at school, and about the party and the events that had followed it. Many traps lay ahead if they did not keep to the agreed story, many triggers for suspicion in a mind that must already be worried about the decisions it had made. And after that, as conspirators in the lie, how would either of them be sure the other was telling the truth when they faced each other for their talk?

He parked the car in a bitumen area surrounded by floodlights. Similar lights were set around the entrance and at regular distances along the walls. Jenny shrank back in her seat, her eyes empty of expression. After a few moments she shook herself, opened the door and came out to join him on a slow, reluctant walk towards the entrance.

He was surprised to find the interior of the prison more attractive than the outside. No grey or brown paint. No bricks. Pastel painted walls and a minimum of visible iron bars in the area they were allowed to enter. No echoing corridors. Nothing like the movies. Once through the entrance the lights were the sort you'd expect in a pleasant boarding house. There was a small hallway and from there a comfortable looking woman, not at all granite featured and mean, showed them into a large open room scattered with small round tables encircled with chairs. The chairs weren't upholstered but they were comfortable. Katie came in unaccompanied from a door at the far end of the room, smiling determinedly and speaking to several other women, dressed as ordinarily as she was, who sat with their visitors at other tables.

Jenny ran forward into her mother's outstretched arms while Manny held back, making a show of examining the other occupants of the room. A hard-faced blonde with a tattoo on her upper arm was talking to a man with a shaved head. Beyond them an ordinary, middle-aged mother greeted an equally ordinary man and three children. He could imagine several possibilities why the first might be in prison but few for the second.

When he glanced back, Katie held Jenny at arms-length, examining her hair with an expression that said she did not approve. Jenny defended herself. Katie shook her head. She turned and glared at Manny, her eyes steeled. Jenny also turned and, not too enthusiastically, beckoned Manny to join them.

"Hi, Katie," he said.

The greeting was not returned. "Did you approve the hair change?"

He gave her a thin smile and tried not to appear to be answering the question one way or another. "Don't you like it?"

"It's terrible. Why did you let her do it?"

He widened the smile a fraction. "It'll have grown out

by the time you're out of here."

Katie glared at him and then around the room, as if realizing they were standing confronting each other and making themselves obvious. She waved a hand to a table and chairs and they sat. He wished he could have waited in the car and sent Jenny in alone, but the prison had made it clear they would not allow that. They were worried how she might react and wanted an adult with her to take responsibility and appropriate action if she became too distressed and had to be taken out again.

"Looks nice. Not like I expected," he said, looking round the room and speaking brightly to try to break the mood.

"I don't think it looks nice at all." She was glaring at Jenny's head.

"Not Jenny's hair. This place."

"Oh, yes. It's home away from home." Her tone was sarcastic.

"Is it terrible?" Jenny asked her. "Do you hate it?"

Katie's body language softened in response to the concern in her daughter's voice.

Unable to move his chair away, Manny sank into it, retreating from the conversation as best he could. He had no heart for confrontation with Katie, or for Jenny to be witness to it.

"It hasn't been that bad," Katie said. "I read, watch television, come and go from my room just about as I please. It's all right if you stay away from the window and forget there's wire round the outside."

"We saw it coming in. It's horrible."

"Depressing. But never mind that. The last thing I want to talk about. How have you been keeping? How was the party?"

The hair seemed to have been accepted as a fait accompli, at least for the time being. They were coming to the more difficult lies. Manny steeled himself not to show any expression that would make Katie suspicious.

"Everything's fine," Jenny told her mother in a bright chatty voice as if it really was. "I've been back to the house and everything's okay there. The garden's looking lovely and Sweeny is keeping an eye on it. Betty's got a new boyfriend. You know David Clark from the house on the corner near the service station?"

"The tall blonde boy?"

"He's a wimp but she reckons he's fabulous. He's got a motorbike. I think it's a Suzuki or it maybe a Kawasaki. It's bigger than ours and he looks good on it and lets Betty ride pillion. She says she's going to get one of her own as soon as she's old enough to get a licence. I think that's when you're sixteen, isn't it? Anyway, I said I might get one too and we could go riding together."

"That would be nice," Katie said. Manny had the feeling she was not listening but letting Jenny's words flow over her like a soothing balm.

"Jane Devonport had mumps. She was off school for ages but I don't envy her because I think mumps is pretty painful, isn't it? Not much fun being off school if you have to spend all the time in bed taking pain killers. Her face is all lumpy, too. You should see the dress Caroline's mother bought her to wear to her brother's wedding. It's a pale yellow with white ribbon slotted through holes around the hem and the neck and sleeves. Tucked in at the waist with pleat things and the neckline is scalloped, you know. It's hard to describe things so you know exactly what they look like."

Katie nodded. She smiled, her attention focused entirely on her daughter. "I know what you mean. You have to know what all the words mean and I never did learn to sew so I don't understand half of it."

Jenny nodded in return. "It really is nice. I think she's going to look fabulous. She's going shopping to find matching shoes and handbag. She thinks she wants a different shade of yellow except a contrast might be nice and she can always fall back on white. That would be safest, wouldn't it? Do you remember that yellow outfit I had? The slacks and top? Yes, white would be safest. Yellow's difficult. I wonder what happened to that outfit? Do you think it would still fit me?"

Was she gabbling to shut out the reality of their surroundings? Probably not. Katie was acting as if this were normal. The middle-aged woman seemed to be having a similar conversation with her teenage daughter while the two boys argued over something and the husband would go to sleep if they didn't leave soon. Again he wondered why a woman like that was in prison. She didn't seem the type any more than Katie did. He glanced across at the woman with the tattoos and contemplated how biased people were by appearances. The middle aged mother could have run over someone in her car because she was talking on her mobile phone while the tattooed woman had done nothing more than grow a few marihuana plants.

"You haven't put on any weight have you?" Jenny was saying. "I thought you might with the sort of food they'd have here."

Katie laughed. "It's not that bad. Not Weight Watchers but I've been watching myself and I've put on a little of what I'd lost before so I'm about the same now."

Jenny had talked to him about none of this. They had had no chatty conversation about Betty and David Clark with the motorbike. No lumpy mumpy Jane or scallop-necked Caroline. He would have recommended the white accessories if he had been asked. Women chatted with women in a way they never did with men. It was part of their networking, their need to be part of a group in which they felt recognized and valued. With surprise, he recognized that was probably what he was doing with NEMSA. Were the new men's groups, the men's sheds, just a way for men to get together and chat?

Perhaps he should chatter more with Jenny, tell her about the people he worked with, the trivia of his day, stories Tommy told about his daughters or Bobby about his three wives. This could be a significant discovery. If he talked to Jenny more like the way Katie spoke to her, would they communicate better?

On the other hand, the way Jenny was talking to her mother sounded more like a young teenage girl than the sort of conversation she had with him. Did he want that?

"I cried the first night. I was a bit scared," Jenny said, jerking his attention back into focus. This wasn't good. He didn't want Katie to think there was anything wrong.

"Locked herself in the bathroom," he broke into their conversation with a laugh to make light of the incident. "Wouldn't come out until I made her an offer she couldn't refuse – breakfast."

Jenny giggled and Katie smiled. When she glanced at Jenny's hair again and appeared to be going to return to that topic, Jenny jumped in first.

"Mr James asked Manny to come up to the school to see him. He really is a dickhead."

"Manny?" Katie sat back, turning her face towards him.

Jenny giggled again, less convincingly than before. "No. Mr James. I've told you about him before. He says stupid things in class and gets angry because I argue with him. We're not allowed to have brains of our own."

Katie remained studying Manny, ignoring this attempt to deflect her. "What did Mr James want to see you about?"

"Wanted me to smack her bum, I think," Manny attempted a grin to keep it light. "I told him to do it himself."

"You didn't!" Jenny yelped. "I think it's disgusting,

talking about me like that. It's unfair."

"Jenny. I'd like to hear what Manny has to say." This time Katie spoke with the unmistakable tone of a parent. Jenny seemed about to protest, read the expression on her mother's face and retreated into silence.

"What was said Manny?"

"Not a great deal. I told him Jenny's stay with me was temporary and he should speak to you. He said he had."

Some of the tension left Katie's face. The rigidity in her arms eased and her shoulders subsided as if she was accepting something she had already known. She nodded. "He can't handle a female who speaks up for herself and won't be sold a lot of chauvinistic bullshit."

"I don't think that's being entirely fair to him."

Afterwards he thought it was seeing her relax that had made him drop his guard and say what he was thinking without first censoring it.

"Oh?" The sound was loaded.

He contemplated retreating and decided it was too late. "The bloke has a job to do. Jenny can sound off when she's in the mood for it."

"When she's in the mood for it?"

"Yes. She's given me the benefit of her opinions, too. Or maybe they're your opinions, not hers."

"You don't agree with these opinions?"

"Not all of them, as it happens. You know that. It's not the point. She was arguing with James in the classroom and it was disruptive."

"I don't think I like you going up to the school to discuss Jenny. You know nothing about her."

"I didn't go up on my own account. I was asked. I spoke with the school counsellor, too."

"What did she say?"

He thought about that. "Not much. She just sounded less emotional about it than he did. I also told her I would speak with Jenny, and I did. I figure Jenny's intelligent enough to sort it out."

The subject of their conversation was sitting still, studying their faces as they spoke.

"You seem to be making a lot of judgments about Jenny for someone who doesn't know her."

"But I am getting to know her, and I want to know her a lot more."

"Who else have you been discussing Jenny with?"

"The social worker."

Katie hadn't expected that answer. Her question had been sarcastic. "What social worker?" she demanded.

He explained.

"Diane Strickland?" Katie appeared puzzled and suspicious, even a little angry. "It has nothing to…" She stopped "She looked all round your place? What does she think Jenny is going to do? Live there forever?"

"I think she thought the place was all right. She didn't think much of me." There might be an opportunity now to ease the tension. He was aware of Jenny's stillness and didn't want to make it any worse for her.

Katie gave a sniff that suggested she agreed with Diane Strickland's assessment. "What didn't she like about you specifically?"

Manny didn't answer.

"I'm sorry, Jen," Katie said. "You must hate it, having to live with him and listen to such crap. I am sorry."

"No, it's okay." Jenny looked at her mother cautiously, weighing what she could or could not say. "Dad says we can go away on holiday."

Inside Manny two emotions collided and brought everything else to a stop. Happiness because she had called him Dad, apprehension because she had revealed another decision he had made without consulting her mother.

Katie reacted to both.

"Dad? I didn't know you…"

"It sort of seems easiest. It's funny calling him Manny. I call his mum and dad Gran and Gramps." Jenny hesitated, giving her mother a long look. "Is that alright?"

For a moment Katie's eyes blinked shut, as if in denial. She opened them again and nodded a short acknowledgement. "Where are you going on holiday and how long for?"

Jenny looked at Manny as if he should answer, but he chose to remain silent. Let it not be wholly his decision.

"Down to the south coast," Jenny explained. "Just for a few days, touring in a mobile home. I think it'll be great."

"It sounds wonderful," Katie responded, clearly without meaning it. "I was hoping you would come and visit me during the school holidays, as you'd have more time."

Jenny's expression suggested conflict, somewhere between irritation and guilt.

"I thought you didn't want me to come when we talked about it," she pointed out. "I'll stay if you want me to."

Now who was making decisions without consultation, Manny thought, but stayed silent. He was glad he had when Katie softened and said, "No. I'm being silly. You have your holiday."

Jenny reached across the table to touch her mother's hand. "I'll take photographs and show them to you when I come back and I'll ring you every day."

"You may not be in mobile range all the time if you're touring around," Katie told her. "Ring me whenever you can."

There were stirrings around the room. Groups were breaking up, the visitors heading for the door they had entered while the visitees remained. Some moved to the other door at the end of the room as if eager to return to their normal routine. Others lingered, even after their visitors had disappeared. Manny began to rise, eager to return to something which, if not his normal routine, was more comfortable than being where he was.

Katie didn't move and nor did Jenny. He sat back in the chair.

"It will be alright," Jenny assured her mother. "We're getting on okay. We really are. The holiday will help."

Katie nodded doubtfully. The pleasant-featured woman who did not look like a guard was coming towards them.

"I'm sure it will."

This time Manny stood up and stayed up. It would mean more if Jenny could reassure Katie while he was not listening. "I'll see you outside, Jen," he said. "Goodbye, Katie."

As he walked back along the corridor and out through the entrance he felt both angry at Katie and sorry for her and the more he reflected on the scene in the visitors' room, the more the latter took over. Whatever else she was, she was a mother and he was starting to understand what being a father meant. Her anger was at her situation, not him. She was worried sick locked up in this place, no matter how convivial it pretended to be, wondering how her daughter was, powerless and afraid she had done the wrong thing. After they had gone she would go over every word that was spoken, every word that was not spoken, trying to remember looks, gestures, to piece it all together. It would go round and round in her mind. She'd have nothing else to do.

He considered going back to the visiting room, to reassure her that as soon as he and Jenny came back from their holiday they would start ringing the prison regularly and telling her what was happening. They would visit her at least twice a week and bring her flowers or chocolates, or anything else she wanted to make her stay there easier. He would consult her before going to the school or taking any other action that a father would normally discuss with the mother when it related to their child.

He needed to establish a good relationship so that he could continue to see Jenny after Katie came out of prison. That was assuming Jenny wanted to continue seeing him. Perhaps it would be better to go on the holiday first, have that talk, cement their relationship and in the process decide together about how often they were going to come and see Katie.

Consultation. That had to be the key word.

Chapter 24

Manny was not all that surprised to find not one but three cars lined up in his carport and the drive leading into it. Two he recognized. They belonged to Tony and to his mother and father. The third, which was a blue hatchback, he didn't.

"It's Madge," Jenny told him. He wasn't sure that she was pleased to see her mother's friend, or his parents for that matter.

"Are you alright?" he asked. It was becoming his standard formula for telling her that he cared and was not being too inquisitive or critical. It had worked for his Dad.

Jenny gave a quick nod. "I have to see people, don't I?"

"No," he told her. "Not if you don't want to. I can explain that you're too upset, that you don't want to talk to anyone."

She shook her head and bit down on her bottom lip, raised her eyebrows and stepped out of the car.

Still seated, Manny also raised his eyebrows and bit down on his lip. It was becoming a habit to imitate the expressions on her face and feel how they mirrored his own features in similar situations.

His father had come over to the car as Jenny gave her a grandmother a hug and greeted Alice and Madge. "You alright?"

Manny felt his chest and stomach muscles begin first to quiver and then shudder in spasms of silent laughter.

He had to fight to prevent the laughter turning into tears. "Yeah, Dad, I'm alright. Thanks." He slid out of the car.

"I had to bring your mother. Couldn't not tell her."

"Yeah, Dad, I know. It's okay."

"You and Jenny sorted it out?"

He didn't know how to answer that one. "We've just been to the prison to see Katie, her mother," he said instead.

His father was surprised. "Did you now?" He glanced across at Jenny. "She take that alright?"

Manny nodded. "I think so. Haven't had any time to discuss it with her, or anything much for that matter. Just trying to keep things calm. You know."

His father nodded as if he did know. "Seems she's doing the same," he said.

Manny had heard his mother's raised voice and the rapid fire of questions from the other two women. There was nothing he could do to protect Jenny from them, and to a large extent he didn't think he should try. It was her bed, even if he had helped her to make it, and she was going to have to lie in it and make her own decisions.

"Excuse me a minute, Dad," he said and walked over to where Tony still sat in his car.

"Didn't seem much point getting out," his friend said. "Obviously you're busy."

Tony's car was locked in by the other two. He had been the first to arrive. Now he couldn't drive away and Manny didn't want him to. "Could you hang around till I sort this out?"

"Sure." Tony took a newspaper from the seat beside him. "I'll put in some quality reading time. Or I would if the bloody paper had anything worth reading in it." He grinned and Manny smiled gratefully back.

"Robert. Jennifer is going to have to come and stay with me. This sort of thing cannot be allowed to continue." His mother had come across and stood glaring at him.

"We've already discussed that, Mum."

"That was before all this business," his mother insisted. "It's in the girl's best interests."

Manny looked across at Jenny, who was now talking with Alice and Madge. "Did you ask her what she wants?"

"Girls that age don't know what they want." Which was as good as saying the answer hadn't been what she wanted, he thought.

"You're probably right," he said to placate her. "I don't think you should see it for more than it was, Mum. I over-reacted to a situation and Jenny got upset. This situation is difficult for both of us."

"She ran away. Anything could have happened to her."

"And nothing did, and now she's back, thanks largely to Dad, and she and I have to sort it out between ourselves."

"That's another thing. Why was your father involved in it? Why didn't you call me?"

Because you would have carried on like you are carrying on now was the answer. Instead Manny said "Dad has been getting on very well with Jenny and I thought she might respond to him."

That answer didn't get a much better reception than the one he had discarded. "So you're saying I don't get on well with her?"

It was a pointless discussion to continue. "I'd better go and talk to Katie's friends," he said. "They were out searching for Jenny last night, too."

His mother stood indecisively, clearly wanting to say more. It would take a while before her feeling of outrage subsided and her more practical self began to see the situation for what it was. Dad, he saw, had gone over to speak to Tony. They were old mates.

He walked across to where Jenny was talking to Alice and Madge. It was the first time he had seen Madge, their previous communications being all by telephone. She was a year or so older than he had imagined, although the conservative hairstyle and clothes were in keeping with the image he had formed. The hair was straw colour and she wore tailored dark green pants and a pale yellow, high buttoned shirt, the casual clothing of someone who was an office manager or an accountant. Neat and tidy. Not exactly attractive.

Alice was a different matter. She wore blue pants and a blouse of a light floral pattern, something that had intertwining leaves and flowers, possibly lavender or wisteria. It had a bright, summery look to it. It was a pity he hadn't been able to get back to her and take her out to dinner. Events had conspired against that plan.

"You see how much they are alike," Alice said as he

approached. "They even have the same thoughts and laugh the same. Come on you two, show Madge how you do it. Say something the same."

Manny and Jenny looked at one another.

"How do you do?" said Manny.

"Sweeny's an idiot," said Jenny.

They laughed, but it was strained and uncomfortable. Something else events were conspiring against.

"I'm Madge, as you've no doubt gathered. Neither of these two is going to introduce me." She stuck out a hand and gripped his. "Pleased to meet you." The words were clipped, as if she was restraining herself from saying something. When he looked into her eyes, something angry lurked there. She didn't approve of him, he decided.

"Hello, Madge. I have to thank you again for helping me search for Jenny last night," he said carefully. "As you can see, she's alright now. We both are."

"She's being telling us about it," Alice responded, "haven't you, Jenny? And about going to see Katie. We were worried, of course, but it does sound as if it wasn't as bad as you were imagining, was it Madge?"

Madge disagreed. "A real father should have acted more responsibly and be showing a lot more concern about his daughter nearly being raped, running away and being out alone all night."

Manny took half a step back. Despite having half seen the attack coming, he was surprised at the intensity of it. He had hardly had any conversation with the woman and had no idea why she should be so against him. Unless she had read his book and made up her mind from that, as Diane Strickland had done, and Katie. The sins of the book are visited on the author. Had she attended one of his lectures, been one of the women who had attacked his views from the body of the audience? If so, he didn't remember her face.

He thought about a possible quick retort and decided against it. Her criticism of him wasn't that far off things he had been thinking himself.

"You're right," he said to Madge. "I made mistakes, and I think Jenny admits she did too. We're both very new to the dad and daughter business, so while I wish none of it had happened, it did and there's nothing we can do to reverse it. We go on, and we'll talk about it some more when we are alone together." He looked at Jenny as he said this and saw she was looking back at him, her eyes not exactly smiling, but not at all unhappy with what he was saying.

"Jenny tells us you're going away on holiday together," Alice said as if she thought it a good idea.

Madge immediately countered it. "Do you think that's wise?"

Manny ignored her. Madge and her views about him were irrelevant as long as they didn't influence Jenny; forewarned was forearmed as far as that was concerned. It was something else he would have to discuss with Jenny when the moment presented itself.

"I'm going to have to go home and get some different clothes again," he heard Jenny saying, as she, too, ignored Madge's comment. "It's a nuisance not having them all with me."

From the size of the suitcase she had brought back with her last time and the piles of clothing he knew filled the cupboards, drawers and half the floor space in her bedroom, Manny was surprised she had not got everything she owned with her. That was not something he was going to add to the 'talk about' list, however.

"You can come back with us," Alice said. "It'll give us a chance to talk some more. That will be all right, won't it, Manny? Jenny could even stay and have dinner and I'll drive her back later. Or what do you think, Jenny, maybe we can pick up takeaways on the way back, for Manny too?"

Jenny thought that was a wonderful idea although Madge seemed less pleased. His mother, too, was displaying her disapproving expression. She probably wanted more time to talk to Jenny and berate him, he imagined. Jenny going with Alice would get him out of that situation as well as give him the chance to talk to Tony.

"Sure, sounds like a great idea," he said. "Jenny knows what I like."

"Deep pan gourmet pizza with extra anchovies." Jenny laughed.

Alice said "Ugh" but laughed and added "That's settled then. Lovely to see you again, Manny, despite the circs.

I'm a pizza fan too so I'm looking forward to having a bite of yours when we get back." She grinned. "Might even let you have a bite of mine."

Was there a double meaning in the words? Before he had the chance to say something clever and test it out, Alice swept Jenny towards their car, drawing Madge with her.

He turned back to his other visitors, wondering how he was going to get rid of his mother so that he could share some of his confusing thoughts with Tony.

Chapter 25

His mother turned out not to be a problem. As soon as Jenny had gone, she appeared to decide her errand was over and announced she was going home. She did fire one last shot, "I expect to hear immediately if there are any further problems, Robert," to which Manny replied "Of course, Mum," and added another lie to his list.

His Dad appeared reluctant to leave, as if there was something he still wanted to ask or say, so Manny said, "Call you soon, Dad. There's something I want to tell you about," and that seemed to be acceptable.

"Come on." Manny beckoned Tony out of his car and led the way across the small courtyard behind the car port and into his office through its glass door. He went over to the fridge, took out two boutique brewery beers, slid them into stubby holders and handed one across. "Sit."

Tony sat, pointed the bottom of the stubby holder towards Manny and took a long swig, finishing with "Ahhh! Good stuff."

Manny also sat and raised his own stubby holder in a toast, already feeling some of the tension dissipating. "So, what's happening?"

"Nothing much with me. Hell of lot with you, I'd say," Tony answered. "The one in the blue blouse seems a bit of all right. Don't think much of yours."

"You'll have to fight me for Alice," Manny told him. "I've got no show with Madge. She doesn't like me. Can't think why."

Tony laughed. "Now why could any woman not like such a handsome devil as you with your ginger hair and scrubby eyebrows? Maybe she's worried you've got a bit of ginger in some other places as well. Or not. Who knows with women these days?"

Manny flexed his shoulders and felt more of the tension ease out of them. This was what he needed, a cold beer and a sledging match with a good mate. "At least you recognise it's me she would be thinking about," he retorted. "Didn't see any sign of her fancying you much."

"Because I was hiding in my car as instructed and leaving the field to you," Tony protested. "I know you can't stand competition, mate. You can't call me a party pooper."

"Yes I can. You're a party pooper."

There was a silence in which they both grinned at their stubby holders. "Talking of parties…" Manny added, and gave Tony the detail of what had happened the previous evening and that morning.

When he finished, their beers were too, so he fetched a couple more from the fridge. "What are your thoughts?"

"Complicated. Not surprised. It was never going to be easy, was it? You knew that."

Manny wondered if he had known it. "Part of me did," he conceded. "I think the trouble was that another part of me thought it was something any man with reasonable intelligence should be able to handle. I mean, after all, being a father's natural, isn't it? Any idiot can do it, and I don't think of myself as an idiot."

"And?" Tony grinned. "Do you now accept that you are an idiot?"

"Let's say I didn't foresee the pitfalls."

Raising his beer in a salute, Tony grinned even more broadly. "I should say you can say that. So now what's the plan?"

Manny explained about going away for a holiday. "Jenny's going to be off school and that means I'll have to take time off from work to be with her. If we stay here she's going to want to go and see her friends and I'll be scratching my head for things to do with her. There's also meetings of the Society of Architects and the City Heritage Committee. If I'm around I'll have to go to them and that will mean leaving her in the apartment by herself. I don't want to do that after what happened, but I also don't want her to think I don't trust her."

"You don't."

"I don't think it's a matter of trust. Even if she thinks that, it's not what she will do I worry about, it's her ability to deal with situations. She's very mature for her age, but she's still only fifteen. I'm very much beginning to learn that."

"Not the new era man dealing with the new era woman?"

Manny shook his head. "Not an adult woman. That was something I didn't take into account, Tony. It's not just about being a different kind of man, it's about being a responsible parent. I hadn't understood that or seen the difference."

"Understandably, since you hadn't travelled along the fifteen years' learning curve most fathers of a girl Jenny's age would have had."

"Right. So I have to spend my time with her and, apart from anything else, that means I won't get any work done. If we go away it solves a lot of problems. She won't think I don't trust her, we won't be explaining to people about her running away, or about what happened at the party. My mother can't come around all the time interfering, or that social worker, Diana Strickland."

After a pause he said, "I don't plan to do any NEMSA business while we're away. Sorry if that inconveniences you. I won't be taking any phone calls or attending any meetings. I need to concentrate on Jenny. I won't be talking to her about men's issues either, nothing that could stir up any of the feminist views her mother's brainwashed her with. Maybe that way we can talk things through, find out more about each other without all the distractions."

Tony said he thought it was a good idea, but there would still be pitfalls. "There always will be," he predicted. "You've just got to get better at seeing them coming." He studied Manny thoughtfully. "What you're going to do, for example, if she says all men are sexist pigs? Aren't you going to argue?"

Manny nodded. "I have been thinking about that. Generally, not just for the holiday. I think the key would be to find out what prompted her to say it, to deal with the issue itself rather than the preconceived views she applies to it."

Now it was Tony who nodded. "So it's like pro-active listening. The sort of thing you suggested in The Male Conundrum. You don't say all men are not sexist pigs, you ask her whether she really thinks they are?"

"And why. I have to focus my interest on what she's reacting to, not to what her reaction is."

"Sounds good," Tony complimented him. "Something to put in your next book. Are you still working on that, by the way?"

Manny admitted he wasn't. He had found it difficult with Jenny in the apartment and the time that was already taking away from his normal work routine. That and the fact that she would ask what he was doing and that could open a can of worms if he told her what the book was about. The Myths of Misogyny. Even telling her the title could start the sort of argument he was trying to avoid.

Tony agreed. "That Dick James, Jenny's teacher, is a good example of what you're saying in the books and I don't think you want to raise that issue with her," he said.

Manny remembered that Bobby had been talking to Dick at the NEMSA meeting the night before, had in fact been going through a pro-active listening process with him to get him to open up and recognise some of his problems for what they really were.

"You think his marriage has had it?"

"No. It's salvageable if that's what they want. Neal's given him a bit of free legal advice and suggested a lawyer. You know how it works. If you start talking lawyers, most times they see how serious it is and start looking for a better answer."

"So how's he a good example for the book?"

"Hates all females because he hates himself. That's one of your myths, isn't it? Like you were just saying, the cause, not the reaction. He's not a misogynist, he's a malcontent. The reasons for his wife leaving him are about his lack of self-esteem and dissatisfaction with the way his life has gone, and the way he keeps complaining and blaming his wife. The problems Jenny has with him at school are just a by-product of that."

"Have you or Bobby said all that to him?"

Tony shook his head. "We leave that to the psychs. At our level we never deal with specific cases. Too many confusing and unrelated emotions involved. Stay with the general. One of your arguments in The Male Conundrum. Am I right?"

He was, although Manny's views had developed since he had first written them down. He began to explain how he planned to expand them in the new book. It was the sort of discussion he had been missing lately because he had been so focused on Jenny.

After they had been talking to and fro for a while he paused. "The trouble is," he said, almost thinking aloud, "I'm only thinking all this stuff at one level, not at another."

Tony looked at him quizzically. "How so?"

"I'm not sure." He stared at the beer glass in his hand as if it were a crystal ball in which he might see his own muddied thoughts clarified. "I'm not your typical man, am I? Not like Tommy or even Bobby and you, and especially not like Dick James. Not even like my Dad in a lot of ways. I haven't married and don't have children I've grown up with like most men. I've been learning a lot lately about what I don't know about that side of being a man."

"And you think this means you've been wrong about the need for men to take a new direction?"

Manny shook his head. "Not at all. Just that I may need to think more about what that direction should be, and what sort of direction men who are married and do have children might want to go in."

"Maybe it's something you should consider in the new book."

"Not the Myths of Misogyny?"

"It has a ring to it, doesn't it? Keep it as a working title."

Manny nodded. "Something else I've been thinking about. These Men's Sheds? Do you think they are a more practical idea? I'm starting to think we may be too theoretical with NEMSA."

"Not at all," Tony disagreed. "While Men's Sheds are doing a great job, someone needs to be doing the thinking and, in your case, the writing. That's what will grow the movement. Don't forget you're an architect, Manny. You're someone who creates the dream, designs the structure and shows how it should look for the builders to come along and build it.

"With Men's Sheds, men are getting together to find a new way for themselves. It's happening spontaneously and with something they know and understand, getting together to do something with their hands. The next stage is they start thinking about it, asking questions and looking round for answers and that's where NEMSA and your books come in."

It sounded right at a theoretical level, Manny thought, so why didn't it answer the question he was asking himself?

"It's just that I was thinking it would be a lot easier to explain to Jenny that I was going down the shed to make something with some mates than to say we were going to discuss a new paradigm in male/female relationships," he explained.

"I suspect Jenny is quite capable with coping with that sort of discussion," Tony answered.

The sound of a car outside interrupted their discussion. Its subject had returned with Alice Todd and even more clothes than she had collected on her previous trip home.

As they went out to greet them, Tony said, "By the way, something I forgot to tell you. Did you know it was Jenny who made the fake bomb Katie threw into that club? Dick James said she made it at school in her science class."

Chapter 26

The mobile home hummed over a crest in a road that descended into a long downward curve shaded between trees standing like sentinels in uniforms of yellows, greens and greys. Jenny uncurled from sleep on the passenger's side of the centre console.

Manny coasted to a halt on the verge with a view down the hill through endless avenues of trees. He watched with pleasure as her eyes widened and she jumped out of the cabin, impatient to look more closely, her breath almost stopping as her eyes absorbed the impressions of late afternoon sunlight dappling down to the leaf-strewn floor of the forest. He got out of the cab and walked round the front of the bonnet to stand beside her.

After the first five days of their holiday, with long days of sunlit sandy beaches and leisurely walks, meals shared in cafes, picked up from fish and chip shops or cooked in the mobile home and afternoons spent sleeping or reading under the shade of a beach umbrella or a tree, they were relaxed and at ease with other. Both had repeated frequently how much they enjoyed being together.

For the first two days, Jenny had phoned the prison every evening, relating to Katie the details of their day and how much fun they were having. Manny could not know how Katie was responding, but he imagined at least part of her was saddened because she was not the one enjoying this time with her daughter. There had to be a painful anguish in hearing about sunlight and bright open spaces when you were incarcerated in a prison cell.

For the past three days they had been traveling deep in the southern forest among tall trees where there was no mobile phone coverage and therefore no communication with Katie or anyone else in the outside world.

For some, Manny thought, that might seem like being in a prison. For him it was liberating. This was a special kind of freedom and he and Jenny were experiencing it together. Now they needed to move to the next phase in what he had been planning. It was time. That was why he had brought Jenny to one of the most beautiful places he knew.

"Katie would love it here." She stood in satisfying awe and gazed down into a valley in which nature might have provided the inspiration for the first cathedral. The trees were more perfect than marble columns, the light slanted down with greater focus and breathtaking effect than ever was created with high windows.

A log had fallen a little way down the hill. He invited her to sit on it in silence, observing the play of sunlight through the trees. In some ways it was a lifeless scene. No birds or animals. Only the wind and the sunlight and the leaves on the trees. Yet the essence of life itself yearned upwards, offering its beauty to the senses and the hope that all the world could be as beautiful. Jenny rose and moved away along the ridge, looking for something else. Not restless, he thought. Impatient for experience.

"You remember before we left home you said we would have to talk," he began.

She raised her face from a wildflower she had found growing beside the road.

"Yes. Do you want to talk now?"

"Mmm." He nodded. "I think we should."

She returned her gaze to the flower, concentrating on it as if in some way she wanted to understand it and what it stood for. "Do we still need to? We've been having such a lovely time."

"That's why I think it's a good time," he told her. "We were both upset before, still too close to it, not sure of each other because of what had happened. I think we are sure of each other now. I really feel like I am your father, and that you are my daughter, and we will always be that now, for ever. So talking about what happened can't take that away."

"Are you sure?"

"Aren't you?"

She wrinkled her nose and pursed her mouth. "I don't know."

This was harder than Manny had imagined. "Would you like to leave it until you've had some time to think?"

She considered that before placing the flower down on the ground in front of her. "No. If we are going to talk, doing it here would be best." She looked up at his face. "Nothing ugly could happen here."

For an instant he contemplated stretching forward and

taking her in his arms. He resisted because it would be an intrusion on what they were establishing.

"I want to suggest we talk in a special way," he said, "a way I think will make it easier to say what we truly feel and listen to and understand what the other one is feeling."

She waited.

"People don't always listen when you're talking to them," he continued. "You can say something and they start telling you something they've thought of that's related. They're not really responding to what you are saying."

She nodded.

"So what I would like us to do is something different. I want one of us to talk while the other listens and doesn't interrupt. No questions. No comments. Just listening. After that the other one talks and the first one listens. When we have both talked we say, "I now feel… and explain how we are feeling, again without interruption. At the end we each say what we want to happen next and decide between us what it will be.

"Cool!" Jenny turned her head around, looking at the trees, the ground, up at the sky and back at Manny. "Who goes first?"

"You decide."

"I think it should be you, because you know how to do it and I can learn for when it's my turn, and because I think it's you who wants it most."

Manny thought that was an intelligent and adult way to approach it, but he didn't say so, just smiled and began.

"One of my friends said that having a daughter, or any children, was a learning curve and you got better at it as you travelled along it. I didn't make the journey. I didn't know you when you were a baby, I wasn't able to do what other men have told me they have done, which is see their child lying there defenceless and unformed as a person and know and promise that they will always love her, always protect her, always be there for her."

He saw she was looking back at him, eyes narrowing in the way he, and she, did when they were listening carefully, as if restricting vision enhanced hearing or focused thought.

"So I want to say that to you now, Jenny. I will always love you, always do everything I can to protect you, and always be there for you."

As he spoke the words a smile formed on her face like a flower opening to the sunlight and a small tear formed in a corner of one eye. Manny felt an increasingly familiar wave of emotion rising through his body and his own eyes started to mist.

"I can't say I'll always protect you because you're not a defenceless, unformed baby, you're a growing person with your own personality. I can't protect you from decisions you'll make, unfair actions that will be taken against you, or disagreeable, even dangerous situations you may confront. All I can promise is that I'll do everything I can to protect you when those things happen. I will always be on your side."

For a moment Jenny leaned towards him and it seemed

as if she was going to say something. He held up a hand to ask her not to and she shook her head, pulled her shoulders back and settled again into her listening position.

"It's hard, isn't it, just listening?" he said.

She nodded.

"When Katie brought you to me, I didn't instantly become a father and think like that," Manny continued. "A part of me did. Some of those feelings were born at that moment and grew later. I was shocked to find out you even existed, angry at Katie for not having told me before, distrustful and suspicious about why she had brought you and unprepared and confused about what I was going to do with you."

"So was I. I…" Jenny interjected, then stopped. "Sorry."

"That's alright." He smiled at her and went on. "I was worrying about how we would get on, what you would want for breakfast, about getting you to school on time and fitting my responsibilities towards you into my work and my life. Then I began to realize you had a personality of your own and that I had to relate to that, you had doubts and fears I had to recognize and respond to, that you were, in fact, a person I had to establish a relationship with.

"I made a mistake, I can see that now. I didn't just let that relationship develop naturally between us, I thought I could be different, that I could use my ideas about men and women to mould something new and special between us. I put unrealistic expectations on you because you were not a blank canvas on which I could create my dream, you were a teenage girl with a lot of conflicting influences and pressures of your own and I wasn't allowing for them.

"I was boasting about my success in creating this new kind of relationship at a meeting I attended the evening of the party. When I came home and found what was happening, I felt as if my dream had shattered. I reacted badly, reverting to some half-baked idea of what a traditional father should do, laying down the law and not stopping to consider what you were feeling and what I should be doing to protect and help you in that situation.

"I can't blame you for running away. I was not offering you somewhere you would want to stay and be comforted, not giving you a chance to explain. I see all of that now, and I apologise.

"If it is not too late, and only if you want to, we can talk about the things that happened that night. I don't want to know what happened with Shane and Grant, but if you want to talk about it I will listen, and help if I can. If you don't want to talk to me about it because of how I reacted, or just because I am a man, we can discuss who you might want to talk to. Perhaps we could persuade the prison to waive their policy and allow you to have a private visit with your mother. If there is no-one else, I could ask Claire O'Connell to talk to you. She's had experience with Dallas and her other children. I'm just making these suggestions to show I want to help. What you do is entirely up to you."

Jenny had been sitting silently and he could not be sure she had listened to all or any of what he had said.

Without the feedback of normal conversation, he realized, there was no way of being certain how the other person was reacting. Perhaps it had not been such a good idea, but he had committed them to it now. "Your turn."

Jenny straightened and smiled.

"That was very interesting," she said. "Not just what you said. Listening to it, making an effort to think about it. It's hard because my head keeps wanting to put in its own ideas, to respond to what you've just said instead of waiting to see what it's leading to, do you know what I mean? While you were talking there were lots of things I wanted to say. Now you've finished I'm not sure I want to say them anymore, which is weird. Perhaps they weren't that important, just sort of quick responses, the sort of thing you expect to say, or think you are expected to say. Can we go for a walk? I need to stretch a bit, and I'd like to think some more before I do my bit."

They left the log and found a track along the ridge of the hill. Level with the crest in the road it turned and ran parallel with itself lower down the hill and then zigged and zagged again, carrying them deeper into the dappled colours of the forest where the sunlight disputed the shadows to reach them.

A struggling creek found its way down the hill and crossed and recrossed the track several times. The lower they went the higher the trees rose above them and the further away was the sky, as if they were descending into a cave beneath the earth.

"Walking seems to make it easier to think," Jenny said. "Can we keep walking while I talk?"

Manny nodded and gestured for her to lead the way.

"I hated you before I met you," Jenny began.

Chapter 27

"When Mum told me who my father was a long time ago, she didn't tell me I looked like you. Perhaps I didn't so much when I was little. I imagined you as taller, with dark hair and a pointy nose. She said she chose you because you were a nice person at the time, but then you changed and weren't so nice any more.

"I thought it was because you weren't nice that you didn't want me. You were one of those horrible people who didn't like children, and I thought it was unfair because I was nice and you would have liked me if you had ever come and met me.

"When I was in primary school there was one girl who called me a bastard because I didn't have a father. I hated her. The teachers blamed me because we used to fight. I didn't like not having a father and being different. They had father's day once and Sweeny came instead. She dressed like a man and she and Mum thought it was funny. It made me sad.

"At high school the other girls who don't have fathers aren't the same as me. Most of their parents are divorced. One's father died in a car accident and another one was a soldier and got killed, but that isn't the same. I never had a father. Not even when I was born.

"I used to make up stories. I told other kids you and Mum were divorced, or you were someone very important who had to go away all the time on business. I even said once you were a spy and we couldn't talk about you or your life would be in danger.

"I used to feel guilty about telling lies and worried that someone would find me out and think I was stupid, and I used to blame you for it. It was your fault because you didn't like me and didn't want me.

"Then Mum said you'd written that book and how terrible it was. You were attacking women and saying horrible things about us. It made it even worse. If those other girls knew about that they'd do worse than call me a bastard. And my friends wouldn't want to be with me. You were sort of like the devil, you know? Evil, and I had your blood in me.

"It was all confusing. Sometimes I thought I hated Mum because she had let you be my father, then I hated you because you were so nasty. Mostly I think I hated myself because I was your daughter and I must be nasty and evil too.

"When we came to see you I was even more confused. I hadn't told Mum any of what I just told you. I was terrified of meeting you.

"And then you were there and instead of being this terrible person you were you and you looked like me. Suddenly I was just scared you wouldn't like me. I wasn't pretty enough, or intelligent enough, or anything.

"I thought you'd want your daughter to be really smart. That's why I said all that stuff about Jane Austen and that. I wanted to sound intelligent. But at the same time I didn't want to agree with you. I wanted to show you I was different, had my own ideas. Pretty silly, eh? Most of it is stuff Mum says. She's really intelligent. And she's good looking."

She had been walking ahead talking more to the trees than to him. Now she turned back. "Since I've got to know you I don't worry about those things so much. I'm sorry about the party and being a problem at school."

They had reached the crest of the hill long ago and turned up along it, away from where they had parked the mobile home. Now they turned and walked back towards it.

"I didn't mean the party to get like that. Boys just started turning up with beer and stuff and someone had weed. I think that was one of the girls. At first I thought it was terrible and then it seemed exciting. It was my party, you know? I was the one they were all there for. It made me feel important and interesting.

"Shane didn't rape me. I mean, he sort of tried, but I don't think he would have. Grant stopped him anyway. I'm not saying it was my fault. Just because you flirt a bit doesn't give the boy the right to do anything."

She stopped and laid a hand on Manny's arm, the first time they had touched since this conversation had started. "I wasn't going to let him."

He laid his hand over hers and smiled to show he understood.

"But that doesn't matter, does it?" she went on,

frowning. "I shouldn't have let the other kids bring in the beer and weed. I shouldn't have let some of the girls go into bedrooms with boys. I shouldn't have let it get out of control."

Manny wanted to say "No, it was my fault. I should have been there," but she had played by the rules when he was talking and he had to do the same now. He let her continue, following as she went on along the track towards the car. More sunlight reached down through the canopy here and it was flashing fiery highlights on her hair. She looked beautiful.

"When you came back I hated you seeing it all. I knew I'd let you down.

"I didn't run away because you were acting like a traditional Dad. I ran away because I didn't like me, and I didn't think you would like me. I changed my hair colour so I would not be like me and I went to that pinball place because it's the sort of place horrible girls like me go."

She stopped again and searched his face. He was not sure what expression to show her so kept it neutral, interested without agreeing or being critical.

"When you came to get me I didn't know what to do. I wanted you to go away so you wouldn't see me, so I said I hated you to make you go away."

She touched his arm again. "I'm sorry, Dad."

Manny fought to stop tears forming in his eyes and squeezed her hand again. "Go on," he said.

"I didn't mean it."

There was no way he could keep to the rules in this situation. "I know," he said.

"When you did go away I was horrified, and I began to get a bit frightened with those men there. Before that I think my mind had been a bit of a blank. I was just not being me, being someone else without thinking who it was. It sounds stupid, doesn't it?"

Nods and shakes of the head were no longer going to be enough, Manny sensed. She needed some verbal feedback to gauge how he was reacting.

"You weren't in danger," he said. "I hadn't gone far and I was watching you. All I could think of was how I could help, how I could get you back."

"I know now," she said. "Gramps told me after he came. I was so relieved to see him. He said you were worried sick and pointed out to me where you were sitting in your car. I told him I felt ashamed and he told me not to worry about anything like that. He said you just wanted me back, and he could see I wanted to go back, so the sensible thing was to go back and let whatever was going to happen, happen. He said he knew it was going to be alright and I had to trust him."

They were almost back to where they had parked. She looked back over her shoulder and said "That's it, I think."

Manny considered what to say. There were things she had said he wanted to follow up on, ask questions, seek to understand more fully. This was not the time.

"Okay. Let's neither of us say any more now. You've

heard how I feel and I've heard how you feel. If it's alright with you I don't think there's anything constructive to be achieved by saying any more. Let's just absorb it and let it become part of the background of our relationship in the future. Maybe one day you'll remember something I said and tell me something you thought about it, and I may do the same. How does that sound?"

"Fine," Jenny answered. Her eyebrows lifted and her face took one of the expressions they shared. "Can I say one thing more?"

Manny didn't need to study her face to know she wanted to say something that was important to her. He nodded.

"What you said about wanting a different sort of relationship," she said. "You're wrong about that. I understand you are trying not to be the old traditional sort of father, and I'm very proud of you for that."

They spent that night parked beside a lake in which they tried unsuccessfully to catch fish. The following morning they drove on through the forest, taking their time. They stopped beside rivers and creeks, watching fish and marron in the tannin-coloured waters, took a cruise on a tourist boat down one of the bigger rivers to its mouth, climbed the ladder round the trunk of one giant tree to the observation tower on its top and lazed in dappled sunlight beneath the canopy of the other trees.

There were more of the long monologues. Jenny loved the idea and revelled in the opportunity to talk without interruption. She seemed to enjoy, too, listening to what he had to say. They told each other more of the things most fathers and daughters don't have to say because it is part of their joint memories. About childhood and the toys they had liked, holidays, friends, school and teachers and books they had read, films they had seen. The programmes they liked on television and why they liked them and the clothes they liked to wear and the cars they wished they could one day own. They came closer together, he growing to know and like her and, he believed, she growing to know and like him. They spoke of things easily, already knowing the other's likely thoughts and feelings, no longer having to wonder or guess.

It was two more days before they drove into a small town where they returned to mobile phone range and were able to access their messages.

The first text Manny clicked on instantly overturned all the good feelings he had amassed on their holiday. Diane Strickland demanded Jenny be turned over to her charge immediately, saying he had broken a custodial agreement by going away without permission.

Chapter 28

Manny rang Neil Blighton and was advised by the NEMSA lawyer to return home and not to answer any phone calls. Specifically, not to talk to Diane Strickland or anyone else from the welfare authorities, courts or police.

"Were you aware of any conditions placed on the custodial agreement? Did you see the document?" Neil enquired.

Manny explained that he knew nothing about any conditions. Katie had told him no charges would be laid against Jenny if she came to stay with him. He couldn't remember her precise words.

"It will be important to know what documentation exists and what conditions, if any, are set out in it," Neil explained. "Until I confirm the existence of the documents and examine them, I can't advise you on that. I assume the girl's mother would have copies of them. Will she co-operate, do you think?"

"We can ring and ask her, "Manny told him. "Jenny's going to ring her anyway, now that we're back in mobile range."

"I'd advise against it. Although I understand that will be hard for Jenny, until we know more it may be best if I make the enquiry through her lawyer. You say you've been out of contact for five days so a few more hours won't hurt."

Manny was not happy with this. When he told Jenny,

she was equally dismayed, but they agreed they needed to follow the lawyer's advice. He gave Neil the contact details for Katie's lawyer.

"Can they take Jenny away from me?" Manny asked.

"Difficult to say," the lawyer answered. "Prima facie you are the natural parent and therefore a legal guardian of the child with no court ruling, prohibition or restraining order to say otherwise. As such you would normally be able to take her with you anywhere you chose without requiring permission.

"Stay in touch while you are travelling back to town and ring me before you return to your apartment. Except for that one call, keep your phone turned off. Don't answer any messages. Will that be alright?"

Manny said it would.

They both had several messages on their phones including from Katie, Alice Todd, several of Manny's clients and an even bigger number of Jenny's friends. They took the lawyer's advice, switched the phones off and didn't reply to any of them.

"Did you know anything about conditions being placed on you staying with me?" he asked as they headed towards the highway and the fastest route back to the city.

Jenny shook her head.

"Did any social workers interview you? Did you have to go to a court before a judge or a magistrate?"

Again the shake of the head.

"Not Diane Strickland, the one who came to the

apartment?"

"No. But Mum knew her. I didn't understand why she wanted to see me. She asked some odd questions."

"Like what?"

"Mostly about you. I think she wanted me to say something bad about you."

It took five hours to drive back to the city, with one short stop to buy sandwiches and drinks for lunch which they ate on the way. For the first four hours they travelled at a reasonable speed. From the city outskirts the traffic thickened and they slowed. About a kilometre from his apartment, Manny pulled into a car park and dialled Neil.

"Something odd is going on," the lawyer advised him. "Can we meet at The End of the Earth?"

Manny pointed out he had Jenny with him and suggested they meet in the cafe on the ground floor. As it was only a few minutes away, he and Jenny arrived first and were drinking a coffee and a Pepsi when Neil arrived.

"What dealings have you had with this social worker, Diane Strickland?" the lawyer asked as soon as he sat down facing them.

Manny explained that she had come to his apartment on two occasions and asked why it was important.

"Had you had any previous dealings with her? Did she have any reason to have taken a dislike to you or to distrust your ability to provide proper care for your daughter?"

Manny began to say no, then recalled the Women's Service League meeting.

"She was in the audience. She said men only wanted power over women, that we controlled all the institutions and we would never allow women to be equal."

"That may be what's behind this," Neil reflected. He turned to Jenny. "When Ms Strickland interviewed you at Manny's apartment, what did she ask you?"

Jenny looked puzzled. "Dad already asked me about that. I think she wanted me to say Dad was not being nice to me, even that he was doing something bad. It was weird."

"Did she ask about your father's views and whether he tried to impose them upon you?" He was writing her answers on a legal pad.

Jenny glanced at Manny. "Shouldn't I have talked to her? Did I do something wrong?"

Neil assured her she hadn't. "It's what Ms Strickland asked you, whether she made assertions concerning your father that may be important, Jenny."

"She said she thought my mother was wrong to let me live with him, and she asked if anything had happened that I wanted to tell her about."

"I see."

"I told her there was nothing, and that my mother had explained why she wanted me to live with him. She seemed surprised at that and asked what it was. I told her Mum said I had to stay with someone and she thought he was the best person."

Neil sat back and looked from Manny to Jenny and back again.

"Thank you for that, Jenny. I am going to write down an account of what you have told me. After it is typed up, I am going to ask you to sign it. Do you understand?"

Jenny nodded.

Neil studied the pad in front of him and thought for a few moments. "What my enquiries so far have indicated is that after the second incident at the men's club, Jenny's mother confessed and said she had done it alone. The child welfare agencies were not involved, but Ms Strickland seems to have tried to intervene on her own initiative.

"When she was told she had no jurisdiction as there was no minor involved, she raised it within her department suggesting there was an issue of potential neglect if the child were not being cared for while her mother was in prison, and that the department should intervene to recommend a non-custodial sentence.

"All of this was unusual, if not irregular, but an inquiry was made as to who would be caring for Jenny. It was ascertained that it would be you, Manny, as the natural father.

"That should have settled the matter, but my informant within the department says it seemed to have the opposite effect. Ms Strickland became even more obsessive and lodged a formal submission that you could not be considered an appropriate person to have custody of a young girl of impressionable age.

"This was over-ridden by her superiors and she was advised there was no legal or welfare-related issue that would argue against you having custodial care of a child which was, in fact, your natural child and to whom you had a right of legal guardianship provided it was with the mother's clear consent."

He looked at Jenny. "Are you following what I am saying?"

Jenny appeared affronted that he should think she wouldn't. "Yes, thank you."

"So we come to the visits to your apartment, Manny," Neil continued with the hint of a smile. "It would appear that they were not officially requested or sanctioned and that no formal record of them was kept. In effect, it would appear Ms Strickland went on a fishing expedition to try and find something nasty to be held against you. She may genuinely, even if erroneously, hold the opinion that your views make you an unsuitable custodian for a young girl. More likely is that she wanted to discredit those views and in some way have you condemned for espousing them."

Manny was stunned. "So there was no custodial agreement, no conditions I violated?"

"Not as far as I can ascertain, and therefore no justification for Ms Strickland to order you to bring your daughter back from your holiday. She appears to have been acting without authority and for reasons that have not been fully explained.

"However, what I have outlined to you here is my interpretation of information I have been given. Ms Strickland has not been officially challenged over this matter and may, although it is not immediately apparent how, have an alternative explanation for her actions. What I will now suggest is that I proceed on your behalf to lodge a complaint with the department and request an explanation. On receipt of such a complaint an automatic interim order would be placed on Ms Strickland not to have any further contact with you or with Jenny until an inquiry is conducted."

"Good Lord," Manny marvelled. "You have been busy. This is not a NEMSA matter. You will bill me accordingly?"

"If you wish me to do so. I could also do it as your friend."

Manny shook his head. "No. Charge me. I wouldn't design a house for you for nothing."

"So we're agreed." Neil stood up. "I will lodge the complaint first thing tomorrow morning and a prompt restriction on Ms Strickland can be expected. Until that happens she is at large and unaware of this discussion. It is not impossible that she could turn up at your apartment, which could lead to further unpleasantness. Perhaps you should stay in a hotel tonight."

"We don't need a hotel," Manny answered, "do we Jenny? We've still got our mobile home. We might find a quiet park or somewhere along the river with a big parking area. Down by the ocean would be good. How about it?"

"Awesome," Jenny replied, making Neil laugh.

"You sound exactly like my daughter," he told her. "In fact I'd like you two to meet one day. I think you'll get on. For now, Ms Frank, I'll bid you goodbye. It has been most enjoyable and, I might even say enlightening, to have met you. I have no doubts whatsoever that you took in and understood every boring word I uttered."

He left the café with Jenny smiling after him.

"So now," Manny said as she turned back to him. "The river or the beach?"

"Beach," Jenny decided. "Can we turn our phones on now?"

Manny wasn't sure and pointed out that Diane Strickland might still be trying to reach him.

"You can hang up," Jenny countered. "You don't have to listen to her."

She was right, so Manny switched his phone back on, and five seconds later wished he hadn't.

Chapter 29

The phone rang, somehow sounding urgent, even angry at having been switched off for so long. He answered it, prepared to hang up on anyone they didn't want to speak to.

"Mr Youngman? Chloe McQuinn. I represent Kate Frank."

It didn't make sense. Neil couldn't have called Katie's lawyer already. He contemplated not responding, of hanging up before he caused any more complications, but curiosity overcame him.

"Yes. Is she all right?"

"Very well, thank you Mr Youngman. Is Jenny with you?"

"Yes"

Chloe McQuinn spoke to someone in the background, but he could not make out the words. She came back on the line. "Mr Youngman. Ms Frank wishes you to return Jenny to your apartment to retrieve her clothes. She will call there herself to collect her daughter. It shouldn't take you more than three hours to drive back. Can I tell her four o'clock this afternoon?"

"Call there herself? She's out of prison?"

"She has been for twenty-four hours, Mr Youngman. She has been considerably distressed that we have been unable to reach you."

Jenny had gone over to another table to use her own

mobile phone to talk to one of her friends. Manny waved a hand to attract her attention. She frowned and said something into her phone before flipping it closed and coming over to sit down opposite him.

"Your Mum's out of prison," Mammy told her, which produced a look of shock and then a huge smile. Into the phone he said "That's wonderful. Jenny is delighted. We'll drive straight over to see her. Jenny can pick up her clothes later."

"No, Mr Youngman." The voice on the other end of the phone was steel hard and unyielding. "Ms Frank wishes to collect Jenny herself, with her belongings. She does not wish you to be there and she does not wish to speak with you."

Manny stared at the phone as if he might be able to see an explanation for what he had just heard. "Why? Why doesn't she want me to be there?"

Chloe McQuinn sighed as if he were being obstinate and uncooperative.

"The reasons are immaterial, Mr Youngman. Please do as my client asks."

"It isn't reasonable." He was aware of the bewildered expression on Jenny's face and realized she could not follow the conversation.

"Does that mean you refuse?" the lawyer said.

"No, it means what it says. Hang on a minute." He held the phone away from his ear and said so that she could hear, "I'm not sure what's happening, Jenny. Your mother is out of prison and wants to come and get you. She doesn't want me to be there."

Jenny took the phone from his hand. "Chloe, it's me. Is Mum there with you? Can I talk to her?" As she was speaking she switched the phone to loudspeaker so that Manny could also hear.

In the silence that seemed to have fallen, they could hear muffled sounds as Chloe McQuinn consulted someone in the room. After a while she said. "Hello, Jenny. Are you well? Is everything alright? Katie has been concerned about you."

"I'm fine," Jenny answered. "There's nothing at all to be concerned about. What's this all about, Chloe? Why is Mum out of prison? I'm very glad she is, of course, but…"

"Your mother will explain when she sees you, Jenny. She is looking forward to that very much. Right now I must speak with Mr Youngman."

Jenny had a worried frown on her face as she stared at Manny. "Why are you calling him that, Chloe. Why don't you say you want to speak to my father? There's something wrong, isn't there?"

The lawyer had picked up on her distress because her voice was softer and a lot less authoritarian when she replied. "It's alright, Jenny. Nothing is wrong and nothing will be if…" she hesitated before continuing as if she wished there were a better word, "your father does what I have asked him to do."

"What is that? He hasn't told me. What's happening?"

Jenny was showing increased signs of distress.

"I have asked him to take you to his apartment and leave you there while you collect your clothes and anything else of yours that is there. Your mother will come and collect you."

"We can't," Jenny said "it's not possible," and there was a silence at the other end of the phone while the lawyer absorbed that.

"Why not?"

"Because Diane Strickland is behaving weirdly and we're worried about her being at the apartment so we're staying away until Dad's lawyer friend sorts it out."

This brought another long silence.

"Ms Strickland has been in contact with you?"

"Yes. She ordered Dad to bring me back from our holiday. She claimed he had broken the conditions of some custodial agreement, but Dad's lawyer says there isn't one."

"I see." The lawyer sounded as if she didn't see at all. "Please let me speak to your father, Jenny." She said the word this time without hesitation.

"I'm here," Manny announced. "I can hear you."

"Mr Youngman, what I have just heard only serves to convince me that my client has justifiable concerns about her daughter's welfare and the deleterious effect of her being with you."

"What deleterious effects? What's Katie saying?"

"Is it in fact possible that Jenny could be placed in an unpleasant situation if she returns to your apartment?"

"It's possible, not certain."

There were more muffled sounds as if the woman had put her hand over the phone and was talking to someone else. Manny decided he had had enough of it.

"If Katie is there and you're talking to her, tell her this stinks," he said. "Tell her she has to tell Jenny and me to our faces why she's behaving in this totally unnecessary manner. She put us both in a situation we were not prepared for and have had, in our own different ways, difficulties in dealing with. We have dealt with them and we've come to an understanding between us. I'm not prepared for Katie to come back in and disrupt everything without a full and thorough explanation."

Jenny leaned forward and said into the phone, "Me too!"

Again the silence and then, "Mr Youngman. Is it necessary to put Jenny through this? I'm afraid it confirms our fears about the influence you've had on her and further justifies our resolve to obtain a court order restraining you from ever seeing Jenny again."

Manny lost what remained of his patience. "Go to hell. You and Katie."

"Mr Youngman. I caution you to exercise restraint in your language and in your behaviour. You have no rights in this matter. You must return Jenny to her mother."

"How did Katie get out of prison?"

"That is no concern of yours."

"I'm making it my concern. If you want any cooperation

from me you're going to have to answer my questions. How did she get out of prison?"

"An application for an appeal was lodged and she has been released on bail pending a further hearing."

"Hearing into what?"

"I am not at liberty to say. This is pointless, Mr Youngman. Katie wants Jenny back."

"Why won't she talk to me?"

"I imagine she feels it would be unproductive."

With growing dismay Manny saw she was right. This was pointless. It didn't matter how Katie had got out or why she was being difficult. He grimaced at Jenny. "I think you will have to go back to your Mum."

Jenny nodded glumly. "We can sort it out later," she said. "Get Mum to explain."

He said into the phone, "Tell Katie to be at my apartment in one hour. Jenny will be ready. I won't be far away because I'll be watching to make sure there is no problem with the social worker. I won't approach Katie. She won't have to speak to me."

He flicked the phone closed without waiting to hear the answer. He and Jenny sat and stared at each other for several minutes. There was nothing to say. It was unfair, unreasonable, irrational, any word you wanted to call it, but Katie was Jenny's mother.

The cafe which had been comfortable and welcoming now seemed garish with its competing soft drink signs, chocolate bar stands and brightly-lit food displays. A large truck pulled up outside behind their mobile home. The young driver climbed down from his cab, stretching his back and leg muscles. A short time before, Manny thought, he and Jenny had gone through similar uncramping motions after their long drive. Now that and all that had gone before it seemed as if it had happened long ago. All he could think of was the single, devastating fact that he was about to lose Jenny.

Chapter 30

He watched the little pink car drive up and park in his carport. Jenny came out with her bags and got in beside Katie in the front seat. They drove away. A small shift in the shadows of the passenger seat window had to be Jenny waving. He drove his own car back into its rightful place. The mobile home had been returned to the company they had rented it from. He was still not crying, not on the outside, not yet.

Without Jenny his apartment echoed emptily. Not only sounds were missing. Vibrations. Fragrances. A presence. He sat and thought about their holiday together, fixing it in his memory so he could never forget.

He smiled sadly. There had been so many smiles over the past few days. Lots of laughs. Lots of happiness. Now all was sad and silent. He went to bed and lay through the night without sleeping. In the morning he started phoning.

"I'm sorry, Manny. This is the first I've heard of it. I had no idea." Neil Blighton was apologetic. "I'll get onto it right away and get back to you as soon as I have something."

"Please do that, Neil. Katie's not getting away with this."

His assurance on this remained firm while he made his next call, to Diane Strickland.

"What did you tell Jenny's mother?" he demanded. "Why has she taken Jenny away from me?"

The reply came in a dry, official voice that bore him no goodwill. "You should not have taken Jenny away, Mr Youngman. You effectively denied Ms Frank access to her daughter, and this department any opportunity to monitor her situation."

"Why did you come here and interview her? What authority did you have to do that?"

There was a little intake of breath. "It was my duty as a welfare officer."

"I don't believe it was. I believe you were interfering where you had no authority to do so, and I believe you have further interfered by setting Jenny's mother against me. What lies did you tell her?"

The welfare officer seemed to consider that and choose her words carefully when she answered. "I did not tell lies to Ms Frank, Mr Youngman."

"Which is like saying you've stopped beating your partner. You did talk to her."

She remained silent, not confirming or denying it, but he was certain.

"Do you know she is out of prison and has taken Jenny back? Have you had any part in that?"

Again the pause and, when she did speak, a careful selection of what to say. "I believe it is the best outcome."

"Did you advise her to do it?"

"I'm afraid I can't help you any further, Mr Youngman."

Manny was incensed, and suspicious.

"Can't or won't? Is this about me and Jenny or because

you disagreed with that talk I gave to the Women's Service League?"

Again there was that intake of breath. "I'm sorry, Mr Youngman. I no longer wish to continue this conversation." The phone clicked into silence.

As Manny put it down it rang back at him. Neil Blighton had kept his promise and been busy.

"This Chloe McQuinn is a very smart cookie, Manny. She lodged an application for a grant of appeal against Katie Frank's sentence on several grounds. Katie has withdrawn her confession and says she was coerced into it by the threat that her daughter would be taken from her. She is citing Diane Strickland as the person who made the threat. McQuinn further claims that the judge should have declared an interest in the case as he is a former member of, and has several close friends who are members of, the club in question. She also submitted the sentence was too severe and based on an error in law and that there were grounds for reconsideration of the matter of natural justice based on the undue hardship the sentence had caused to the accused as a result of consequent events involving her daughter. The court ruled sufficient issues had been raised which need to be considered as an argument for reversing or amending the original judgment. On that basis, Katie's release on bail was appropriate."

"So Katie is now saying she didn't throw that fake bomb in the club?"

"She is saying that she confessed under coercion and it

was therefore inadmissible. That is a different matter. If the court now rules that is the case, the prosecution will have to supply firm evidence that Katie did throw the fake bomb. I have no idea whether they can do that. It would require an eye witness or other corroborating evidence. None of that has any effect on your immediate situation, Manny. Jenny's mother is out of prison legitimately and in that situation is entitled to take back custody of her child."

"Don't I have any rights?"

"Basically, no. Katie gave you temporary custody of Jenny of her own free will and under no compulsion from the court or any other authority, although she is now claiming there was coercion. As such she has the right to terminate that arrangement and take Jenny back."

"I'm her father."

"A grey area I'm afraid. Biologically it would appear you are and I have no doubt that a DNA test would establish that. However, until recently you had not been a father to her in the sense that you have lived with her, raised her or even provided for her financially."

"Can't I get access rights, like some fathers do after a divorce?"

"Those rights are granted as a condition of the divorce settlement; they are in effect a division of rights and properties resulting from the marriage. You are not in that situation. I'm sorry, Manny."

"What do you suggest I do?"

Neil considered that before asking cautiously "Is your

relationship with Jenny as strong as I suspect it is after seeing you together yesterday?"

Manny said it was.

"Good. In that case I would rely on Jenny persuading her mother to let her see you. I would let it rest for a time, Manny, to allow Katie to calm down and for Jenny to realize for herself what has happened."

It was an unsatisfactory answer, but Manny could think of no arguments to raise against it. He told Neil that he would follow his advice. Privately he intended to find out a lot more about what had happened and why.

What information had Katie learned in prison that had made her retract her confession? There were still too many unanswered questions. Neil might be right that the answers made no difference to the fact that Katie was Jenny's mother and had all the legal rights on her side, he still felt he had moral rights. Jenny had rights too. Katie was wrong to stop them seeing each other. If he found out what had made her do it, perhaps he could persuade her to change her mind without waiting for Jenny to do it.

He thanked Neil and promised to keep him informed of developments.

Then he rang Alice Todd.

Chapter 31

Alice's voice sounded wary and uncertain when she came on the phone. He feared she was going to hang up as soon as she realized who it was.

"Have you seen Jenny," he asked. "Is she alright?"

There was a silence, then "I think so, Manny. Yes, she's alright. She's not very happy, but she's alright."

"Do you know what all this is about, Alice? Why has Katie done it?"

Another silence.

"I'm sorry, Manny. It was Madge."

He held the phone away and stared at it, bewildered. What did Madge have to do with anything? He pressed the phone back to his ear and listened.

"Madge rang Katie at the prison. She told her about Jenny running away and about the party and the dress and Jenny nearly being raped."

"Why?" Manny exclaimed. "Jenny and I have talked through what happened, Alice. What good did Madge think it would do telling Katie?"

"I tried to stop her." Alice sounded distressed. "I told her she was making things worse and it would hurt Jenny. She wouldn't listen. She called me a slut."

Again Manny stared at the phone, not understanding what he was hearing. "Why?" he demanded. "Why did Madge say that?"

"She said you were coming on to me. I said she was

being silly, but she said I had responded to you, that I encouraged you."

"Why would Madge ring Katie because of that?"

This time the silence had a different quality, a surprised stillness. "Madge is my partner, Manny."

For a few seconds he didn't understand. Then it hit him how blind and stupid he had been. "I didn't…"

"We're married. Didn't Katie or Jenny tell you?"

Manny found himself shaking his head and then realized that was pointless over a telephone. "No," he said. "I should have realized. I'm sorry."

"It isn't you who has to be sorry. I should have made it clear. Madge is right. I was flattered. I… I thought it was funny making her jealous, so it is my fault. I should have realized how upset she would get."

"So she rang Katie and told her I was unfit to care for Jenny?"

This time Alice's silence was its own answer.

"What exactly did she tell her, Alice? I need to know."

"She told Katie you insisted on Jenny wearing that green dress and that it was provocative and inappropriate. She said you supplied beer for the party and left Jenny unsupervised with a lot of drunken louts and she was nearly raped, that she ran away from you because she feared you would be violent and you sent a lot of drunken men out looking for her, and you made her go away with you when she didn't want to. I'm sorry, Manny, I heard her telling all these lies to Katie and tried to tell her she was causing trouble. She was angry and pushed me away from the phone. I tried to call to warn you but your phone wasn't answering."

Appalled by what he was hearing, Manny could understand why Katie had acted the way she did.

"Have you spoken to her since Katie brought her home?"

"No. It was just a few minutes ago. Madge is over there. She wouldn't let me go with her."

While Manny wondered about the relationship the two women had that enabled Madge to prevent Alice doing anything she wanted to do, he resisted asking the question. From the sound of it he had done enough damage in that direction.

"You said Jenny wasn't happy," he reminded her.

"I saw them getting out of the car. I didn't have to talk to her, I could tell."

Questioning her further told him nothing that made the situation any better. Madge had damned him completely in Katie's eyes. It seemed clear that Alice had no way of countering what her partner had done. All he could hope for was that Jenny could do what Alice couldn't.

As he hung up the phone there was a knock on the glass door of his office. Tony stood outside.

"Neil rang me," his friend said. "I came round straight away. Are you alright?"

Manny said he was, just. He explained what Alice had told him. "Based on that, Katie's justified in what she's done. There's nothing I can do unless Jenny can convince her it isn't true, that it didn't happen that way."

"I'm sorry, mate. No way of lodging a claim for access to Jenny or anything like that?"

"No. The way Neil explained it there is nothing before the court for me to appeal against."

"What about Katie's appeal against her sentence? That still has to be heard. Can you oppose that, tell the court there was no basis for letting her out because Jenny wasn't in danger?"

When Manny explained in more detail what Katie's appeal was based on, Tony's brow furrowed. "If the court dismissed her confession and they don't have other evidence, she could get off?"

"It seems so."

"So why did she confess in the first place?"

Manny had been wondering about that for some time.

"And Dick James said Jenny made the fake bomb," Tony added. "Wouldn't that be evidence to convict Katie? You should tell them."

"Imagine the consequences. Katie would go back to prison and then there is no way she would return Jenny to me. She would make some other arrangements and take out a restraining order to stop me seeing her. And in the second place…" He stopped. He had been going to say that Jenny would hate him and would not want to come back to him. Instead a new thought had struck him. "What if Katie confessed to protect who really did it?"

Tony didn't seem to see the logic at first. Then he understood. "Jenny."

"It makes sense of quite a few things," Manny told him. "I was always surprised that someone as intelligent as Katie would do such a childish thing."

"And you think Jenny did, and Katie chose to say she did it and go to prison to save her daughter?"

"Yes. The more I think about it. Yes."

"Okay." Tony frowned. "But why did she then bring Jenny to you? Couldn't she have found someone else? This lesbian couple, for example."

Manny had no answer for that. Perhaps it was because Katie knew how unstable Madge could get, or even thought living with lesbians would not be good for an impressionable young girl. He didn't know and it didn't make a lot of difference.

"All I want is to get to a point where I can see Jenny again and have a relationship with her for the rest of my life," he told Tony. "In a way I'm glad Katie is out of prison. I know Jenny wants that and I know that if she was asked to decide whether she wanted to live with me or her mother, she would choose Katie. That's natural and I'm okay with it. I don't want to punish Katie or cause any trouble for either of them. I just don't want to be without Jenny in my life again."

Tony nodded. "I hear that, mate, believe me I do, you poor bastard. Okay, so what's next? What can I do to help?"

"Take me to The End of the Earth," Manny smiled

thinly at him. "Help me focus on something else. For the moment I'm leaving Jenny to work on Katie. Meanwhile I need to get on with my life as normally as possible."

Tony stood up, came across and hugged him. "Sounds like a plan, mate. Let's go and get normalled out of our minds."

When they got to The End of the Earth, Neil was there with Bobby, Tommy and several others. The lawyer called Manny to one side. "After you had a word with Diane Strickland, she lodged a post-dated report to justify her actions in making those unsanctioned visits to your place and interviewing Jenny. My contact in the department let me see a copy." He held out a piece of paper.

Manny didn't think it mattered any more. Whatever Diane Strickland thought or didn't think had been taken over by events. She wasn't likely to have any more influence. Still, he read the report anyway.

"Due to extreme concern at the significance of the radical sexist views expressed by the postulated father, Mr Robert Youngman, into whose care the subject, Jennifer Frank, had been given, the interviewing officer questioned the subject to ascertain her ability to withstand the impact of such views and the potential they indicated for this to be an unsuitable environment in which she should remain.

"The decision was made to allow the subject to remain with Mr Youngman on the basis that she had a degree of ability to evaluate such views and not be unduly influenced by them. However, this degree of ability was perhaps not as high as the subject herself assesses it to be and some degree of influence has to be assumed. The officer weighed this against other factors:

"1. That the timespan involved was relatively short and would probably not be sufficient for any influence to have a lasting or damaging impact.

"2. The subject herself expressed a desire to remain with her father whom she had met for the first time only a short time previously. It was considered that it was not appropriate at that point in time given (1) above for an order to be made which would remove the subject from a situation which she herself desired.

"Given the above, the officer formed the intention to monitor the situation closely and at regular intervals, maintaining the option of making other more suitable arrangements for the subject's care and custody if it was deemed that this was warranted and requisite for her physical, emotional or psychological protection. The intention to maintain such a monitoring stance was subverted by Mr Youngman's act of removing the subject from his home to another location, the officer being unable to determine her whereabouts. As required by the department's policy of due diligence, numerous attempts were made to locate the subject and/or Mr Youngman. However, these proved unsuccessful.

"Also in the spirit of due diligence, contact was made with Ms Katherine Frank, the subject's mother, to alert her to the situation and apprise her of the officer's concerns.

Ms Frank appeared grateful for this information and indicated that she would be taking action to re-establish her custodial rights in relation to the subject and return her to a more secure and appropriate environment as soon as practicable."

So Katie had received a blast from two barrels, Madge and Diane Strickland. Manny shook his head in disbelief at the extent to which both women appeared to have lied, or at least distorted the truth, to accomplish their own agendas without considering Jenny's own desires and welfare.

That didn't change the course of action he had chosen. He thanked Neil for providing the copy of the report and asked him to make no further enquiries for the time being. "I don't want to stir the pot," he explained, "Let the mud settle for the moment, I think, and see what comes to the surface."

The lawyer smiled at the metaphor, agreeing it was a wise course of action. "There's now the question of whether Strickland coerced Katie into confessing," he pointed out. "That opens a whole new can of worms. I have a suspicion she did herself damage by interfering without authority and going to Katie to malign you. If she is accused of coercing Katie into confessing and it comes down to who believes who, Strickland is not going to be seen as a person who can be believed." He smiled. "I think she might be in very deep shit."

Manny felt a little better as he began to circulate, asking Tommy how his daughters were going and Bobby what news there was of Dick James. The English teacher, it appeared, had taken the advice he had been given and had contacted the men's helpline. What the counsellor on the other end had told him appeared to have eased some of his tensions. He had been to see his GP, been given a referral to a psychologist and was now embarked on a course of counselling which included Mrs James with the agreed intention that they might get back together and, if not, would at least part amicably.

Sol Garfwicz was a different matter. No-one had seen him for several days and the last time Bobby had been seen him, soon after the search for Jenny, Sol had been in a much deeper and darker mood than was usual, even for him. Bobby planned to go round and see if he could find him and spend a bit more time with him, be there in case he needed it.

Manny moved on, talking to other members, having several more beers, remembering how he had not been drinking the last time he had seen Sol, because he had to go and pick up Jenny afterwards.

He stood near the hotel door and looked around at the men talking and laughing together. For no particular reason his father's face came into his mind. Did Dad have someone to go to and share his problems with when Mum was giving him a hard time? Did he ever have the same sorts of doubts about what a man was these days? If he did, a Men's Shed would be the place for him. He'd have to suggest it to him. Mum and Dad didn't yet know that Katie had taken Jenny back. He would have to tell them, and not over the phone. It was not something he looked forward to.

Chapter 32

"You've got to get her back," his mother insisted. "That young woman has no right to barge into our lives, present us with a beautiful granddaughter we naturally fall immediately in love with and viciously snatch her away again. It shows a total lack of compassion and understanding. Obviously she is not at all a nice person. I can't imagine what you ever saw in her in the first place, Robert. If you had been a little more discerning, perhaps we wouldn't be in this devastating situation."

Manny sniffed back half a laugh and gazed at her in awe, not sure whether to be shocked by her revelation, for the first time as far as he was aware, that she had immediately fallen in love with Jenny, amused by her reference to Katie as 'that young woman' or angry because, as usual, she had turned it around so that it was all his fault.

From long experience he didn't try to defend himself or even try to explain how he felt. She wouldn't listen and it would fuel the fire of her dissatisfaction. He'd hang on to the positive fact that she had liked Jenny and wanted as much as he did to continue having her in their lives.

He didn't have to make that decision with his father. The older man's disappointment was etched deep in the creases that already lined his face. He would probably go out to his shed soon, Manny thought, and work out his feelings by making something. It was one of the ways the two of them were alike, except that his outlet was his architecture.

There were many drawings in his office spawned by an emotional response to some event in his life, happy or sad. Some had translated into buildings.

His mother sat at the table in their kitchen, her hands fussing with a cup and saucer, trying very hard not to cry. "It's not fair," she said. "It's like someone's given you a present and taken it away again."

Without knowing he was going to do it, Manny moved round the table, wrapped his arms around her and hugged her to him. As she frowned up at him in surprise he said, "Jenny loved you and Dad, too, Mum. She's very smart and very tough and she'll find a way to see you again."

The frown changed to a small smile. "Yes, she will, won't she?"

He nodded, glancing across at his father who was also smiling.

The two men walked together to the door as Manny was leaving.

"I think I'd better stay with your Mum a bit," his father said. "Reckon she needs a bit of comfort. I won't go down to the Men's Shed."

Manny stared at him in astonishment. "What Men's Shed?"

"A few mates of mine have been going for a while so I gave it a go and I'm enjoying myself. A lot of the blokes there think along the same lines as you even if they don't express it the same way. You should come and meet them."

Thinking what an incredible coincidence it was when

he had been thinking about suggesting such a thing a short time before, Manny said he would be happy to go along one day. He was getting into his car when his father stopped him again. "Anything I can do, son. You know that. We need her back."

Tears pricked the back of Manny's eyes. He had to wipe a hand across them to see the road as he drove on to Claire O'Connell's office, the next stop on the day he had planned for himself. Getting back into his normal work and life routine was essential. Without it he would be mooning around and more likely to do something stupid like ring Katie or go round to her house and have a confrontation with her. Either would be unproductive and probably disastrous, making matters worse instead of better.

His plan was not to tell Claire what had happened, to proceed with business as usual and not let his personal troubles spill over into his work. He should have known better. She took one look at his face and asked what was wrong.

After listening to his story she picked up her phone. "I'm texting Dallas. Although she's not in the office right now she'll check the message and call me back. She may be able to help."

Manny hadn't thought of Dallas O'Connell as a conduit to Jenny. While they had seemed to get on well together he had not considered them close friends. He expressed this view.

Claire told him he was mistaken. "Our daughters have

been spending quite a lot of phone time together. Dallas will know how to find her."

They spent the next two hours with Claire updating Manny on developments while he was away. He returned to his office to arrange appointments for the next couple of days. Several clients had left messages saying they wanted to have meetings.

He tried hard to concentrate but found it impossible. In the short time she had been with him, Jenny had managed to leave an incredible number of reminders of herself around the office and the apartment. He found himself staring at them, his heart crumbling and his eyes misting over. Eventually he gave up and went back out to his car, taking his diary with him. He could make calls on his mobile, visit clients in person instead of ringing them. It would be more direct, show a personal touch and emphasise that he was back on the job.

It worked for about two hours. Late afternoon he was parked on the other side of the road a hundred metres from the school gate. No closer because Katie would be picking her up and he didn't want a confrontation. All he wanted was to see her, to make sure she was alright.

He watched all the other children coming out. Betty and Grant Polson. The boy Shane. Many more faces he recognized from the party. No Jenny.

He drove home very slowly, debating whether to go round past Katie's house, to ring Alice Todd again. Anything to find out what was happening.

He heard the phone ringing in the office as he got out of the car. He ran across, fumbled with his key, swore, jerked the door open, and was just in time to pick the phone up before it stopped.

"Jenny?"

There was an awkward pause. "No, Mr Youngman. It's Dallas. Dallas O'Connell."

"Have you spoken to her?"

"She's very upset, Mr Youngman. Her mother wouldn't listen when she said the party and everything wasn't your fault. I'm sorry, Mr Youngman. Jenny says you mustn't call her because it is only going to make it worse. She made me swear I would tell you that. She said I had to tell you that she's alright. Her Mum's angry and being stupid. She hasn't been hurt or anything."

"Why hasn't she rung me?"

"Her Mum's taken her phone, and disconnected the one in the house."

"You spoke to her. How could you do that?"

"I didn't actually speak to her. She can still use her computer. Her Mum's blocked her emails but there's a chat line we've used before."

"Katie's blocked her emails?"

"She won't even let her go to school. I think she's afraid you will go there and meet her. Jenny said her Mum keeps saying she's been brainwashed and they have to reverse it."

"That's fucking ridiculous!" The exclamation was involuntary and Manny instantly regretted it. There was no point in making Dallas any more upset than she already sounded.

"Please don't call her, Mr Youngman. Jenny made me promise."

"Is your mother there, Dallas? Can I speak to her?"

He heard her pass the phone to her mother.

"What do you think?" Manny asked. "What should I do?"

"Do what Jenny says," Claire said. "Don't imagine it is worse than it is, Manny. Jenny's mother is behaving like this because she has been under stress. Being in prison can't have been easy let alone being told her daughter was nearly raped and ran away from you. You took her away where she couldn't reach you and she was hearing all these terrible things. It must have been very worrying for her."

"I have to make her understand it's not true."

"From what Dallas has told me, and from what I am hearing in your voice right now, you are not the person who can do that."

"So who can?"

"Katie is not in a vacuum, Manny. She has friends around her, people she talks to who will hear what Jenny has said to her and will help to make Katie see things more logically. Focus on two things. Jenny says she is alright, and she doesn't want you to go there or call her. That sounds to me as if Jenny understands very well what is happening and thinks she can work her way through it. I have a lot of faith in her and I think you should too."

She was right, but it was still difficult to take in and deal with. Manny told her he would take her advice and asked her to thank Dallas for her help.

He replaced the phone and spent a long time sitting in silence. His thoughts raced like an express train on a circular track that went nowhere.

The phone rang again.

He grabbed it up, not saying "Jenny?" this time although it was the name that was on his lips.

"Manny? It's Tony. Sol's committed suicide."

Chapter 33

The group waiting when he got to The End of the Earth included Tony, Neal, Bobby and Dick James. The latter had spent the school holidays growing the beginnings of a beard. He also wore working jeans with a wide leather belt and a red checked shirt under a denim jacket, the cowboy clothes celebrating having finally, with their psychologist's blessing and guidance, separated from his wife. This was not the time to make jocular remarks, however. The expression on Dick's face was as glum as the rest of them.

"We should have been able to stop him," Bobby groaned. "There must have been something we could have said."

Tony shook his head. "If someone's going to do it you can't stop them. We did everything we could."

"It still wasn't good enough," Bobby retorted. "It just wasn't bloody good enough."

They all stared at the stubbies they were holding and, as if of one mind, raised them in a silent toast to their lost friend.

"It's bloody incredible, isn't it," Tommy growled, "the way women claim that the world is stacked against them, and when it comes down to it, it's the men who get the short end of the stick? No wonder so many are topping themselves."

"That's more true than you know," Neal contributed, his voice slurring. "In the majority of divorces the women end up better off than the men. Sol's wife ended up with his house, his car, his kids, and he got nothing." He slammed his stubby down on the bar. "Why can't people be more bloody understanding?"

"Do you know," Bobby interjected. "Do you know Sol went to a psychologist and told her he was thinking of committing suicide? She told him she couldn't counsel him if he said things like that." He glared round at them. "What use is a bloody psychologist if she won't bloody listen when you say you feel like killing yourself?"

"Our psychologist wasn't so bad. She was quite understanding," Dick countered, but Tommy spoke over the top of him. "No bloody use at all," and leaned down to fumble in the carton under the table and drag out another stubby.

"Good idea. I need another," Neil said.

Manny felt as if he was standing apart from the others, watching from behind a barrier, able to hear while not relating in any way to what was being said. A separate part of his mind felt a deep sorrow for Sol and for all the troubles in his life, while everything else remained focused on Jenny.

"His bloody car as well?" Tommy said as if he had just then realized what Neil had said earlier. "As well as his house? Mind you, I'm not surprised." I've seen it before. Lots of Yvonne's friends are divorced."

Yvonne was his wife; a small, determined woman with hard eyes and three matching daughters.

"Her friends. Did you hear what he said? Her friends." Bobby was making a new point. "Not his friends. I bet these women's husbands used to be your friends, eh, Tommy?"

Tommy nodded. "Of course they were. Good blokes most of them."

"Not anymore, eh? Not after the divorce. Your house and your car AND your friends. Funny that, isn't it, how the women stay friends and the men are ostracised? The men are always made out to be the villains."

"Absolutely right. That's what happened to Sol," Bobby contributed. "He had no friends except us, and we did everything we could for him, didn't we, eh? We did, didn't we?"

He looked round at them beseechingly and they all nodded back at him, Tony patting him on the shoulder and saying, "Sure we did, mate. You did especially."

Dick was looking around him blearily, shaking his head and giving the impression that he was disappointed and unhappy. "I came tonight to celebrate my separation," he said. "I didn't really know this bloke. What's his name again?"

"Sol," Bobby reminded him. "Sol Garfwicz."

"Sol Garfwicz," Dick repeated, and stared across at Manny. "You know old Sol Garfwicz?"

Manny said he did, and was very sad that he was dead.

"Yeah, but you've got other reasons to be sad," Dick said. "Didn't take your house or car, did she? Took your daughter."

He surveyed the bar and called out in a voice everyone in it would be able to hear. "Bloody woman had his kid without telling him. Stole his sperm."

"Ought to be illegal," Tommy contributed. Others took up the refrain, joking as he and Tony had.

Manny didn't want to hear. He reached out a hand to try to stop them.

"What I'm saying is," Dick added regardless, "she's come back and stolen from Manny again. I heard all about it at school. I'm her teacher, so I would know, wouldn't I? She stole his daughter away from him. I mean, they weren't even divorced or anything."

"For heaven's sake, shut up, Dick," Manny expostulated, but it was too late.

"Let's go and get her back," Tommy suggested. "We'll just go round there and get her back. For good old Sol. So he didn't die for nothing."

Manny had no idea what getting Jenny back could have to do with Sol's suicide. He did know he no longer wanted to be there listening to his friends get drunker and make less and less sense. Joking about Katie stealing his sperm had seemed funny when he and Tony had that conversation in what now seemed like some past age when the world had been very different. Now it seemed sad and somehow disrespectful, although he was not sure who to.

"I'm going," he said to Tony, beginning to move towards the door.

"We'll come with you," Tony exclaimed. "All of us.

Help you get Jenny back."

Tommy sounded less certain. "Maybe I'd better get home to the wife and kids."

"No way," Tony insisted. "We're all NEMSA members and we're in this together. You've got to come too."

Tommy shrugged without looking convinced. "Okay."

"I'm in," Neil asserted. "That bloody Chloe McQuinn might have the bloody law on her side, but the law's an ass, even if I do so say myself."

There was no question that Bobby would not follow. He was grinning from ear to ear. He began to lead the way at a half run out of the bar to where their cars were parked outside. Manny called after them and told them to come back.

"You're all drunk," he told them the obvious. "This isn't going to help at all."

There were mild protests but they all trooped back inside. Bobby opened another carton and began handing out more stubbies.

"To Sol," Manny heard them saying as he walked out to his car.

He sat in it for a long time going over what had just happened, trying to make sense of it. Were these men his friends? Was he even one of them? Had he become some other person since Jenny had come into his life?

He had no idea whether the alcohol was talking or some other chemical churned around inside his brain. Then he remembered Sol had committed suicide. That was all this was about. Not him. Not Jenny. It was like women howling their grief at a funeral. He got out of the car and locked the doors, his thoughts sobered enough to know he should not drive. It was not a long walk and he had a lot to think about.

It was like déjà vu when he got to the entrance to the driveway and heard the office phone ringing. He stumbled as he ran across the courtyard and fumbled with his keys before he could open the door. Again, he got to it before it stopped ringing.

"Is she there?" Katie's voice wailed at him from the earpiece.

He didn't understand, the alcohol still fogging a part of his brain.

"Have you got her," Katie screamed again.

"Jenny?"

"Of course, Jenny. Is she there?"

"No." He was bewildered.

"You're lying," Katie shrieked. "I'm coming round to see for myself."

Chapter 34

Katie must have been in her car on the way to his place when she phoned because she arrived a few minutes later. From his upstairs window he saw the little pink car swerve into the driveway and slam to a halt. She was out of the driver's door instantly, crashing it shut and sprinting across the courtyard. He barely had time to open his front door.

"Where is she? Where have you hidden her?"

Manny stood to one side as she flung herself through the door and began running from room to room, calling "Jenny! Jenny!" Only after she had searched the bathroom and toilet did she slow down and come to a halt, distressed and breathing heavily, back where she had started. "Where is she?" She burst into tears.

It was pointless answering until she calmed down and it would not be a smart move to put his arm around her. Instead he pulled a chair forward and placed it where she could sit if she wanted to, went through to the bathroom, ran water onto a yellow face cloth under the tap and took it back to her in a red plastic bowl he picked up from the laundry on his way through. Seeing she was now sitting down, he placed the bowl on the floor in front of her and perched himself on the edge of another chair, ready to offer more aid if she needed it. She bent forward, shoulders slumped and heaving with the rhythm of her sobs, hands covering her face and muffling the strangled wailing coming from deep inside her. It took about ten minutes before the wailing quietened and the heaving lessened. Her hands came away from her face but remained holding her head.

He saw a flicker of her eyelids as she looked down and saw the bowl at her feet. The sobs ceased and she froze, as if unable to understand what she was seeing. Her hands came away from her hair and her face tilted up towards him.

Manny sat still, working hard at keeping his face impassive, not judgmental, not sympathetic, not anything that she might think she needed to respond to. Behind that mask he wanted to scream, "What has happened? Why are you looking for Jenny? Where is she?" but he knew if he wanted the answer he had to stay calm.

Katie took the face cloth out of the bowl, held it like a veil over her face, pressed it into the hollows of her eyes and rubbed it across her forehead where it left a streak of displaced mascara.

"She's not here." It was a statement, not a question.

Manny shook his head.

"I thought she would be. She wanted to see you. She kept saying it."

Part of him wanted to shout 'hallelujah', but he was attuned to Katie's emotions and knew better. It was a strange feeling, almost of detachment, as if he were over in a corner, or up near the ceiling like a departed spirit staring down at its own body. He could see Katie in one chair and himself facing her in the other, and he was observing first one then the other as if waiting for the next move.

"Can I have a drink?"

It was not a move he had been expecting. "Sure," he said. He wasn't a distant observer any more, he was part of the action again, getting to his feet and going through into the kitchen. "What would you like?"

Before she answered he knew she what she was going to say. She had said it once before, maybe more than once before, a long time ago. At least fifteen years ago. Had she been pregnant then and he didn't know it?

"Something strong," she said.

"I've got brandy," he told her. "Dry ginger with it?" He recalled the evening she had brought Jenny to him and even beyond that, a much older memory from when they had been together. Brandy and dry with a slice of lemon and a sprig of mint.

"Just the brandy for the first one."

He poured it and passed it to her.

She held it in her hand and examined it. "What am I doing?"

"Having a drink to calm yourself so that you can tell me what has happened. You don't seem to know where Jenny is." He was being calm and wasn't sure why. Oddly he was now feeling as if his Dad was watching him from the corner, or up near the ceiling, or somewhere inside his head.

Katie shook her head. Searching for a place to put the untasted brandy, she sat it down on the floor next to the red plastic bowl and stood up.

"I've got to go and find her." She went out through the door which was still open from her abrupt arrival.

Manny followed. "I'll come too."

"No." The reply was loud and immediate. "You've done enough damage!"

For a second he was stunned. Then the anger he had been suppressing burst out of him. "It's you she's run away from this time," he yelled after her. "You're the one doing the bloody damage."

"Just stay away." Katie screamed and got into her car, screeching the tyres as she reversed out of his driveway and into the road, narrowly missing a passing car. She turned around it, ignored the gesticulating driver and burned more rubber as she sped away. The driver was still there, his car stalled, shaking his fist, wanting to vent his anger on someone, when Manny ran out into the road.

"Our daughter's missing," Manny shouted at him, opening the passenger door of the man's car and jumping in. "Take me to The End of the Earth."

The man stared back at him, bewildered.

"My car's there," Manny explained. "I need it to look for her. Down by the docks. I'll direct you."

The man seemed to unfreeze, jammed on the ignition and brought the car back to life.

"Straight ahead, second left," Manny told him.

As he gave the man directions he tried to think where Jenny could be. Obviously she had run away again, this time from Katie.

"There," he pointed, and the man pulled to a stop behind where his car was parked. "Thanks." He jumped from the car and into his own, swerved out into the road and sped away. Behind him he heard the man call "Good luck".

There was no point trying to find where Katie had gone. She had no idea where Jenny was. Not that he had any better idea, but there was one possibility. A few minutes later, heart pounding, mind praying, he pulled to a stop outside the shop with the pinball machine.

There were very few people there. None of them were Jenny.

"Lost your little girl again, mate?" said a voice, and the young man from the previous occasion turned from the machine and grinned at him. "You should be more careful."

The next thing, the young man sprawled on the floor, yelling "Oy!"

Manny backed towards the door, his expression daring any of the others to come near him. None did. He ran outside, stood on the pavement, tried to think, to decide what to do next. Was there another shop like this one, nearer to her home and Katie's? He got into the car, began driving in that direction, then stopped as the rational part of his brain told him it was pointless.

After sitting staring out of the car window for several minutes he pulled out his phone and called Claire O'Connell's number.

"Claire. Is Jenny there by any chance? Is she with Dallas, or does she know where she is?"

"One moment." Claire's voice was brisk and practical, not asking any questions.

Dallas came on the phone. "Mr Youngman. Is Jenny missing?"

"Yes. She seems to have run away from her mother. We're both out looking for her."

"I thought she might. She was very unhappy when I last spoke to her."

"Her mother thought she would come to my place, but she didn't."

"No, she wouldn't." Dallas hesitated. "That wouldn't be loyal to her Mum. She loves both of you."

Manny stared at the phone. "You mean she's running away from both of us?"

"I'm sorry, Mr Youngman. I think she is."

If she was fleeing from both of them, the chances were she had gone a long way away. It was like it had been before. He should have seen it straight away. The sensible place to be was back at his apartment, not driving round the streets with no idea where he was going. Jenny could contact him there if she wanted to, or the police or anyone else who found her. He could make more phone calls from there, to Betty Polson, to the boy Shane, to the school counsellor Ursula Bronson. He began driving in that direction.

He could get the details of the chat room from Dallas, see if Jenny was there, leave a message if she wasn't. He'd leave text messages on her phone, send her an email, put a message on Facebook or twitter or whatever else you could put messages on. Somehow, somewhere, he would get a message to her.

He had a plan. He wouldn't just be sitting there waiting. He would be doing something.

He was almost humming a tune as he turned into his driveway and saw the pink car back in his carport.

Chapter 35

"This is all your fault." Katie was standing at the top of his steps. "You turned her against me. She wouldn't have run away if it wasn't for you."

"Why the hell have you come back here?" He didn't bother trying to be calm and detached any more, didn't care what Katie's feelings were.

"Because this is where she's most likely to come," Katie retorted. "Because you've stolen her from me."

"That's just bloody stupid. You're the one who's made her so hurt and angry she's run away this time. You're the one who started it all by getting yourself put in prison."

"I didn't."

"What, make her angry or go to prison?"

"It was for her."

"You wanted to get yourself on television, show what a real feminist you are, waving the flag, mouthing the slogans, promoting the cause."

"I didn't get on television."

"Bad bloody luck. You stuffed that one up, didn't you? Need a better publicity agent."

"Like you? You're the one who's been in the newspaper articles and on television, spouting your men's bullshit. I thought…"

"You thought what?"

"I thought she might get… forget it. It doesn't matter. I didn't think you would be so stupid and irresponsible you would encourage her to have a drunken party at your place, let her dye her hair green and take her off somewhere where I couldn't contact her."

They were still standing outside his front door. Manny glared at her, put his key in the lock and opened it.

"I'm going in," he said. "You can stay out her screaming for the neighbours to hear if you want to."

She glowered at him with hate-filled eyes as she followed him inside. He lifted the chair she had been sitting on earlier back into its normal place, picked up the red bowl and the glass of brandy, considered whether to hand it to her and decided against it.

"I'll admit I was wrong not being here to supervise the party," he said. "I thought Jenny was mature enough. Obviously she wasn't. Maybe if I had known her better, if I'd even known she'd existed for the past fifteen years, I wouldn't have made that mistake. To make it worse I made the same mistake you seem to have made. I played the paranoid parent and tried to discipline her. She doesn't take well to that, as you should know since you were the one who raised her."

"I raised her well."

"How clever of you, and all by yourself. Not just a clever little feminist. A clever little mum as well."

Katie's eyes were hard and shining. "You're not seeing Jenny. Ever. Do you understand? You stay away from her or you'll be the one in the bloody prison. I'll see to it. You hear me?"

Manny laughed. "Didn't work when you tried to put her in a prison, did it?"

Her eyes took on a defensive expression. "I kept her out of prison."

That didn't quite make sense, but Manny ignored it. "You've taken away her phone, kept her out of school, locked her in her room for all I know, all because she still wants to see me, and it hasn't worked, has it? She's escaped."

"I won't let you see her."

"She's my daughter and I'll see her if I want to."

"No, you won't."

"I will. I'll get a court order."

"They won't give you one."

"They might if I tell them that you lied when you withdrew your confession, that you not only threw that fake bomb in the men's club toilet, but you involved your daughter by getting her to make it for you in her school science class."

He couldn't quite read the expression on her face. Anger, contrition, bafflement? It all seemed to be there.

"For your information," she spat at him. "Your wonderful Jenny not only made that bomb, she threw it. I wasn't even there."

Manny stared at her. "Why did you say you did?"

He already knew the answer. She had told him a few minutes before. She had kept Jenny out of prison. "I'm sorry, I didn't..." he began.

Katie reached for the table behind her, picked up a heavy glass ashtray and hurled it.

Manny dodged, watched the missile crash against the wall above the television, turned back to see her reach for something else. He leaped forward, grappling with her.

"Stop it, Katie. For Christ's sake! You'll damage something."

"Let go of me." She clawed at his face, pushing him away.

He clung to her, pinning her arms to stop her picking up anything else. A shift in her balance warned him the instant before her knee rose between his legs. He twisted, saving himself from a lot of pain. Their legs tangled and they fell, rolling across the carpet towards the television.

Her fingers found flesh on the outside of his thighs. She pinched savagely, forcing him to let go of her arms to defend himself. She swung her arms wide and brought both fists crashing round on either side of his head.

He had to stop her. He spun on his hips, whirled his body round to knock her legs from under her and rolled. She lay beneath him, spreadeagled, his hands pinning hers to the carpet while his knees kept her legs immobile. Her head came up to butt him, teeth snapping. He saw it coming and dodged.

"Stop it! Stop it, both of you!"

They both froze as a voice penetrated through the haze of their frustration and anger. Manny rolled sideways off Katie and they sat up together.

His mother stood in the doorway, staring at them with a horrified expression on her face. Standing beside her was their daughter.

Jenny hadn't uttered a sound. Not a word or a cry. They saw the pain in her eyes overwhelm her spirit and send it fleeing to some dark inner place in search of safety. She turned and hurled herself into the arms of her grandmother.

Chapter 36

Manny's father came into the room behind Jenny and his mother.

"Pair of you having fun, are you?" he asked.

"For heaven's sake," his wife exploded. "How can you be so flippant?"

"Because there's not much point being anything else," his Dad said, walking across the room and sitting in a chair.

Manny struggled to his feet and stood sheepishly in front of him, to be told "Help Katie up too, son."

He offered a hand and, after a slight hesitation, Katie took it, hauling herself up to stand beside him.

"I'm sorry, Jenny," she said. "I really am."

"Where did you find her?" Manny asked.

"Curled up under the bench in my shed," Dad said. "It was lucky I went in there. Was on my way to the Men's Shed and remembered I promised to show one of the blokes what a spoke shave is. Went in to get it and there she was."

"She came to us," his mother said, and Manny blinked in surprise at the tears in her eyes. "She came to her grandparents. She knew we'd love her."

Katie gave a small cry. "I love you, Jenny. You know that."

Jenny looked from Katie to Manny and back again, then walked over to her mother, reaching out a hand to squeeze his as she passed. Katie's arms enfolded her while tear-filled eyes shone a smile of relief and thankfulness.

Manny waited and was rewarded. Jenny left her mother and came to him. In seconds she was in his arms. No words had to be spoken.

"That's all right then." Dad said.

"No, it's not." The tears had gone from his mother's eyes and she glowered at Katie. "You deserve to be punished for what you've done."

Katie reacted as if she had been stung. "What I've done? What about your precious son? It's what he's done."

"Him too," his mother responded. "Both of you have behaved badly."

"Oh, for heaven's sake," Katie snapped back at her. "Even if you are Jenny's biological grandmother, that gives you no right to talk to me like this. It's not as if you did a good job of raising him, is it?"

"I didn't run away and have him in secret and not let his father know. I raised him knowing who his grandparents were, God rest their souls, and loving them and knowing they loved him. You didn't only rob Robert of his daughter, you did it to all of our family."

"Well, I'm sorry," Katie retorted. "That's hardly the point now, is it? Your son has turned my daughter against me and I want her back."

Manny decided it was time to intervene. "I didn't turn Jenny against you and I have no objection to her going back to you, provided I still get to see her and spend time with her. That's not unreasonable, is it? To let us spend some time together?"

"So you can tell her more of your misogynist bullshit?"

"So I can give her a different view of the facts of life than she has received from her mad, man-hating mother who gave her such distorted values that she threw a fake bomb into a men's toilet and frightened some poor old men out of their wits."

There was a silence. His parents stared at Manny in disbelief.

"Hang on here," his father said. "Are you saying she went to prison to save Jenny?" He frowned at his granddaughter. "Is that true? Did you do it?"

"I never heard such nonsense," his wife interjected. "Jenny wouldn't…"

"No. Hang on. I want to get this straight. Jenny?"

Jenny nodded shamefacedly.

"It was still my fault," Katie defended her. "I took her the first time to nail up the door, which didn't have the effect I hoped it would. Jenny decided she would help me by going one better." She had an expression on her face that mixed guilt with something that was almost pride. "She wanted to do something to show she was as committed as I was. She didn't expect all those men to be inside. She didn't even know it was the toilet window she threw it through."

"So you said it was you?"

"I wasn't going to let her go to prison, or detention centre or wherever they send girls her age. I told the police I had done it. Then I had to think of someone for Jenny to stay with."

"And you brought her to Manny?"

Katie shrugged. "I thought it was best."

Manny was still confused. "Why not someone else, one of your friends?"

She gave him a look of scorn. "It doesn't matter, does it? I made a mess of that, too."

"Seems to be what you're best at," Manny retorted. "You've made a mess of taking Jenny away from me, you're making a mess of stopping her from seeing me. You just keep on, don't you?"

Katie bristled. "If only you had…"

"Shut up, both of you," Jenny said into the pause while Katie gathered her thoughts. "I know what you think about each other. I don't want to hear it anymore."

"You go, girl," Manny heard his Dad say in the background. The old man was grinning. Even his mother showed signs of being impressed.

"I think it's my turn," Jenny said. "I think it's time you both listened to me." She turned to her grandparents. "Do you mind if I speak to my parents alone?"

His mother made a move as if she was going to resist, but his father tugged at her arm and she followed him out of the door. They heard them pause at the top of the steps. His Dad said something and they went down.

"Now," Jenny said, turning back to them. "I think I'd like you to sit down." She looked at Manny. "Your rules, okay? No interruptions."

Manny nodded.

"That means you can't say anything," Jenny told Katie. "You just have to listen."

Katie also nodded.

"Good," Jenny began. "I've been thinking about it a lot, what I want to say to you, so it may take a little time."

Chapter 37

"I know this is all my fault," Jenny began.

Katie started to protest and was stopped by a raised hand.

"No interruptions, Mum. Those are the rules."

Katie subsided without looking convinced.

"What I did was silly and I wish I hadn't done it and I'm so sorry Mum because you went to prison when it should have been me."

She directed herself to Manny. "I wanted to tell the police but Mum wouldn't let me. She said it would ruin my life and made me promise I wouldn't tell anyone."

There was a pause while she studied them both as if trying to make up her mind about something. Manny half expected Katie to speak into the silence but she didn't, seeming to have recognised the need for Jenny to say her piece.

"I'm sorry about what has happened," Jenny said when the silence seemed to have stretched so thin it must break. "I'm not making excuses. I want to make it right again. The thing is, everything has changed. It's not like it was and I don't even think I am the same person. I wouldn't do that again, or anything like it. I don't know what is going to happen. I hope I don't have to go to a detention centre, but I will if I have to."

Again she paused.

"Whatever happens, I know one thing. I love both of

you.

"I have lived with you, Mum, and you have raised me and that means a lot, but you have to understand that now I have met Dad, and know what a nice person he is, I love him, too, and I want to keep seeing him.

"I said I think I am a different person. Before I met Dad I thought I knew who I was and then I found out I wasn't, or I didn't have to be, anyway.

"That sounds wrong, so I'll try to explain. I wanted to be like you, Mum, because that was all I knew. I mean, I knew other people, like Madge and Sweeny and our other friends and people at school, but you were the person closest to me, the most like me, who loved me. So you were the person I loved and admired most and wanted to be like. Not just a clone of you. I wanted to be me, but a me that had a lot of you. Do you understand?"

Katie nodded. Jenny turned to Manny.

"And then I met you. I've tried to explain to you already some of how I felt. First I had this dream about who my father was, some sort of wonderful fairytale person like I suppose every girl who doesn't have a father wishes. Then Mum told me I did have a Dad and he was this man who had written that book, The Male Conundrum.

"I hadn't even read it, because I thought it was too terrible, all about men hating women. I didn't even know what conundrum meant! I thought it was something like a contraceptive. I was horrified. I didn't want my friends to know that monster was my father."

She turned back to Katie. "And then you said you thought I should go and live with him. Why did you do that?"

Katie lifted her shoulders uncertainly. "Am I allowed to answer? I thought I…"

"The rule is that you're not allowed to interrupt," Manny told her, making it up on the spot. "You are allowed to answer a question, but have to limit your answer to the subject of the question."

"I see." Katie thought about what she was going to say for a minute. "When you threw that fake bomb, Jenny, I realised that it was my fault. You were becoming something I didn't want you to be. I know you say you wanted to be like me, but that wasn't really me, only a part of me, and I didn't want you to be like that. I had to find someone you could stay with. I thought about Madge and Alice, and other friends too. I decided I needed to find someone else, someone who wasn't part of my life, who would show you something different."

She frowned at Manny. "I heard that you were speaking at the Women's Service League so I went along to see what you were like. I wasn't going to say anything, but you were too smart for Diane Strickland and that red headed woman. I felt I had to get up. It was strange. I was arguing with you and suddenly I saw that you were the person Jenny should go to. You would give her a different set of values, counter the damage I had done." She turned back to Jenny. "That's why I said you should go and live with him."

"So why did you take me away again and stop me seeing him?"

"Because Madge and Diane both told me he was filling you with anti-female propaganda, that he was letting you run wild and that you had nearly been raped because he was not looking after you properly. You have to understand, Jenny, I was in that prison, unable to do anything, and I thought you were in danger and it was my fault. I couldn't ring you because you were out of mobile range. I panicked. I had to get out and get you back, to reverse all the trouble I thought I had caused. I see I was wrong now, about all of it."

"Good," Jenny asserted. "So you'll let me see him?"

There was the briefest hesitation. "Yes," Katie agreed.

Manny felt a deep sigh of relief well up inside him and thought for a minute he was going to start cheering. The look on Jenny's face stopped him.

"I haven't finished," she said. "You two. You infuriate me. I'm happy we've got that over and I can now see my own father when I feel like it, which I would have thought any daughter had the right to do, or son for that matter. I still don't want to go on with my mother and father fighting each other all the time, acting as if they are enemies and have different ideas about things when they really don't.

"Your trouble is, Mum, you still think like the feminists did years ago. You still hate all men, still protest and carry on as if there haven't been any changes, any improvements. I know there are still women who can't get top jobs, but some can. I met Claire O'Connell and if she can do it, I can do it, and so can other women. We just have to find a better way of making it happen, and happen quicker. I'm sure there are plenty of smart women around who have ideas about that, and they don't go around saying all men are pigs.

"I know, I know," she said to Manny. "I said things like that. I was just trying to stir you up, show you I was different, be loyal to my mother, I don't know. It doesn't matter. I'm not thinking that now.

"And you," she turned back to Katie. "You and your feminist friends should have seen long ago what was going to happen. Of course the men were going to react to women changing the rules. Why wouldn't they? You became obsessed with the idea that men would attack you, that they would try to stop those changes and reverse them. Instead you should have seen that men would want to change, too, and that that was what you wanted, wasn't it? You wanted men to change, so why didn't you support them and help them when they did? Why aren't you supporting them and helping them now?"

Manny's eyebrows rose. He felt very pleased how this was developing. That was a mistake.

"Don't raise your eyebrows like that," Jenny growled at him. "I know what it means, you know."

He removed the satisfied look that had been in his eyes.

"You're all words and no action," she snorted. "Don't think it's all Mum's fault, her and other women like her.

You go round mouthing about how men need to change, how they need to establish a new relationship with women. I was taken in at first. I thought you were trying to be different.

"But what woman have you tried to establish a new kind of relationship with? The women you've had in your apartment who come and go so quick you have to keep spare nightdresses for them? How many of them have stayed more than one night, or is that the only sort of relationship you can cope with? No real commitment? All your real relationships are with other men, so you can talk about how things should change without changing yourself.

"You know what? Men should have understood women better, too. Men should have seen the stresses on women, how hard it was to assert themselves and be something different, and that it would be better for men as well as for women.

"All of you. You fight each other like sects in the Middle East who kill each other over stupid beliefs when they are all just people, just human beings. Why can't people live together and love each other?

"Be different, Dad. Live what you preach, don't just keep preaching it. And you, Mum. Be you, not some tired old feminist slogans."

She stopped and looked around the room as if looking for a cue sheet to tell her what to say next. When she didn't find one, she shrugged her shoulders and said. "That's it. It's all I want to say. I'm finished."

Chapter 38

"Chisel's a bit blunt," his Dad said. "Always a problem when you're not using your own tools. Wonder where they keep the stone, if they've got one?"

They were in the Men's Shed, a large building containing areas for woodworking, metal working and general repairs and maintenance, with a screened section at one end that had chairs and tables, a coffee-making machine, refrigerator, audio-visual equipment and rows of shelves filled with DIY books and machinery manuals. About a dozen men worked at the benches, mostly in twos or threes. A similar number socialized in the coffee area.

An enquiry of one of the men at a nearby workbench provided a clue to where the sharpening stone could be found. Manny went in search of it.

"Don't forget the oil," his Dad called after him, bending over the piece of wood they were about to turn into the head of a rocking horse. The two men at the next bench were making the rockers. Over in the general area, an ancient individual who had once been a saddler showed two younger men how to make reins and saddles from recycled belts and leather handbags.

The tools were kept in an enclosed, lockable area in one corner. Manny selected a sharpening stone and some oil and carried it back to his Dad.

"Know how to use one?"

He shook his head.

"Right. You finish marking this up while I do it. Bring the oil?"

Manny handed the can across and watched as the oil dripped onto the stone. His father ran the blade backwards and forwards. So many of these old skills were being forgotten, he reflected. If nothing else, the Men's Sheds kept them alive for a few more years, perhaps even a few more generations. He turned to the piece of wood and took up the template to finish drawing the horse's head. A stack of finished blank heads stood on a table to the side, ready for the next stage of carving out the eyes, flared nostrils and curving hair of the mane. They were going to be quite something, these rocking horses. Each one was going to provide a thrill for some deprived child next Christmas.

"Jenny's doing a good job finding us kids to send them to," his Dad said as if he had read Manny's thoughts. "She seems happy doing it, even if it is meant to be a punishment."

Manny nodded, using the template to draw the curve of the horse's muzzle onto the wood. After the courts had listened with sympathy to the story of Katie's false confession to save her daughter, she had been reprieved.

Jenny had received a stern reprimand and had been ordered to do community service. She worked three hours every Saturday morning in the office of a children's charity which distributed the toys the Men's Shed made. Neil Blighton and Chloe McQuinn had worked together on getting that result.

"She says she understands what she did was wrong," Manny said, raising his voice over the scraping sound of the chisel, "but she can't see any point in feeling miserable or hard done by about it. She's been out with some of the older volunteers to some of the homes they visit. I think it's been a bit of an eye-opener for her. Talking about studying to be a social worker when she finishes school. Been looking to see what subjects she'll have to do at uni."

"Pity she has to do it at weekends," the older man responded. "Means we don't get to see her so often. Your mum'd like to see more of her."

Manny would, too, but he was learning to be satisfied with the times he did see his daughter. Once a week she came to the apartment for a meal. They either went out to a movie together or stayed in and found something to do. Her most recent idea was to take out a jigsaw from the local library and there was half of one completed on his dinner table. When finished it would depict the interior of a man's shed with all its tools and paraphernalia. Her plan was to invite his Dad round for their final evening on it, so that he could lay the last piece in place.

They had a loose arrangement for him to see her every second weekend, too, which she found more difficult because the community work left little time to spend with Dallas O'Connell who had replaced Betty Polson as her best friend. She was staying at the O'Connell house that weekend. He wasn't sure what Katie would be doing. Going somewhere, she had said, and when Jenny had asked if it was with a man, she had laughed and said that was her business. Manny had been picking Jenny up from their house at the time and knew it was not his business, except a small part of him thought he might perhaps like it to be.

"How's Katie?" his Dad asked, showing again how often their minds seemed to be in tune. What was it? Some secret communication between the wish washy eyebrows? Jenny also seemed to have it at times.

"She's fine," he said. "Well, I think she is. Jenny says she calmed down a lot since the court hearings. She was pretty worked up before that."

"She sorted out things with those friends of hers, the one you fancied and her partner?"

Manny smiled. "Madge and Alice have gone on a second honeymoon. A cruise ship up to Singapore and Penang. Away three weeks, I think." It had been a small surprise in his life that his father and also his mother had accepted with equanimity the fact that Alice and Madge had a lesbian relationship. In a lot of ways his parents were turning out to have more tolerant and understanding views than he had expected them to have.

"And what about the other woman who got Katie stirred up, the social worker?"

"Suspended from her job during an inquiry. Subsequently reinstated with a warning."

"Funny business that."

"When she heard Katie was going to prison she seems to have got it into her mind that she could get her off, then got angry because Katie didn't go along with it. When she heard Jenny was with me she decided she had to stop that. Everything she did was unofficial. Katie seems to think her heart was in the right place and she was trying to help."

"So what's Katie doing now?"

"Gone back to writing her Sybil column in that magazine. Jenny thinks it's a good sign. I'll have to get around to reading one after I've prepared the talk I'm making next week to Claire O'Connell's Executive Women's Conference."

"I heard your talk to the State Men's Shed Association conference went down well," his Dad said. "Women executives might be a tougher audience."

Manny nodded. He'd been thinking the same thing. "Did you know Bobby is thinking about nominating for the board of the association? He thinks we should be part of it, and maybe even change our name to include Men's Shed in it. Tony's not so sure. He thinks NEMSA has a separate role to play."

"Not much point having your own Men's Shed when you can come to this one. My vote would be with Tony. Stick to the talks and the books, Manny. You've got a job to do there." He had finished sharpening the chisel and began to carve lines along the pencil marks on one of the horse's head blanks. "Bit like sharpening a chisel, or these days using a computer. Someone has to show you how."

He was right. Some of the NEMSA members, Tommy Bloffwitch for one, and possibly Dick James, might be more at home doing practical things in a Men's Shed like this one, except Dick had quit teaching and was working in a book shop. Perhaps that was all the therapy he needed. Coming to a Men's Shed might have been a good thing for Sol Garfwicz. It was too late for him now. Like it had been too late for his widow and children to cry at his funeral. If he meant that much to them it was a pity they hadn't shown it a lot earlier. Still. Who was he to judge? Who was anyone to judge?

Looking around the Men's Shed, he wondered what the story was for each of the men there. Most were retired, with a few younger men. There because they had problems at home? Because they had no-one at home? No-one else to talk to?

Perhaps he should walk round and talk to a few of them, find out why there were there. It might give him some material for his talk. Even for his book.

"Someone here named Manny Youngman?" A man in a checked shirt and jeans was calling from the far side of the shed near the entrance.

Manny held up his hand.

"Someone outside wants to see you," the man called. "On a Harley Davidson. Sportster 1200 by the look of it. Nice looking machine."

Putting down the horse's head he was working on, he gave his father a puzzled look. With a shrug he walked across to the entrance where he found a figure in black leathers and helmet sitting astride a blue motorbike with high chrome handlebars and mudguards. Gloved hands rose and removed the helmet.

"Like to come for a ride?" Katie said.

Chapter 39

The Harley Davidson cruised over the crest in the road and descended into the long downward curve shaded by the soldier trees, their uniforms greener now with the change in the season. The afternoon sunlight's angle was lower and less of it dappled down to the leaf-strewn floor of the forest.

They coasted to a halt and stepped the machine back on its stand. Removing their visored helmets, they stood together looking down the hill through the endless avenues of trees.

"It's so beautiful." She moved forward and stopped on the edge of the slope, as if mesmerised by the mystic beauty of the scene before her. He walked across to her. She had asked him to bring her there. To share it with her.

"Jenny was right," Katie said. "It's breath-taking. Can we walk down there? You and Jenny did, didn't you?"

Manny eased the back of his jeans where he was tender from the long ride on the pillion seat. Katie had proved to be an excellent rider. He had been nervous at first until he'd relaxed and enjoyed the experience of having his arms around her, the scent of her hair strong in his nostrils, the warmth of her pressing back against him.

They found the top of the zigzag path and began the easy sideways descent.

"Jenny has told me a lot more about you," Katie said, dragging his thoughts back into the present with what almost seemed like clairvoyance. "At first I didn't listen because I don't think I wanted to hear. Still a bit hung up about sharing her. Then I started listening. Now I ask her questions."

She had turned at the end of a zig and was starting on a zag, lower on the slope, looking upwards at him.

"Jenny explained about the way you talked without interrupting, the way she did to us that day after your mother and father brought her back. She said it made her listen to what you were saying. She felt as if you listened."

"Sometimes I think I didn't always say the right things," Manny admitted, stepping carefully where some stones had been disturbed and spilled across the path, perhaps when he and Jenny had passed that way.

"Not according to Jenny. She said you talked about things she wasn't expecting to hear sometimes. That was part of what made her listen. She said she realised you must be talking about things that were important to you, because she was talking about things that were important to her." She laughed. "What she actually said was that when you had such a wonderful chance to say what you liked and the other person had to listen, it would be silly to waste it on something that wasn't important." She paused. "Can I go first? Same rules?"

A fold of sunlight had surrounded the glade into which they were descending.

"Sure," Manny said a hundred times more casually than he felt.

"I want to tell you about me. Because I've heard so much about you, I suppose.

"You said something once about my father. I suspect you think he abused me or something. It wasn't as simple as that. He didn't want me. He wanted a boy and he said so, frequently. Nothing I ever did was right. He wasn't violent, just snide and negative. I hated him and I despised my mother because she let him do it.

"As I grew up, I found girls were always treated as inferior to boys, even by people who weren't nasty like my father. It was always there. At school, sport, dances, everywhere. At dances we were supposed to wait for the boys to ask us to dance. I used to sit there getting angry because no stupid boy would ask me.

"Finally one did, and I didn't know how to handle it. I became all tongue tied and clumsy. Scared I was going to put my feet in the wrong place or say the wrong thing. All because of a boy. I hated him. But I was even more frightened he wouldn't like me. That's what it seemed being a girl was. Being good enough for boys to like me."

She bent and picked up a twig from the path, snapping it between her fingers into smaller and smaller pieces as she walked.

"I knew girls in my class at school who pretended not to be bright because the boys wouldn't like them.

"I knew what the boys were interested in, of course. Not just the boys. Men. You couldn't help it. Walk down the street and you felt them looking at you. Staring at your breasts and pretending they weren't if you stared back at them. Even men old enough to be my father. It didn't even matter if you wore clothes that made you look flat chested. They still seemed to look at you all the time. In the end you just had to try to ignore it.

"I remember thinking to myself, they're my breasts and I'm proud of them because they mean I'm a woman. I'm not going to hide them just because some dirty-minded men keep looking at them. It was a bit better after that, but you never get rid of the feeling. You're always aware of the stare.

"I wanted to be a woman. I wanted to wear great clothes and have my hair done in exciting styles. I wanted to feel elegant and sophisticated and sure of myself. But they were all the things that seemed to go with the other side of it - of being stared at by men and put down as some sort of brainless twit who was interested in frivolous things and couldn't be taken seriously. I was very confused about a lot of that. I think most girls of my age were."

She had to come to the smallest piece of twig and threw it away. Her hands twisted as if they wanted something else to do. As they walked on she touched her hair, the side of her face, laced her fingers in front of her and clasped them behind her back.

"Discovering feminism was wonderful. Here were all these other women, all over the world, the same as me. I read book after book thinking, yes, it's true; that's how I feel.

"The more I read the angrier I became, too. A lot of what I had been feeling was made clear to me. How women were put down by society. It was my father all over again, criticizing my mother and sneering at me."

A creek was busily washing away a wide section of the path. Katie stopped speaking while she picked her way across a line of stepping stones still above the surface of the water. The tops of the stones wouldn't be dry much longer. With a little more rain the creek would flow over them and cut the path completely.

"This is harder than I thought," she said as she waited for him to join her on the other side. "Talking like this is a bit like crossing the stream. You have to pick your way, saying what you need to say to make your point without making it too confused."

"Would you like to take a break?" Manny offered. "Gather your thoughts together? I could talk for a while or neither of us has to say anything."

Katie shook her head. "No. I'll keep going, if that's alright?

He said it was, smiling because it was true. It was more than alright. Her spoken words were helping him unravel what was unspoken in his own thoughts.

"You want to know what a woman is? A woman is deep, deep down inside being very gentle. It is being soft and loving and wanting to spread that love everywhere, to everyone, to wrap it around you and everyone so that you carry the world, safe and protected, like you carry a baby in your womb. It is nurturing. Holding the world to your breast, giving from yourself like you give milk to your baby. Being a woman is wanting to be open and loving and caring. Wanting to be honest and fair and just. Wanting everyone to love each other and the whole world to be a much softer, sweeter, lovelier place. Wanting to understand and be understood. Wanting to give, and to be given. Wanting to relate to the world. To be absorbed into it and flow with it, not to fight it and be fought by it.

"That's what it feels like, deep inside. The essence of being a female. To me, anyway. And I think to other women because when I talk to them that's what they seem to be saying.

"But that's not what being a woman is in the world. Being a woman in the world is protecting that inner self from the real world - which seems to mean from men. Being a woman is having to fight, because if you don't you get trodden on. Being a woman is trying to care and nurture in a world where caring and nurturing can leave you weak and defenceless. Being a woman is yearning to be that inner femaleness in a world which doesn't allow you to be. And the stupid thing is that, to protect your inner self, you have to become hard on the outside.

"That's what I've discovered after all these years. I thought I had it worked out, but all I've done, all I think women are doing, is becoming what they didn't want to be, building shells around themselves which make it harder and harder for the real selves to get out, to be expressed."

She turned. He was walking behind her.

"Do you understand what I'm saying?"

"Yes, I think so," he said. And he did. While she had been talking he had been thinking how much the same sorts of things applied to men. Both built shells around themselves. Not just men. Women executives. That was an idea he could develop for his talk. Perhaps Katie and he could even work on it together.

"Perhaps I should stop while I'm ahead." She laughed. "No. There is something else. "Jenny. I do want to say something about Jenny.

"You see, I realise now that I was selfish keeping her to myself. I was selfish to her and to you and to your mother and father.

"That's the sort of way we go wrong, do you see? If I was the sort of woman I spoke about, caring and nurturing and all those things, how could I be so selfish?

"To try and prove that I was an independent woman who didn't need a man, I denied her a father and you a daughter. I denied you both a chance to be caring and be cared for. Does that make sense?"

The path was starting to rise. They had crossed the lowest part of the valley where the undergrowth was most dense and were moving back into the more open forest on the upper slopes.

"I also denied myself an opportunity to be caring and nurturing towards a man. That's one of the biggest things I've realised. Women and men have to relate to each other.

Otherwise there's no sense to it. I thought I could somehow cut myself off from men, but it's not possible.

"I have to come to terms somehow with men, not run away from them. I still want to be a woman. I still don't want to be dominated by men and live in a man's world which doesn't treat me equally or allow me to be what I want to be. Now I'm no longer sure the path I've been walking along is going that way."

She stopped and looked around her, laughing.

"Damn it, I don't even know where this path we are on is going. Are we lost?"

Manny shook his head. "Up ahead there is a ridge and over it we come to the road ahead of where we parked the bike. It'll be easier to walk this way than go back the way we came.

"Good. Up there?" She let him move ahead and lead the way. "What happens now? I think I've run out of words."

Manny turned back to her and grinned. "I get to have my say. You have to listen."

"That's what worries me. Are you going to disagree with what I've said? I feel as if I haven't said it right and need to explain it better."

"No," he said. "The rules are that I can talk about the same thing, but I can't say you said this or that and disagree with it. Anyway, I don't disagree, so you don't have to worry."

They were walking side by side now.

He began talking.